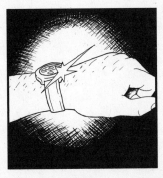

"If you could have one superpower, what would it be? Leaping, of course! I always say that. Only I didn't know what to call it until reading *Leaper*. Insightful, humorous, well-written, with a lemony-fresh smell, *Leaper* delves into faith, its many questions and quagmires, inside the crazy world of an erstwhile superhero trying to make sense of his life and his newfound gift. This book is a gift to every single one of us who finds Jesus at our side and doesn't quite know what to do with Him. I can't wait to get a peek at what Geoffrey Wood has up his sleeve next."

—LISA SAMSON, award-winning author of *Straight Up* and *Quaker Summer*

"A friend will recommend this book, and you'll think you can maybe just dip your toes in to discover whether the water is as inviting as it looks. Be warned. By the end of the first page, you won't get out. The book will sweep you into its currents, and you'll enjoy every moment of the ride."

—SIGMUND BROUWER, author of *The Last Disciple* and *Fuse of Armageddon*

"*Leaper* has it all: a great hook, compelling writing, and a real look at faith in an unreal world. It's fantasy, it's reality, but best of all, it's a fabulous read."

—MAY VANDERBILT and ANNE DAYTON, authors of *Emily Ever After* and *The Book of Jane*

The Misadventures of a
Not-Necessarily-Super Hero

LEAPER

A NOVEL

geoffrey wood

WaterBrook
PRESS

LEAPER

PUBLISHED BY WATERBROOK PRESS

12265 Oracle Boulevard, Suite 200

Colorado Springs, Colorado 80921

A division of Random House Inc.

All Scripture quotations or paraphrases are taken from the King James Version of the Bible.

ISBN: 978-1-4000-7343-6

Published in association with the literary agency of Alive Communications Inc., 7680 Goddard Street, Suite 200, Colorado Springs, CO 80920, www.alive communications.com.

Library of Congress Cataloging-in-Publication Data
Wood, Geoffrey, 1969–
    Leaper : the misadventures of a not-necessarily-super hero / Geoffrey Wood. — 1st ed.
        p. cm.
    ISBN 978-1-4000-7343-6
    1. Heroes—Fiction. I. Title.
PS3623.O6256L43 2007
813'.6—dc22

                                        2007000456

Printed in the United States of America
2007—First Edition

10 9 8 7 6 5 4 3 2 1

6147 06337

For Claudia and Tim

When they heard these things,
they thrust Jesus out of their city
and led him to the edge of a hill
that they might throw him off the cliff.
But passing through their very midst,
Jesus went his way...
—THE GOSPEL OF SAINT LUKE

Hotel reserved under alias, "Gabe Oates." Payment made in cash. No record concerning that name. Police alerted when personal items found in abandoned room after checkout time. Window open overlooking river. Video surveillance cameras at front desk identify above-mentioned same as missing person, and concierge confirmed identification from police photo. Remarked as to the suspect's agitated, dazed demeanor—said that suspect had "wandered the hotel, barefoot, talking to an empty ice bucket."

No evidence of foul play. Room clean with bed made. Notebook, keys, handwritten note to one Father Chavez. Note reads: "In Care of Father Chavez: Please donate '88 Volvo to church. Half the time she won't start, but it's better than no ride at all."

No body found. No eyewitnesses of the jump. Likely trajectory from a window leap would put body in river. No plans to drag the river due to the width and turbulence of that spot. No body likely found in any case. Evidence often irretrievable, washed away.

The tape recorder mentioned in the notebook entries not found.

Just a three days' diary and an open window.

—Captain William Goss

Part 1

1

The first time it happened, I had pins sticking in my back.

I don't believe the acupuncture had anything to do with it. But in a way, my acupuncturist, she's a witness of sorts. Ask her. She can tell you. Although she doesn't really know what she witnessed, but then neither do I.

So she's not a *real* witness-kind-of-witness. Not an official, legal sort of witness, you know? Circumstantial at best. She didn't actually *see* it happen, just the aftereffects, and I'm sure she explained all those away.

She wouldn't have believed me even if I *had* told her what really happened.

Who would? Anyhow...

I'd gone to my acupuncturist for my regular appointment. Every three weeks for my back. Spasms, mid- and lower back, nothing out of the ordinary. I work in a coffee shop; I open the store most mornings, and I'd opened it that day. Not too much espresso, maybe six, seven shots. Nothing unusual. But working on the espresso bar, pulling drinks, fetching gallon jugs of milk, lugging out a sack of trash, it wears on your back. So she sticks a few pins in, and it feels better. Unblocks the chi, or whatever. I don't know, I don't go for the metaphysical bit, and there's no mystical confusion about my experience. It's alternative care, but she wears a white coat just like a real doctor.

She did what she always does, no more, no less. Pins in the back and neck, one or two near my thumbs. No strange sensations or anything. I'm perfectly aware of myself. No mumbo jumbo, incense burning, or whatnot. There's a ceiling fan on way low, barely moving, I remember. She dimmed the lights when she left the room and made it relaxing. The same as always.

So I'm lying there under the sheet with her *Sounds of Rippling Water* CD playing, and my mind starts to drift. This is what it's supposed to do; it always does. I'm not some mind-drifter. I focus, I'm aware. I'd had my coffee. But I'm daydreaming because you have to lie there. Not quite asleep, just really relaxed, half-dreamy, half-thinking of what I'm doing for the rest of the day.

Phone bill, got to mail that off. Run back by the coffee shop, pick up the book I'm reading, *The Great Divorce,* C. S. Lewis, it's wild stuff. I took it in to work because I always take a book everywhere, although I never have time to read at work. And if you take a book and don't get to read it, chances are you forget it's there.

I'm not flighty or forgetful. I know what happened to me. Or at least that it happened. But you take a book and don't read it, you forget it. That happens to most people.

Anyhow, I'm drifting and thinking that the name of the book is *The Great Divorce,* and I snort a chuckle. I guess I chortle while I'm lying there because I'm thinking, *Now that's an oxymoron—a great divorce.*

My wife and I recently got divorced, so I'm sort of sensitive to the title. I guess she's not my wife, but you understand…my ex-wife. I'm sort of chuckling because our divorce was anything but great. I guess most divorces are less than superlative, not the kind of thing you look forward to, or look back on and say, "Gee, swell times."

She'd called the night before, looking for something. Actually, she'd called to accuse me of being why she couldn't find something. A cutting board. A cheap, white plastic, $6.99 cutting board that she swears was hers, though I remember buying that board back in college. A cutting board, a sharp knife, and three pint glasses. I made it through college with just those things: no plates, no cutlery, no napkin rings. She has all the plates, all the cutlery, all six sets of napkin rings we got as wedding presents.

She divorced me. But she got everything. Don't take that wrong, she's peaches; but the fact is that I moved out for a song, and she's still in the house. She got the dogs. Yet the night before, she's calling about that stupid cutting board, right?

I live in squalor. Most of my stuff is still in boxes, and I haven't even moved all the boxes to my apartment; some of them are still in our garage. Excuse me, *her* garage. And I know I haven't seen that cutting board. I haven't had time to cut anything in my apartment.

"You know how much I liked that cutting board," she says. "Besides, I brought it to the marriage."

Brought it to the marriage. She says this like she had arrived with a huge oaken hope chest, like her people felled trees for timber and built our house from scratch and moved us in. Like her father pulled the clapboard wagon up in front of the house and dropped off the blushing bride with her stupid cutting-board dowry.

"If it's in a box," I say, "I don't know about it."

"Well, if it's in a box, find it," she says.

"When I get to all the boxes, I'll let you know if it turns up."

"Well, your concern doesn't help me cut an onion tonight," she says.

I say, "No. No, it certainly doesn't do that."

"James, there's no call for rudeness," she says. "I just hope every time I find something of mine missing I don't have to call you and wait for boxes to get unpacked."

"I haven't had time…"

"That's right, you never did. Half your boxes are still in my garage. And half those half are ones you never unpacked when we moved into the house five years ago."

Ten, maybe a dozen boxes, are still there, certainly not half. My back just shoots spasms every time she calls.

So I say, "Honey, if there are any five-year-old unpacked boxes in that garage, you can have everything in them."

Truthfully, I meant to cover up the phone for the next bit, but it's one of those tiny little flippy cell phones, and you don't know where the speak hole is. You can hardly see it, so how do you cover it up?

She hears me when I mumble, "Might as well, you took everything else."

There's this silence. Oh, for silences that remain silent.

"No, James, I didn't *take* everything else. I didn't *take* anything. I *kept,* perhaps that's the word you were looking for, *kept* what was mine. Those things I bought when my job was the only one paying the bills and buying all the pretty little boxed-up things that now crowd *my* car out of *my* garage. Did you know some people actually call them carports? They drive their vehicles into them at night, these ports for cars? They keep cars, not their ex-husband's boxes, in them."

My wife's an attorney. I got nothing.

I say, "Honey—and I mean that in the most condescending way possible—honey, that cutting board is actually mine."

"So you do have it?"

At this point in the conversation, my chi is so wadded up in the small of my back a million little pins wouldn't liberate it.

"No, Meg, I don't have the cutting board. At least I don't think I have *my* cutting board. Like I'm saying—and I shudder to say it to you again—but it could be in a box. My cutting board, yes, could be in a box, so I can't see it with the naked, un-cardboard–penetrating eye. It could be in a box in this apartment or in your very own parking garage. I really don't have the foggiest. After you run over the pitiful contents of my remaining boxes with your Jeep, you're welcome to look them over and see if you come across it. But frankly, I don't know what else to tell you."

She can pitch that sort of fit, but I'm not allowed.

"Is it going to be like this, James?" Her voice trembles, slightly, unconvincingly. "Are we really going to be like this?" she says. "Five years, James, five years of our lives. I know we're divorced, and I know you feel you weren't fairly represented, but do we really have to snip and claw?"

I look around to the walls of my apartment for something to focus on, just to look at, so I cannot think of snippy, clawing, damaging remarks, but the walls are bare.

There's a pause. In her mind, I imagine she's calling a mandatory do-over, because then suddenly she's sweet. It's scary.

"Hello, James... I'm making dinner... I have no cutting board... I have items right now on the counter to be cut, currently uncut. If you find the cutting board, will you please let me know?"

"Absolutely, Meg. I'll look for it right now."

"Thank you. And I'll just make something else for dinner."

"Good. What are we having?"

That took her a little off guard. Took us both, actually. I hear her lay the knife down.

"Good-bye, James."

On my cell phone, even after she hangs up, the little digital numbers keep counting for five, maybe ten more seconds as if she's still there.

"Good-bye, Meg."

That's where my mind drifts while I'm lying there with pins in my back. And I'm really not mad anymore, with a bunch of little pins in my chi. I mean, a little mad goes with the landscape these days. A general simmer of madness that never quite resolves. That's divorce, right? Come to think of it, that's marriage.

But here's the thing: I look at my watch.

I always wear a watch. (This is important, so let me assure you it's no exaggeration. In fact, it's an occupational hazard for someone who opens at a coffee shop, a reliable watch with a nasty alarm. People want their coffee first thing. Addicts. So you have to be earlier than first thing to get ready for them or you're in for an earful—a cranky, unkind, uncaffeinated bawling out. I always wear a watch.)

I am down to my skivvies under that sheet, lying there on the treatment table, and I don't even lift my arm to check the time, just sort of roll my wrist toward my head. The watch face is right there—close, almost too close to see it.

My eyes are a bit blurry without my glasses. The room is dim, the bulb above glows barely orange like a steady ember, and a little afternoon light seeps in through the blinds even though they're shut. The CD switches from "Bubbling Mountain Stream" into "Placid Meadow Rivulet," a distinction I've learned to make over months of alternative care. And I squint at my watch face because that's an eyeglass wearer's instinct, to squint. But then I have to open my eyes wide, wider than normal, just to see the watch face, it's that close.

August 19, Friday, 3:16 p.m.

I remember this moment exactly, glasses or no. No mistaking that.

I close my eyes again. I'm thinking, *I'll get out of here around four o'clock.* I wonder what time Meg gets home these days. I should go by the house and pick up another round of boxes. I don't have keys anymore, so Meg has to be there. But hopefully, I can get in and out before her new boyfriend, Doug Something-or-Other, shows up. He's a financial consultant with two kids, eight and five. His ex-wife is crazy. My wife tells me so, repeatedly, tells me all kinds of crazy things Doug's ex-wife does. I guess so I'll appreciate what kind of a pearl she's being to me. Tells me that and how much money he makes. And I think I can go by and grab a load before he gets there, then stop at the post office on the way home, and forget the book till tomorrow.

I drift a little and wonder what Meg will be wearing. We used to be married, so this is inbounds. I'm wondering if good ol' Doug has told her she can't cook yet, or if he still smiles and takes her out to dinner a lot. I'm thinking about her hair. Wondering if she'd straightened it that day. That was my favorite, even though her curls, which are natural, are excellent. But I've always liked it straightened, the way it smoothed across her forehead. The way, when straightened, she'd tie it back in a ponytail to work on dinner. Her awful dinners. She'd tie it back like she was about to knead bread for an army even if she was just opening cans and dumping them in a boiler pot. She worried about her hair getting in her way, like it was expensive silk she didn't want to have to dry clean. Even when she was slicing a boiled egg.

That's when it hit me. Something about a boiled egg. We had two of those egg-slicer contraptions. Absolutely essential, these. A blue one and a white one, both wedding gifts. You wouldn't think two completely different people would spring for the egg slicer. You wouldn't imagine Shoppy Mart would actually have two on the shelves. The white one, hanging in the dusty carton since the store opened, and a three-week wait for them to special order in blue. Somehow we got two.

And I remembered. The afternoon Meg told me she'd filed the papers, I stood over my first box in the middle of the kitchen with an egg slicer in each hand, thinking whether I should take both or just one. She rarely used them. I don't think she understood them, probably afraid her hair would get caught and shredded in one.

But I remember thinking, *No, Meg likes blue. She should have the blue one.*

I returned the blue egg slicer to the drawer by the oven and walked back over to the box. I'd written "Essentials" on the flap with a black marker. This was early in the moving process, when I still wrote things on the sides of the boxes. I'd just thrown junk in there—it was full, not what you'd call properly packed. Just a pile of stuff that happened to be piled inside a box.

I knelt down over this box thinking, *They'll never be together again.* And I was sad for the egg slicers, you know, for the blue one and the white one. I held the egg slicer up a second before I put it in, giving it a last good look at the kitchen. Then I laid it down.

On top of the cutting board.

That's when I remember. The cutting board. Lying on the acupuncture table, I could see it in the box so clearly, at such an angle. On top, inside the box marked "Essentials." Being the very first box I packed, I moved it to the garage, and surely, with all the boxes that came after it, it hadn't ever been moved. In fact, I knew exactly where it was. Anticipating so many boxes, I'd put it in the far corner. I was sure it was still in that corner by itself; I could see it.

And I want to give Meg that cutting board, even though it was mine. I want her to see I don't care about any of it.

That's when it happened. Water rippling, a lazy breeze wafting from the ceiling fan, and my eyes are closed. It felt like two, maybe three minutes since I'd checked my watch. Lying there, eyes closed, and I'm seeing down into that box, with the flaps open, the one marked "Essentials." I could see the egg slicer, slid to a corner next to a turkey baster, both of them on top of the cutting board, plain as day.

I want her to have this, I think. And I reach down…

The cutting board.

I'm standing there. Reaching down into the box. Touching that cutting board. I mean I'm actually there, in her garage. My eyes are open; there's a cutting board in my hand. It was my garage so I recognize it. My boxes, that dartboard, the hook where I used to hang my bike. See what I'm telling you? Suddenly I'm standing in my ex-wife's garage in my underwear with a cutting board in my hand. I have no idea how I got there, how I even got in. (I mentioned her changing the locks, right?)

I look at my bare legs sticking out of my skivvies. That's my hair on my chest. I check my watch, squinting because I don't have my glasses.

Still August 19, Friday, but now 3:19 p.m.

That was the first time it happened. This afternoon. And this is my first entry documenting my strange gift.

I slipped across space without using time.

I leapt.

have no pants.

Strange to say, once that moment or two of immediate shock of having instantaneously leapt across space wears off, no pants is still no pants. No matter how fantastically you got there, you're there with no pants.

"Oh, hey, Meg, oh, um, yeah, seems I found the cutting board..."

That wouldn't do. Not pantless.

I pad across the garage to the mail slot in the garage door. It's an old house, an old garage with an old garage door. Meg and I didn't find that mail slot till the second year of our marriage. Along with old bills from some very angry people. We could never figure why anyone would put a mail slot dead smack center in a garage door. Mail gets run over, slips under cars, or is drowned in oily puddles. Sometimes mail takes a fun ride around town on the car bumper. Most of the time we got mail in the mailbox like the rest of the neighborhood, but other times it was shoved recklessly into the least-tidy, least-lit, and least-used room of our home.

But Meg and I found other clever uses for the garage-door mail slot: we watched the neighbors, looked to see which unwanted person was ringing the doorbell, checked for cars parked in the drive.

So I creak open the mail-slot door and crouch to look out. No sign of Meg's Jeep. I had time.

I open the door to the kitchen, stick my head through.

"Hey, Meg!" No answer.

The dogs come bounding around the corner, thrilled to have a guest. Perhaps they still recognized Daddy's voice, but I've often suspected they'd greet uninvited dogcatchers or invading assassins with the same unbridled glee.

"Down! Get down!"

Without clothes, a man shies from large, happy dogs prone to jumping up and flopping a paw on either shoulder.

"Down, buddies!" I hide behind the garage door. They slam into it merrily.

Ponzy is a seventy-five-pound German shepherd known for jumping through the den window at the appearance of the meter man or the sound of thunder. Through, not out. Those windows don't open. Unless a German shepherd shatters the glass. Chunky is a ninety-pound chocolate Labrador who earned his name as a pup by decimating a can of Chunky soup. One morning I found a very thin, shiny, tooth-punctured piece of aluminum on his bed. After looking two hours and finding a couple of stray English peas, I figured out that flat piece of tin was once a full can of Chunky soup left too low in an open pantry. He'd eaten it, label and all, leaving no stew juice anywhere as a clue.

My brutes claw the door and whine affectionately.

"Hold on, boys!"

I sought pants at any cost and pick up a screwdriver to open a few of my boxes. Luckily, I had wrapped a vase in an old pair of jeans so it wouldn't break. Meg had thought this a poor way to pack, but then, she couldn't have foreseen the pants paying off in this particular manner. I pull on the jeans. The vase drops and cracks.

"Hey, buddies! Good boys!" I swat the dogs down with the cutting board as I walk through the kitchen.

"I'm home."

Meg could be home anytime. Fridays were her short day. I still need a shirt, so I go to our bedroom. (Sorry, divorce very recent, my ex-wife's bedroom.) Call it instinct or perhaps desperation, but under the circumstances, looking for a shirt in my old closet wasn't the oddest thing I might have done. I wasn't spying.

And I find one: a white oxford, pressed and starched. I take it off the hanger. I was touched, really, she never did my shirts. Deeply touched and almost willing to forgive a multitude of snips and claws. It was so...

Then I realize: It isn't my size. It isn't mine! It's Doug's. Five white, starched shirts hang in my wife's closet. She'd picked up the man's laundry. She never folded my socks, not once in five years. I ravage the shirt in my hand, wrinkling it mercilessly, cracking the heavy starch until I find the cleaner's tag. "Williams."

She had taken Dougie's shirts to the cleaners, not just picked them up, but dropped them off under her name! Picking up somebody's laundry, you might do that, you know, even for someone you barely knew, if you were going anyway and they've asked, "Hey, can you grab mine?" But dropping off and picking up! Paying to have his shirts cleaned. His shirts under her name.

Her maiden name.

"Down, boys! I'm not in the mood!" I yell.

And my dogs know this other mood. They give up on me and roughhouse each other down the hall.

I pull on Dougie's shirt. Even if it's a bit small, it's better than no shirt. *I'll just roll up the midget's sleeves,* I think. But strangely, the shirt hurts. Yes, it's small under the armpits, but I mean it actually hurts me. Sharp pains up and down my back. Like the financial consultant with the crazy ex-wife cast a spell on his shirts so that only he could wear them. Like how only the Lone Ranger could ride Silver.

When I drop my arms and take a step, pain shoots through my back like a bunch of little pins sticking...

(Of course, I'm an idiot, but this is proof! I didn't black out and wander over to the house after my appointment. On a treatment table, then the garage. No pants. Pins still in my back. I didn't imagine a thing.)

I take the shirt off and hunch toward the bathroom mirror. I rummage the sink drawer for Meg's round face mirror, the one she used to pluck her eyebrows or to check how her hair looked from the back.

I turn like Meg, the mirror in one hand looking for the bathroom mirror behind me. I strain my other arm around to pull out the pins, dropping them one by one into the sink. I get the ones on my neck and the two by each thumb. After a thorough visual check, the best possible without my glasses, I take down a towel. There's no other way. Courageously and suddenly, I dry my back.

No more pain. I had them all.

That's when I hear the front door unlock. Dogs run and skid across the hardwood to greet Mommy's return. Putting on Doug's shirt quickly, I button it up wrong, one button off. I tuck it in anyway.

"Meg?" I call out.

The scream of an ex-wife startled by her ex-husband is a chilling, razorlike event. I hear dogs running for safety. Things from a flung purse scatter and roll. I hear Meg gasping for breath.

She catches that breath. "Holy mother of…James!"

I come out of the bathroom, hands raised somewhere between a conjured ghost and a captured fugitive.

"Honey…"

"You…you! James, I swear…what the…"

"Honey, I can explain." Then I hear myself. "No. No, honey, I can't explain."

"That's not your shirt!"

"I cannot even begin to explain this, but I can tell you what happened."

"Who do you think you are?"

"Meg, I need to tell you what happened."

"Yes. Yes, James, you do!"

"I need to tell you because I think I might be crazy."

"Are we voting? Because if we are, it's unanimous. You're completely crazy if you think you can walk in here while I'm gone and…"

"Honey…"

"How did you get in here?" She looks down the hall, back into the den, up at the pull-down attic door.

"Honey…"

"I changed the locks!"

"Honey…"

"Did you break a window?"

She goes in motion. Rushing all through the house, yelling and checking doors.

"Meg?"

"Did your dog break that window again, and you thought you could just crawl on in?"

She yanks at the sliding patio door, mugs the knob on the back door, double-checks the den window, circles back, and crouches by the front door to see if the lock has been jimmied.

I'm flattered that she thought, even briefly, that I could jimmy a lock. "Honey…"

Standing in the entryway, she glares at me. "How did you get in here?"

I open my mouth to start the impossible answer, but she goes in motion again. "That's not your shirt!"

She shoves past me and positions herself in the middle of her bedroom as if she were a wrestler challenging all comers.

"What have you been doing in here?"

"Meg, I don't know how to tell you this, but…"

"Where are your glasses?"

A car honk causes both of us to stop. I practice innocent blinking. Definitely honking, from the driveway. Three polite taps. Short separate taps, annoying ones. From her face, I could see Meg and I still agreed on some things. Who honks politely?

"You stand right there. Do not move! Do not touch or look or walk! Stand."

I move.

As she marches out to the driveway, I walk over to the front door. It was Dougie, in his Lexus. He was the polite honker. Watching through the door crack, not the door-door, that wasn't at all safe, but the crack-near-the-hinges crack, it seems Meg clarifies to Douglas a thing or two about honking at women from driveways. She spins to come marching back, twists a heel on her shoe, and stumbles. With a hand balanced on Dougie's hood, she takes off both her shoes and throws them at a tree, one by one. She nails it on that second try.

I scurry back and put my feet in the exact position they had been when she left.

She throws open the screen door. We apparently no longer own dogs. Not a peep, nor a paw. I surrender my arms up again.

"Get out of here!"

"Meg…"

"No!" She lunges toward me, stops, rethinks, then turns and slams the front door, locking it from the inside.

"Tell me how you got in here—then get out of here."

"I came in the house from the garage." See, I've never lied to Meg.

"Your garage-door opener still works?" she yells. "They promised me they changed that, too! Give me that garage-door opener."

"You have my garage-door opener."

"Apparently not!"

From an outside perspective, she would still seem to be screaming. Her voice is loud. It is shrill. It's definitely still angry. There are arm motions—dangerous, unhappy arm motions. But her hair had begun to loosen, to fall from its pins. I know this sign. Her hair is not unconnected to her anger. She pinned it up, but the pin was giving way, bit by bit, like a taut rope fraying. Curls were breaking out, coiling and rising, stretching and loosening, and though one would not say this is unlike Medusa, I could tell she was calming down.

"Honey…"

"Apparently not!"

Repetition. Not for effect, but for gathering air. I knew this too. She was definitely cooling.

"Apparently you can open the garage door, unless you crawled through the mail slot."

There is this curious pause where we eyeball each other blank-faced, breathing, pondering that strange possibility.

"Meg, can I tell you something?"

She puts her hands on her hips, drops her chin. Having assaulted a tree with her shoes, she's barefoot. She wraps one foot over the other. "If you tell me you love me, I swear I'll crush your collarbone with that brass lamp."

I have always feared that heavy brass lamp.

"Just listen. Okay, Meg? Listen to the whole thing till I hold up three fingers, and then you'll know I'm done. Three fingers. Like a Boy Scout. Okay? But listen to the whole thing before you choose how to hurt and destroy me."

She stops blinking.

"Like a Boy Scout. Okay?"

Her nostrils flare.

"Good. I'll take those flared nostrils as you saying the letters *O* and *K*."

I squint at my watch. 3:42 p.m.

"Where do I go on Fridays between three o'clock and four o'clock? Semi-rhetorical, Meg, do not speak. I go, as you know, to acupuncture. From three all the way to four, I lie on a table with pins in my back. Not an outpatient sort of deal. You don't get to leave before they take out the pins, and I believe they may reuse them, but let's not think about that now. My point: it takes the whole sixty-minute hour. That's where I was approximately twenty-three minutes ago. I was lying on a table with pins in my back. Then, Meg, something happened, and this is the strange part. I was lying there, and I thought of you. Oh—not that I thought of you! That's not the strange part. Stay with me, Meg, stay with me. You're doing great! Anyway, I thought of you, not in the least bit strange for me. I thought specifically of being here, in the garage. A little strange, but it gets stranger. And as I was *thinking* about being in the garage, suddenly…I was *in* the garage."

She's blinking again, but otherwise unresponsive.

"That's the strange part, Meg."

She just stares.

"Oh!" I hold up three fingers.

"How much coffee have you had today?" she asks.

This is good. Quietly insulting, Meg was back. I pick up her cell phone from where it had fallen on the floor.

"Call her?"

"Call who?"

I grab the phone book off the shelf and start thumbing through it.

"We'll call my acupuncturist. You ask her."

"James…"

"Here it is. Two-six-eight…" I start dialing.

"James…"

"Two-six-eight-one-four-five-five."

"James?"

"Here, Meg," I hand her the cell phone. "Ask her where I am right now."

She listens. When she hears that it's actually ringing, she slams the phone shut.

"Good heavens, I'm not calling your doctor."

"Acupuncturist."

"You think she thinks you're still there?"

I flinch. "Wait! What if I am? Here and still there too? Impossible…"

"James?"

We both turn at the polite knock on the door. Three short knocks. Then Dougie's muffled voice from the outside.

"Darling, the kids are getting restless."

He punches up that *darling* whenever I'm around.

"Sorry," she says to me, "we were going to the park. We just stopped to get Doug's laundry."

His laundry. I couldn't speak.

She opens the door a crack, whispers to her boyfriend, then returns.

"I'm sorry, James. I have no idea what you're trying to tell me, but there's no excuse for you breaking in—"

"Meg, I didn't—"

"No, James. No!"

She holds up three fingers, which she points and shakes at my head as if to strike me with silence.

"Now you listen to me! It doesn't matter how; it's still basically breaking in. I wouldn't break into your apartment just because I could, even if I thought I had a good reason. It's not right. And I'm sorry if you missed your appointment, and I'm sorry I yelled at you about your boxes. I know that's what you were doing, trying to get those boxes, and yes, you need to get them out of there. But no, James, no, it is not all right for you to sneak in here, even if it was once your house. It's not now. I'm sorry. That's what happens when two people divorce. Okay...okay?"

I nod.

"Okay, then." She withdraws her pointed three fingers as if to release me.

"You did the finger thing backward."

"What?"

"You were supposed to hold up three fingers after you were done speaking."

"I don't like the whole three-finger thing..."

"No, you just did it wrong."

"Maybe I did, James, but so did you."

"Right, but I was just trying to show you..."

"I don't like the finger game, okay? It's dumb."

"Right, it's very dumb. I'm sorry, Meg."

We ended up here too often. I think this is why we got divorced. Too often, two people exhausted over whatever they were arguing about.

"Look, I have to go," She says. "Doug's waiting. And James—"

"Do you really understand what I've told you?"

"And, James, you have to go too."

"I'm telling you I leapt here."

Meg tucks her hair behind her ear. "You what?"

"I didn't break in! I was in one place, I thought of you, and bam—suddenly, I'm in the garage."

"You were thinking of me?"

"At the acupuncturist's. I was thinking about you and the cutting board."

"So you found it?"

"Well, yes, actually, but that's sort of off the point."

I walk into the bathroom, grab the cutting board, and hand it to her.

Holding it, she frowns and cocks her head as if she just remembered missing something.

"Where's your car?" she asks, opening the door and going out onto the porch.

"Don't you listen? I didn't drive here. I just…sort of…showed up."

"Yes, I've been meaning to say something about that. You've got to stop just showing up. Call first. It makes Doug jumpy."

"I don't mean I stopped by unannounced. I mean I appeared out of thin air."

"Without your car?"

"Meg, now you're just not trying. You can say I'm an idiot, I have years of practice with that. But don't act like I'm not saying what I'm saying."

The screen door opens a crack, and Doug sticks his nose inside.

I say, "She heard you, Doug, she's coming."

"Oh…I didn't see your car, didn't know you were here. Excuse me."

He shuts the door behind him. He shuts it hard for Doug.

"Thanks, James," Meg scowls at me. "Thanks a lot."

She opens the door. Meg can open a door louder than Doug slams one.

"Doug!" She calls out to him. "I'll be right out."

He doesn't turn around as he walks back to his Lexus.

"James, I have to go."

"Margaret." I put a hand on her arm. It was the first time I'd touched her since she'd announced she wanted a divorce.

"Tell me, please. I need to know. Do you believe me?"

Meg stares at me, unsure if she wants to be angry again. "I don't know what else to say to you right now." She walks past me into the bathroom, to fix her hair.

"I've never lied to you, Meg," I say, but I knew the conversation was over. All over. As I walk out the front, I say, "Not once, Meg. Not once."

On the porch I can hear her say, "There's a bunch of little pins in my sink?"

But it was over.

I start walking. I pass Doug's Lexus, and his kids wave at me. I wave back. Doug pretends he doesn't see any of that. At the end of the drive, I start walking in the direction of my acupuncturist's. I suppose I need to go back, pick up my clothes, my glasses, my wallet, my car. I'm guessing those will still be at my acupuncturist's. But who really knows? I'm not where I'm supposed to be.

As I walk, I try to flatten the bulge in my shirt and realize it bulges because I misbuttoned it, so I leave it be. The sidewalk is hot. I have no shoes.

And Meg doesn't believe me.

I hear one long blare of a car horn. I turn and see Doug's Lexus slowing behind me, Meg's hand reaching over to the horn. Her window slides down.

"If you really don't have your car, we can take you." Meg offers this, though neither she nor Doug look overly pleased.

"Get in back with the kids."

I get in. Doug's kids look at me as if I were a criminal. Between the driveway and now, someone has explained who I am.

Meg looks in the rearview mirror and asks, "Where do you want us to drop you?"

"My stuff is still at the acupuncturist's, I guess."

"Tell Doug where to go."

She says this, and that's all. She won't speak to me again the rest of the ride. But her eyes look back at me in the mirror, and occasionally I catch them. Her eyes and my eyes. Something is lost between them. We both feel it. Something no longer there. Some good thing, one last good thing, lost.

3

I decide to see a priest.

Perhaps not the obvious choice. But then, I sort of defy anyone to pop out the obvious protocol for bodily transspatial meta-hiccups of the personal sort. Slows opinions down a bit, huh?

For the record, riding in Doug's car between the kiddies, I also consider consulting a psychologist or a doctor. But I figure, a *doctor* doctor would pretty much only prescribe me a sedative—a family-size, Sam's Club box of sedatives to calm my undeniably overwrought condition. And I wouldn't have passed on a round of that right then, had it been handy. But I didn't think a doctor would believe me. Wouldn't even drive down believing-me street, let alone park there. Even Meg thought I was crazy.

If a *doctor* doctor thinks you're crazy enough, dangerous enough, he might ease his finger under the desk and press the hidden red button. Alert the proper authorities. Or better yet, his nurse might slip you a stack of papers to sign, and before you've retracted the ballpoint, bam—you're strapped to a cot with an endless supply of the happy juice pumped into your arm, and for the next five years you're peeing in your personal Ziploc baggie Velcroed around your waist.

No thanks.

As for the shrink, well, I figure that would be the same song, second verse. There's even more likelihood for alarmed professional retribution—sedation and explanation. Sedation for the crazies, explanation of the crazies by digging into my remarkably uneventful, but nonetheless nervous, childhood, my stunted-to-the-point-of-dwarfed emotional maturity, my exceedingly bad marriage, my fault for the exceedingly bad marriage, my fault for most exceedingly bad things in the world, my penchant for abusing the word *exceedingly*.

No, definitely a priest. A candle-trimming, discreet, bound-by-God-not-to-blab-a-word priest. Besides, priests already believe a stack of impossible things, right? Whether or not I believed them myself, I wanted someone to believe me.

Regarding belief: I'm mostly Catholic. Okay, Catholic most of the way. The way I see it, there are degrees of belief. I suppose that wouldn't be the sort of thing that would sink an eightball with a priest or a nun. It's not information you'd just pony up unless you genuinely wanted a rather lengthy, disapproving lecture on belief, replete with a personal guilt trip for your aiding and abetting the crucifixion of God. I don't just tell priests any ol' idea that pops in the brain, nor should you. But we've all got a little notched knob when it comes to believing in God. Even if you don't intend to, we all do, every day. We calibrate.

So I'm definitely more Catholic than I am anything else. More Christian than I am, say, Buddhist or Communist. In fact, I don't have any idea what a Buddhist is supposed to believe to get the Buddhist club card. Or a Communist either. Seems like you'd have to read a few key, very dry books about those subjects and be pretty impressed,

impressed enough to implement an idea or two on some personal scale, great or small. Meditate on your lunch break. Deny the individual. Buy a loaf of bread and distribute one slice into all your neighbors' mailboxes.

I do know I was christened. I know I was forced to comb my hair and go to Mass once or twice every month until I learned to drive a car. After that, I took myself to Mass less regularly. Groomed less regularly. I recognize Latin. I know when to stand, when to kneel. I don't fear grown men slinging water on a crowd of well-dressed people. I don't just pile out; I wait politely for the priest and procession to leave first. I think candles are holy and magic because they're so quiet, because they stand in for someone's prayer.

After college, for a long while, I only went in for the big Masses: Easter and Christmas. Felt a little fat and depressed, marginally lascivious during Lent.

But for the past year, I've been going to Mass every week. Maybe because my marriage was going sour? Nonetheless I went. One might say I've been attending Mass "religiously." So that's not simply redundant, what I mean is that I made myself go like it meant something.

And sometimes it did. I can remember days when the Lord's Prayer—recited out loud and holding a stranger's hand, a stranger who in turn was holding the next stranger's hand—felt like something bigger than all of us. Better than just everybody's decent intention to show up and make it through the "Go in peace." I remember a Mass or two where the wafer seemed to melt on my tongue, and I wondered if God could actually be absorbed into a body, into a life, like a divine vitamin. I don't mean that stupidly, frivolously. I mean the thought that I might actually, suddenly, be a better person because of proximity to God. A surer person, one more apt to do a good turn. A person less consumed with how it confused me to be me—and more thoughtful of how confusing it might be to be you.

I remember a moment or two from a homily; bothered me for a whole week. I remember something about a tax collector told to get up from his tax table and follow Christ. That's it. Impossible. For all this guy knows, a crazy, prophetic Jewish peasant walks by—this crowd of riffraff around him—and stops just to tell this guy to up and leave his job, leave his money right there on the table and come along.

"Follow me."

That's it, that's all he gets. Get up. You. Come along.

And the crazier part is—he does it. He leaves everything he's doing and tags along for the rest of his life. And the twist? Come to find out he's Matthew. He's the one writing the book. "The Gospel according to…" That guy. I kept thinking, *That guy made saint? Him? What about all the others?* How many times did Jesus pull that maneuver on some stranger, that sudden eyeball-to-eyeball "Follow me." Of all the times the Gospels record that he does do that, how many more times are not recorded? Was he doing it all the time, like hourly, and how often does it work? In a couple of spots, Jesus adds, "Sell everything you got and follow me." That doesn't pan out, of course. Matthew tells you it doesn't, but sometimes it works. When a guy actually follows, I've wondered, how often does he stick with it? All the way? Do they all become saints in the end?

That's been going on in my head for a while now. And I guess if you puzzle a homily out that far you're further along than the God's-Name-in-Vain sort and a little past the Beg-God's-Help-Only-When-in-a-Pickle sort. Further down the believing road, I'd say. Not much, but a bit. I definitely don't cross myself after meals or when I see a serving tray with a picture of Mary on it.

So I guess I believe. Or I'm certain that I don't *not* believe. I'll jump on the Christians' team over the Communists' any day. If I'm going in the game, I know which way I'm kicking, right?

That's what I mean by degrees of belief.

Meg and Doug drop me off by my car in the acupuncturist's parking lot. I've never been so happy to see an '88 Volvo. They drop me out, keep the car running, don't stick around for my reappearance. As they're backing out of the space, Meg puts on her darkest sunglasses, bites her top lip, and adjusts the radio. She can't even look out the window at me.

And it's better that they don't stay because I'm going to lie to my acupuncturist. I have no intention of trying to explain the truth to her. This is way beyond alternative care. I just hope she isn't the kind of lady to pilfer a wallet. She'd never struck me that way, but then again, her job is just a hop-skip up from voodoo. And there's important stuff in my wallet.

Quietly, slowly, I open the front door to her office.

But it doesn't matter how quietly I do it. I've forgotten about the little electric bell that goes off every time the door is opened. An electric chime dings like you're in a department store. Often she's in one of the treatment rooms sticking folks when clients come in, that's why the bell.

Hearing it, she comes out of the second treatment room, smiling.

A note about acupuncturists: They smile. Often and unrelentingly. This isn't a bad or a fake thing. Of the few I've met, they're all smilers, placid, peaceful sorts. Like whatever kinks they had in their chi, they smoothed out years ago. They're so relaxed, so "in-tune," it's like they can smell a wadded chi and see right through you into your tangle. I've seen my acupuncturist flinch when she looks at my back; it's that tangible to her. I think she flinches when I drive up.

She's smiling now. "Hi, James."

Completely happy, poker-faced. Whatever she thinks, she's not tipping me a glance.

"Sorry," I say. I haven't worked this speech out. I should think these things through before I open my mouth, but I just start talking.

"Sorry. I had to come back. I have to get my stuff…in that room? I didn't mean to leave my stuff for you to…how much do I owe you?"

It's a dumb question. I always pay the exact same amount, every time. A ten-dollar copay. Then again, dumb—but not out of the ordinary. I always ask her how much I owe, although it's always ten bucks. Acupuncturists don't go in for rate charts. They live simpler, same rate per visit. I've a more pay-by-the-pin mentality.

"I hoped you'd come back for your things. I didn't quite know what to do with them."

She picks up a plastic shopping bag by her desk. She'd folded my things neatly and put them in a bag. My glasses lay on top. I put them on; I can think better with them on. They smell funny. She'd cleaned the lenses with rubbing alcohol.

"Yeah, I'm real sorry about that," I say, setting down the bag and fumbling through it for my wallet. I take out a ten and hand it to her.

She smiles and nods appreciatively.

"Yeah, something sort of happened, and I, um, had to take care of it right away."

"Sure," she says. She's completely unaffected by my disappearance. Perhaps worried *for* me, but not about her money. *She* is a placid meadow rivulet.

She walks to her desk to write me a receipt.

"I would have said something, but I was gone so quickly, when I thought about telling you…I, uh, came right back."

"No worries," she says. "Have a good afternoon."

And she means it. Nothing fazes this woman. Not that she isn't bright, just nothing bothers her. For a moment, I think, I should tell her what happened. Try my crazy story out again, give crazy another shot. Maybe even if she didn't believe me, she wouldn't treat me like a criminal. Like an ex-husband.

Instead, I blurt out, "Do you reuse the pins?"

I don't know why I asked. Yes, I do. I've always been mortified to think she reuses the pins. Disease just itching to spread. Even if you drown them in rubbing alcohol, it seems unsafe.

She doesn't answer. She seems to contemplate the motive for my question, perhaps connecting it to my sudden flight. Perhaps she's frightened by the invisible malignancy of knots she sees in my chi. We just stare at each other. She smiles. I notice my poorly buttoned shirt again. Dougie's shirt. I wait to see if she'll ask me for her pins back.

She doesn't. She's way too peaceful for that. But I can tell she's wondering about them.

I can never go back there.

The Volvo starts, so let's not pretend the entire day was unlucky. In fact, alone now, with my glasses back on and my wallet safe, I begin appraising things differently.

I corrected my metaphysical mishap with minor casualties. I mean, think about it: I could have been lying, all pinned up, and thinking about speeding traffic. I could've been thinking about the mall.

Cincinnati.

Helicopters, what about those?

What if I'd been thinking about cooing pigeons on the ledges of the bank downtown? Or what if I had been daydreaming about a nice cup of espresso and beamed my mostly naked self to my very public workplace? For a moment, I count my blessings and I am calm.

Now it's 4:32 p.m. Rush hour in this city is not the worst in the world, but the priest I'm headed to see works downtown. I speed up and merge onto the interstate. The notion of talking with someone besides myself, someone who might at least hear what I'm saying, who won't throw me out on the lawn—well, it feels like a step toward something positive. I was doing something about my problem, and that felt good. I punch the gas and think, *Right. You definitely should speak to someone. Before it happens again.*

Pure heart-stopping panic. Who said it would happen again? I have no precedent, personal or historical, scientific or hallucinatory.

Neither CNN nor comic books nor Dial-A-Prayer nor Google has any wisdom on this matter. What are the warning signs? I experienced no tingling in my left arm, no sudden weight loss, no curious blotches to my peripheral vision. I didn't rub any old Arabian lamps, hadn't broken a chain letter, wasn't bitten by a radioactive cutting board. It just happened.

The thought that I didn't know what came next, when it would come next, whether or not the impossible would happen again, horrifies me. Who lives their lives moment by startling moment?

Then I think, *Hey, Ace, what if it happens while you're driving?*

Immediately I jam the car into second gear, lurch over into the slow lane, and take the first exit off the interstate. The Volvo makes new and interesting noises. But if a driverless Volvo suddenly careens off the road, it won't be going seventy miles per hour. I put on my hazards and drive like my grandmother after she sips a daiquiri.

Like that I drive, miserably slow, holding my breath. You have no idea how far things really are until you drive somewhere in first gear. Like watching tea steep. I'm driving, thinking, *Man, I wish I was already there…no. No, I don't. Time-out. Recall. Uncle. I do not wish any such thing.*

I park at a meter outside the cathedral. Into this meter I pump all the change in my pockets, and I only get fifty-two minutes, leaving me still twelve minutes shy of the six o'clock cutoff. It's been that kind of day, you know? Like dropping your keys three times trying to lock your front door when you're late for work and you just know in your bones you should go back to bed? The whole day like an inside-out sock.

There's no more change on the Volvo's floorboard, not under the mats, not in the ashtray. I spend nearly twelve minutes looking for more change, so if I'd only waited to put my original change in…that kind of day.

Not one fuzzy nickel.

Father Chavez is a good man, a reasonable one. He's been at Saint John's for fifteen years or so, as long as I can remember. We've been chatting quite a bit lately—sometimes after Mass, sometimes when I stop by after an early weekday shift and bring him a hot chocolate. He's the kind of priest who'll sit down anywhere with you: on a pew, outside in the grass, on the cathedral stoop, at the kitchen table in the church refectory. He's a quick sitter, crossing his legs and leaning forward to hear you better. He nods and scratches his head, pulls at his ears. I like that about him, that he doesn't make you go into a box, the confession box, or his office. He's always busy, but always stopping what he's doing to sit down and chat with somebody. That's probably why he's always busy. I guess people bother him a lot with their troubled stories, but this story was a doozy. Good guy or no, I feel I'd better ease him into this one.

Father Chavez sees me. "James!" He stops preparing the altar for evening Mass.

"Father," I say.

He walks down the steps, turns, kneels, and crosses himself. All priest, this guy. He stands for just a moment to whisper something, then he turns and shakes my hand.

"James, how are you?"

"Can we speak for a minute, Father?" I ask.

"A few minutes, yes. I've Mass at six o'clock. What can we do?"

I wonder if he means God—"we" can do? It's like he's bringing God to our meeting, and I'm not sure I like that.

"Something's happened to me, Father," I say.

"Sit, sit."

I walk him down the center aisle to a pew a few rows from the front. Four rows back, to be exact. I don't know why no one ever sits on the first pew, but it's just not done. Too close to the action. What if they ask for audience participation? Too close to the God area.

"Father," I start. "We can speak, right? It's like this. Just a couple of hours ago, I…"

He does that cross-legged bit, leans, his face turns instantly intense. Instant fervor, this guy.

"Whoa! I didn't shoot anybody or anything," I say.

He was a priest, after all. I don't want him to ready himself for something murderous. We are not technically in the confession zone, so I'm not sure if we're covered by the no-disclosure clause.

"I haven't done anything wrong—or not that I know of. I mean, yeah, I've probably screwed something up this past week, but that has nothing to do with what I want to tell you. In fact, I don't think any-thing about it classifies in the sin category, so don't worry."

"I'm not worried, James."

"Okay. Good. Stay just like that. You might be worried, in a minute," I say.

People are already coming in for Mass. You know, old ladies who feel they need to show up way early or it won't count. Maybe they're just inverterately early. Old people do that, their whole day: a half-cup of coffee, the paper, lunch, Oprah, Mass, and time spent getting places early.

And I don't know how to start: do you just blurt out a crazy, impossible thing, or do you chitchat first? I don't want to freak out a priest right before he has to do Mass.

So I say, "The Bible's full of fantastical elements, right?"

"Some," he answers.

"Healing the blind, right? There's a pack of that going on, huh?"

"Some."

"Fish and loaves, right?"

"There are several accounts of feeding a multitude with very little capital," he says.

"Right! Fantastic stuff."

I just sit there watching the old people creep around and slowly fumble with the kneelers.

"Fantastic," I repeat. I sound like I'm giving a pep talk, like three cheers for the Bible, as if I'd just read the book and had no idea how much crazy stuff would be in it.

"How about imperviousness to fire?"

"Old Testament. Daniel would be your book."

I knew that one; I'm just feeling him out.

I say, "How about flying?"

"Flying?" he asks.

"Yeah, flying."

"I take it you don't mean birds?"

"No, like people. Look, up in the sky, it's a bird, it's a plane, no…it's Habakkuk…that bit?"

He scratches his head, crosses his legs the other way.

"No. I can't think of any humans flying in the Bible."

"Perfect. How about, say, special aquatic powers?"

"Are you asking me if there are good swimming passages?"

"No, I mean like talking to fish."

My comic-book reading was very limited as a child. My mom never bought me the cool ones because there must have been some discount, generic comic-book rack at the grocery store. Those are the ones my mom would have thrown in the cart. I got *Archie, Betty and Veronica, Aquaman,* and that man in the iron suit. I can't remember his name.

Father Chavez says, "Jonah was swallowed by a whale, but I don't think they discussed it."

"Right, but being swallowed by a whale, that counts? At least, semi-fantastic. Recovering from that, doing a fish-break, and walking back to town. And there are seas parting down the middle, right?"

"Yes…wait a minute… Jesus talked to fish."

"Really?" That I didn't remember. Of course, I'm thinking dolphins, and Father Chavez, he means trout or whatever fish are indigenous to the Dead Sea. Tilapia, maybe. If the sea has *dead* in the title, are there fish? Living fish?

Anyway, he's getting into it now. He's bobbing back and forward with his legs crossed like he's fine with this game.

"Yes," he says, "Jesus talked fish into swimming into his disciples' nets."

"Just like Aquaman!"

I say this with a flair of surprised discovery and actually slap the priest's arm like we're buddies, like we just realized we were at the same baseball game years ago and saw the same home run.

"Technically," he says, "I don't think Aquaman talked fish into the fishermen's boats. Against his Aquaman code. I think he was generally too fond of fish to send them off to be eaten."

"Good point. Jesus was on the fisherman's side."

"Right. Not Aquaman," he says. "Definitely on the fish side. But the same fish-talking ability, in a way. And then there's the water. The Bible says he talked to the water; Jesus spoke and calmed waves. Technically, again, Jesus was probably talking to his Father about the waves, not so much at the waves."

"I don't think Aquaman could do that one."

"I believe not."

A little elderly lady across the aisle scowls at us. Perhaps we are talking too loudly. Perhaps we are talking too stupidly. She rattles her rosary at me.

"Sorry, Senora Alvarez," Father Chavez apologizes. He lowers his voice. "What's this about, James?"

"Right," I say. I look around and lean in close. I whisper, "Father, what about leaping from place to place?"

"You mean like superhuman jumping?"

"No, Father. Not jumping. And, for reference sake, that'd be the Incredible Hulk. No, I mean more like beaming. Instantaneous transport of one's body to another location. Like *Star Trek,* but without the molecular static mumbo jumbo. Just snap"—I snap for effect—"and you're there?"

"Just snap?" He snaps with his right hand, then suddenly opens his left, palm up. That was much better.

"Exactly. I call it leaping."

There. That's where I mess up. I say "leaping" with far too much intensity. I roll the word out there like it's a gold coin, like leaping means out the window with the stolen microfilm. Even Mrs. Alvarez could tell I thought I leapt. I stare at her hard until she bows her head again.

"In the Gospels," says Father Chavez. "I recall something of the sort."

I'm surprised. That's craziness. No, really. I had no idea. All this blah-blah was merely my lead-in to asking if I'd come unglued.

He says, "Once Jesus was cornered by a mob; they intended to kill him. And the Gospels say he suddenly wasn't there. He shows up next in another town."

"No way," I say.

"Yes, it's in there," he says.

"Get *out* of here!" I say.

Mrs. Alvarez thinks I mean her. She's appalled. She says something in Spanish. I cross myself and apologize.

"James? What's this about?"

"So it's possible?" I ask.

"Well. It was a moment of life or death; so it seems, it was necessary."

"And you believe that?"

He smiles at me. "I don't believe in Aquaman or Santa Claus, James. But yes, I believe the miraculous surrounded the Son of God while he was on this earth."

That sounded like a priest. That's what I wanted.

"Do you think it happens to anyone else?"

He looks at me puzzled, and can you blame him? I barely tithe. I'm probably not the best Mass-goer he's got. I've never bought one raffle ticket.

But he answers, "I don't recall any mention in the Bible of anyone else doing so."

"No, I mean…" I check to make sure Mrs. Alvarez's lips are muttering, that she's praying, not just bowing and eavesdropping.

"No, I mean, do you think it could happen again? To anyone today?"

Again, I blow it. Too crazy, too whispery, too genuinely concerned. I wiggle my fingers in front of me too much like I'm casting a spell on my own chin. I might as well have come to church wearing a cape and tall shiny red boots. Strapped a cat on my head and asked if anyone liked my hat.

Father Chavez's face turns a worried corner. He leans back, folds his hands together. His forehead furrows, and he seems unsure.

It's a bad feeling, worrying a good priest.

"I don't know for certain, James," he says. "Why do you ask?"

I can't speak. I remember Meg's face when she threw her shoes at the tree. I think I hear Mrs. Alvarez praying for me. My shirt is buttoned wrong.

"No reason."

More people are coming in the cathedral now because the Mass begins promptly at six. Other people in robes are trying to get the Father's attention.

"Stay for Mass, James." Father Chavez says. He stands up, signals to the others that he's coming. He presses my shoulder in that priestly way. "We can talk afterward."

"I have to go," I say.

"No, James, please. I have to catch one or two folks after, but then we can—"

"No, no. Thank you, Father. It was just a silly question."

He looks at me. He doesn't seem to know how to help.

So he offers, "Like I've said, there is some record of such a thing. Leaping, as you called it. After his resurrection, Jesus did it all the time, but that's different. With resurrected people, you can imagine, it's a whole new ball game. But there's the one instance I mentioned, maybe others. Of Jesus, I mean, of an unresurrected Jesus, doing that."

"Okay. Great. Thanks for your help, Father."

"Would you like to finish our talk after Mass?"

"Oh no. Thank you though, Father," I say. My voice lilts, and I wrinkle my nose cutely, like he's offered me a finger sandwich or a meatball on a toothpick.

But he's still looking at me. I'm afraid he's going to ask me something too direct, and I don't want to lie to a priest in a church. He knows I'm trapped, so he simply leaves the invitation open.

"Have a good evening, James. Take care."

He walks away and steps through a door behind the altar, comes back out in his robe. He's quick at that. As I sit there in the pew, Mrs. Alvarez's courage grows now that I am alone. With no priest to protect me, she grunts and stares freely. I smile at her, give her a kind wave, and she scowls. Sensing she'd be happier if I acted more churchy, I pull down the kneeler.

Lowering myself, I think, *How do you pray about this?*

Regarding prayer: I've prayed before, right? But they were mostly the stock prayers, borrowed prayers mumbled like passwords or the Pledge of Allegiance. I've said words *toward* God. I've shot requests God-ward. But I've never had a question, not a *real* question, that I didn't already know how I wanted God to answer. I usually tell God, more or less humbly, what I've already decided.

If things go well, sometimes I give God credit, but I don't usually ask for a thing, then wait to see if God answers. I'm not sure you should. And I've certainly never asked God about impossible things. Why bother God? And I don't even know what I want now; it's just that what's happened makes no sense.

I bow and press my forehead on my folded hands resting on the pew in front of me—a lot like praying but without using words. Plus I keep my eyes open. It seems safer. I can't really think of anything to say, so I look down and I see it: in the rack, at my pew, a slip of a bright yellow ribbon hangs out of the prayer book, marking some place. I stare at this ribbon. Being bright and yellow, its color is striking in an otherwise gray and dusty world. I smile at how yellow it is. That it would be brave enough to do that.

"God, forgive me," I say, not even sure why. Nothing happens, not then.

I cross myself, getting up. I hadn't intended to stay for Mass, and I certainly don't want to pick up my conversation with Father Chavez later, so I figure I'd better go. Mrs. Alvarez will be happy there's an open pew for the kind of people she likes. And I am way too close to the front.

I walk down the aisle and I open the big wooden door, stepping out onto the portico. I hold the door for a couple entering. But I don't even make the first step down. I stand there and see the sun setting over the horizon. The cathedral faces west, so it's the last bright sun of the afternoon, and it's in my eyes. I squint. It's brighter than it seems it should be that late.

I think, *Do I really want someone else involved?*

If anyone, a priest would be good. I think fondly of Father Chavez: how he hums when he picks up hymnals, the way he'd talked about Aquaman, the way he'd pressed my shoulder and invited me to stay. Going home, I think, *I'll be completely alone.* For a moment, I desperately want to go back inside. I want to go to Mass. It wasn't too late. What's too late for a Catholic going to Mass?

Standing there, I tilt my head.

The sun reflects in a funny way off my glasses, that special way that makes a mirror of your own lenses and a ghostly eye appears on the inside of your lens. You see your own wet, rolling, glaring eye, far too close. And, of course, it's looking at you because you're looking at it, or none of that would be happening. I'm trapped there, blinded by seeing my own too-close, focusing eye.

And suddenly I think of that silky slip of yellow ribbon. So yellow, so silky, it too looked wet. Looking down on it, that yellow ribbon directly below my bowed head. Yellow. The bright, brave color of it...

"James!"

Father Chavez is talking to Mrs. Alvarez, but he turns and finds me praying.

"James," he says. "Good! I thought you'd gone."

He grabs my shoulder again. Me there on the kneeler, four rows from the front. I leapt exactly where I'd been maybe a minute ago. Me staring at that yellow ribbon. I knock on the wooden pew just to hear the hollow sound. I grab the ribbon between my fingers to be sure.

"I'm glad you decided to stay." I watch as Father Chavez walks up the steps to the God area. Part of me wants to stay, but there are too many parts. How can I just sit through Mass as if nothing...

I cross myself again and go.

That was the second time it happened.

4

My car now sports a parking ticket.

I get in the Volvo and file the ticket on the backseat floorboard with all the other trash. I've decided I need to get somewhere I can observe what's happening to me.

Maybe I should tell Father Chavez. Maybe he could help me; maybe he can fix this parking ticket. I think he can do that—fix parking tickets. I don't mean supernaturally—rather, he knows people. But I can't wait around because who knows where I'll leap next?

No, I'm going to put myself away for the evening, watch myself scientifically, see if it happens again. I could use a trusty assistant, but I only know one guy in my building. He talks to me. I don't think anyone else in the building will talk to him, and I don't know why I do. He's usually drunk, and I'm usually caffeinated; we both mumble and drool, me quickly and him slowly—a gorgeous couple.

No, I'm on my own. I'll need a tape recorder and duct tape—lots of duct tape—a controlled experiment. I will, very empirically, lock myself in my apartment, barricade myself inside, duct tape the doors and the windows so no slipping out without injury to the tape. If you come home after a long night of leaping and the door's still taped shut, you know you've used the superpowers, right?

I'll buy some groceries, stock up on coffee, won't leave the apartment until it happens again, and I'll catch myself this time. Get clear, solid, irrefutable data on what's happening to me. I've always prided myself on my ability to outrun my own insanity. A very controlled experiment.

"Perfect timing, James! I'm clocking out right now."

The moment I enter the coffee shop, Kevin says this. This guy. We work together. I mean, he works there, I work there, and he thinks we're friends.

"What?" I ask.

"It's Friday. We should probably go now, to beat the traffic," he says.

"I'm sorry?"

"It's Friday. Are we still on for tonight?"

I still have no idea what he's talking about. And I have no idea what Friday means to Kevin. I probably promised him something, but I don't care what he's talking about, I'm not going. He's in my way, though, not letting me get to the espresso machine. I've got needs just then.

"Sorry, no. Not going to be able to make it this Friday. Today, that is. Not making today at all. Sounds good, though, doesn't it? We'll have to do it some other time."

"Oh...I guess we could do something else. When's good?"

As I don't remember what I'm saying I can't make it to, I'm a little leery of issuing a rain check, signed and dated. Besides, it seems I'm unstable. Either psychologically or metaphysically, I'm clearly on the verge of not being all there.

"You know, Kev…," I say, and realize I've never called him this before, never called anyone by some snappy shortening of their proper name, and I hate myself. But I say again, "Kev, you know…"

So I push past the guy.

I make it to the espresso machine and shove a paper cup under the spigot, press the button ten or eleven times, just to be sure. I hear the machine whir, then click and start to grind beans.

It's one of those automatic machines, one button whizzes all. Completely inferior to the lovely old grind, tamp, cinch-the-portafilter-on-yourself machines. Sure, my clothes, arms, and face were always smudged beyond repair with coffee soot. Most days I looked like a chimney sweep. But a man feels like he's made a coffee when he's had to wrestle it out of the machine, when the machine would fight back, when it'd viciously steam your eyes, blast off a portafilter, and when it'd bleed black, creeping goo like the *X-Files*. Most customers don't mind the change. Most customers bury espresso in chocolate syrup two inches deep, under twenty ounces of steamed milk and a stack of whipped cream. Most customers are whipped cream–oriented. But for soot-oriented espresso drinkers…

"Hey, James?" Kevin interrupts again.

I take a deep breath.

"Even if we can't get together tonight, do you think you might have a chance to talk?"

I can't fathom what's being missed here. Did I somehow inadvertently seem kind? I don't feel kind. Actually, I feel like my eyes are bulging. I just want coffee, to rub espresso between my eyes, massage it into my temples, but the guy's still standing there, asking me questions.

So I say, "Man, I am really torn out about canceling on you like this, but my crazy wife, she's—"

"You're divorced"—he interrupts, pointing at me—"I mean, you said you were?"

"Right." Note to self: replace default excuse. "She's not my wife anymore. But, boy, she's still crazy, Kev! She wants to go to dinner, maybe a show. Old times' sake, she says. One loopy gal, and I kind of thought I owe her. See? So…sorry, Kevin."

"I'm okay," he says, but he looks sick, like my Labrador did after he'd eaten most of the throw rug in the front hall. Gave me a whole new perspective on the term "throw rug."

"Hey, why don't you two use the tickets?" He fishes in his shirt pocket and hands them to me. He's carried the things around all day, which worries me. Two tickets to this amazing jazz show downtown, Herbie Hancock and the Headhunters. I check the price on the tickets in my hand. Forty bucks a pop.

Now I remember. Couple of days ago, I was dragging around the coffee shop. Divorced and dragging. Undercaffeinated maybe. And Kevin talking about jazz, how he wants to see this deal, tickets still available for Friday, he believes. He's being genuinely nice to me. I think, *You got to get out and meet people. Can't sit in your apartment again all weekend. Kevin's all right. And there's no huge line of people with invitations.* So I said, "Sure. Let's do it."

This is the promise I'm breaking to poor Kevin while holding eighty dollars' worth of jazz tickets in my hand to show my ex-wife a good time.

"Kevin," I say. "I can't take these. My wife is a jazz hater. Childhood trauma with a saxophone. As I said, so very crazy."

Kevin just smiles, waves, and walks away. He's done with his shift for the day, on his way out for good.

"Hey, Kevin!" I shout. I follow after him a few steps, but he ignores me. I feel awful.

"Give me a call, please." I say. "We'll talk!"

He's gone now, but all the customers, my fellow employees—even the homeless guy who basically lives in the store's bathroom—everybody thinks I'm desperately trying to get Kevin to go out with me. Everyone knows my wife left me. People stare in that trying-not-to-stare way. I hate being divorced.

I collect myself, grab a couple of coffee timers, a pound of ground coffee, and my ten shots of espresso. I drink a big glass of water because that's good for you. I don't say good-bye to anyone, just head for the door. I didn't say hello to anyone so I feel I'm exempt.

"See you tomorrow, James!"

This from a girl named Monica. She also works there.

Regarding Monica: a truly beautiful person. Without question, she is the kindest person I've ever met. Everything makes her happy. Everybody's worth being nice to, and in Monica's world, everything is just about as good as it needs to be. Customers who ask for their lattes to be stirred counterclockwise on Tuesdays, she sees the good in these people. I've tried to make her angry; she won't budge. Pathologically nice, and she's beautiful—brown eyes, huge smile, long hair that she keeps pulled up in some wispy, fabulous way—but that's not what's attractive about her.

What I mean when I say *beautiful* is that, when she looks at you, there's something about her eyes—they don't want anything. They don't already have a plan. They see you, just you, like she has no idea what's next and she's happy with right now. Her eyes listen.

Monica's a straight line—genuine, smiling, and straight. How can anyone see that cleanly? I've seen her look at a steaming pitcher the same way. And somehow I mean that as a compliment.

I need that in my life.

So when Monica calls out good-bye to me, I turn around, walk over to her, and hand her Kevin's tickets. I take her soft hands, look into her brown eyes and say, "I love you. I always have. I wish I could go to this show with you tonight, but I just don't see us working out."

Then I walk out.

Perhaps this sounds as if I'm burning bridges, but I'm not really. Even though most of my bridges have been highly flammable for some time now and I have barged loudly through the coffee shop in a hypervigilant semi-rage, these people understand I'm an espresso drinker. Chalk it up to happy synapses. I'm feeling better. The coffee's kicking in; the bridge of my nose tingles. So let's just say it was an exit. I thought it graceful under the circumstances.

It's getting dark and I don't know how late things stay open. For a recorder, I need an electronics store.

"Mister…"

The boy genius at the Gadget Town enunciates this carefully as if maybe I'm losing my hearing.

"Mister," he repeats, "you probably want to check yard sales or thrift shops for tape recorders. What do you need one for? A prop for some old eighties play?"

Now, I'm thirty. I'm not that old. Not old enough to have some pimply geek in khakis and a bright blue golf shirt talk to me like my teeth just fell out on his counter.

I ask, "Are those flat screens impact resistant?"

"These? Sure," he says. He looks at the televisions next to his counter as if they are way out of my league.

"How impact resistant?" I ask.

"Technically, these new ones are impact resistant up to—"

I pick up a stapler and spike it off the biggest screen.

"Hey!" The kid recoils as if he's been shot. And they are. Remarkably resistant.

I ask again, "I'm wondering if you could point me toward the tape recorders?"

"Aisle nine!" He screams, then flees his counter.

I know he's heading for security, ratting me out. The stapler thing was completely unappreciated. I don't have much time, so I jog to aisle nine. Recorders, rows and rows of them, all digital. This is the advancement I hadn't kept abreast of in my advanced, doddering state. I'm thrilled when I read the package: up to one hundred hours of recording time. You can download things you've recorded into computer files to save them; you can re-record an infinite number of times; you can send in the bar code on the packaging for free earphones. I look around for the kid to tell him thanks, but he seems uninterested in making up. Something about the security guard he sends my way. The kid stands at the end of the aisle, pointing at me with the stapler.

I head the other way. Not really running, but fast walking. Lots of hips and arms movement. I hop up and down to look over the aisles, locating where they keep the registers. The security guard has a walkie-talkie, and he and the kid are in hot pursuit. Also fast walking, hips and arms. The guard puts the walkie-talkie up to his mouth. Reinforcements! He presses buttons, clicks, and mutters, but something's wrong. He clicks and clicks and clicks. Inexplicably, it appears that the security guard in an electronics store has a dead battery.

The kid looks at the security guy with sheer disgust. "Didn't you plug it in and charge it?"

"That tone right there," I call out. "That's how staplers get thrown!"

But they've stopped pursuit altogether. Here in Gadget Town, a gadget that doesn't work properly stops them in their tracks. They gather around the walkie-talkie like it's a dead body fallen from the sky.

I buy the digital recorder and slip away, but in the Volvo, I'm gasping to catch my breath. All that fast walking. So I try to breathe.

Called a bit of attention to myself that time. So I decide to make a concentrated effort to be low-profile in public places.

Last stop before home, the grocery.

I stop inside the front doors of the Shoppy Mart for a moment to take a breath. I stand casually, very low profile. For groceries, I'm a man who likes to make a list. I like leaning on a cart and glancing at or scratching out, but I've got no list now. I try calmly to search myself for something to write on, but I have nothing.

So I make a mental list:

1. *Paper–for on-the-fly lists*
2. *Notebook–for observation, a journal chronicling my events, and for extra paper*

Immediately, I see the papery redundancy of this list and, mentally, I cross out, then erase:

1. *Paper–for on-the-fly lists*

But now the list starts with the number two. I have to change the two to a one. Just making a list, I get all high-profile:

1. *Notebook–for observation, etc.*

Then add:

2. *Duct tape–too many rolls*

I need food. There's no food in my apartment, and I have no idea how long I'll be locked away. What if there's no leaping when you're watching it? I don't cook. I'm a warm-and-serve kind of guy. I shake and drink. I tear along the perforated edge. I mentally write:

3. *Rations*

Usually, list-making soothes me, but that's when I have paper. There's something about getting it out of your head, where you can see it. I look around for a soothing distraction. Outside, it's night now, and the parking-lot lights cover everything with their orange glow. Instead, I look around the grocery and wonder why so many people are grocery shopping at night. *Don't these people have plans? It's Friday night. I had Friday-night plans. With Kevin. Forty-dollar tickets. I owe the guy.*

As I'm depressing myself with thoughts of Kevin, I see a bird, a brown-and-white bird, inside the grocery, flying over the aisles. He's trapped and confused. The bird flies frantically this way and that, but he can't find where he came in.

Birds don't belong in groceries. It's too bright, with too many people, and there's no sky, just a paint-chipped ceiling. I stand on the mat to keep the automatic doors open, and I wave my arms, but it doesn't help. In general, birds don't fly toward humans flailing their arms.

Then I remember: this self-enforced time-out was called to lower profile, to draw less attention to myself. Now there's an old lady afraid to enter the open doors because of me.

I lower my arms and walk over to get a cart.

This next part is not entirely my fault. I can't unstick a cart. Someone has clearly jammed and welded the shopping carts together. I'm serious—they're welded together, because no matter how I pull the nearest one, the whole line of them moves. Every cart I touch seems to clench its teeth and hold on for its wobbly-wheeled life to the cart in which it's wedged. I try them all, and let's not say noise-lessly, then take a break to gather my strength.

So I'm watching as the old lady steps up cautiously and then, with a slight upward lift, liberates the cart I'd just abandoned. She tries not to look at me, but, oh, she's pleased. I try grabbing the next cart after hers. Completely immovable. There's a trick to doing things normally, and I don't have it.

I kick, I shake, I cajole, I argue, but nothing.

Finally, an old man in a uniform steps up to help me. Grocery-store rent-a-cop. His badge is clearly plastic, but his gun is not. He has a gun, it's a big one, in this huge holster on his hip. He walks off-kilter, like the hip has been replaced or the gun weighs too much. And I wonder why a senior citizen making minimum wage is packing heat at the Shoppy Mart.

He steps up next to me and says, "They stick."

"Good work, Ranger." That comes out before I can stifle it. Proudly, I do stop myself from saying, "Shoot a cart loose for me, cowboy." It wouldn't have mattered, though, because the guy's deaf as a post. A weathered, well-armed, deaf post. If it all goes down one day in meats-and-dairy, do we want this guy waving a pistol?

I slip away as he works on the stuck cart and grab a handbasket instead. I decide to eat less, buy only nutrient-dense items, load up on protein bars and beef jerky. Chewing—I know I can do, and that's the only possible reason for the existence of beef jerky. Chewing without the bother of digestion. But first, the tape. I wander up and down aisles. The chances I'm talking audibly to myself are, yes, very high. I am actually announcing the items as if I'm doing personal inventory.

"Mustard: yellow, brown, sweet, deli, squeezable, and there's the spicy. Mayonnaise: real and the other kind. That's easy. Pickles: kosher, garlic, dill, spears, whole, halved, hamburger slices, sandwich slices, thick, chunky slices, gherkin, sour, fancy, sweet, and, again, there's spicy. So much spicy."

Like making lists, sometimes I inventory. It's calming.

Finally, tape: electrical, packing, Scotch, masking, and duct. No spicy. It's expensive, but I take the duct tape. I'm a firm believer in duct tape. You can never have too much duct tape. I've never taped myself into my apartment, so I guess twenty rolls will do. They have seventeen, and I take them all.

Regarding handbaskets: clearly these are made for someone buying three apples. Or say, two apples and a bunch of celery. A person could just carry two apples to the register, but three? One might juggle, unless there's celery. A cute, cheap plastic, worthless, three-apple basket is therefore provided, complete with an insufficient coat hanger of a handle. And duct tape is surprisingly heavy. The wire handle immediately begins to buckle and bend, and the basket's plastic bottom just sags. But there is no way I'm going back for a second round with the rows of welded carts. I stoop as I walk, partly because the basket is that heavy, partly because you think stooping helps a cheap basket not to break. I begin to realize that seventeen rolls of tape will limit my buying food supplies to the amount of beef jerky I can cram under my arms.

An abandoned cart would be ideal. People do that—abandon

carts. I know that greatly increases the chances of getting a cart with a spastic wheel, or a wheel that doesn't roll at all. And technically, is it still a wheel then? Rolling is fundamental to its wheel-ness.

But I spy one, a seemingly abandoned cart, by the frozen fish sticks. Of course, how can you tell if a grocery cart's been truly abandoned? Sometimes people get a cart and park it cleverly somewhere in the store with every intention of coming back for it. If they've touched it once, they've got dibs on it, no matter where they leave it.

Working on keeping low-profile, I eyeball this cart from a distance for four, maybe five minutes. No bites. It just stands there, but it looks like there're a few things in it. Technically, that's a claimed cart, although the guy could have forgotten his wallet, just left it standing there. I can't see the items, but from a distance, it looks like three things. I figure you multiply the minutes spent unattended by the number of items in the cart and subtract from a hundred. Roughly, eighty-five percent chance this cart was abandoned, which is pretty high. I watch for a minute or two longer, but the handbasket is so heavy the wire handle digs into my hands.

I rush this cart, heave the duct tape, basket and all, into it and push it around the corner quickly. In the next aisle, I slow down and put on as if this cart and I have been together for years. Keep my eyes up, concentrate very diligently on the shelves, lean over the cart comfortably, moving along at an easy stroll.

I find the protein bars and grab a box, tossing them in my cart. Grab a couple of notebooks. I find the beef jerky rack. I spin it, tossing jerky after jerky on top of the duct tape. Now that I have my own items, I think it time to discard the previous cart owner's items. Only one other guy is in the aisle, a tidy, business-looking type in khaki pants and a white button-down, busy reading the label on an oat-flakes box. He seems safe.

There's nothing fishy about taking items out of your very own cart. Put them back wherever, as it happens. From beneath the pile of jerky and duct tape, I dig and pull out a dented loaf of bread and a box of denture adhesive.

And a purse.

As if on cue, the old lady who'd trumped me at the cart game comes around the corner. Her face is flushed, and she's panic-stricken. She walks in short, fluttery steps, as if the tiles are intermittently bursting into flame.

She gasps, "My check! This month's check! It was in my purse."

She is gasping this to the rent-a-cop. She holds him by the elbow, and he's all business, bristling like a dog who's heard a noise outside the window.

"That's my purse. There!"

She means, of course, the purse I am currently holding. The guy in the khakis shelves his oat flakes and turns his attention on us. The senior security man puts his hand on his weapon.

"Here's your purse, ma'am," I say, taking a step toward her.

"Drop the purse, Mister!" says the security guard.

I know he's deaf, so I am certain he mistook my movement for aggression. I stop and hold the purse out.

The lady grabs her purse, immediately opens it to locate her wallet and her check.

"It's still here, thank goodness," she says.

"I just found it in my cart." Saying this, I turn and point at the cart in question. The khakis guy has already closed in and is so close I can smell his Old Spice. He inspects the contents of the cart in question, surely wondering why anyone needs seventeen rolls of duct tape and enough beef jerky to build a child-size beef-jerky cabin.

"I'm sorry. I didn't realize there was a purse in this cart until just now."

"What'd he say?" asks the security guard.

"You just happened to shop using a cart with someone else's purse in it?" This from the oat-flakes guy.

And I want to say, "Yeah, her purse looks a lot like mine," but I don't because right about then, I notice the detective's badge clipped to his belt.

Instead, I offer, "I assumed the cart in question was abandoned, Officer."

"Did you assume she'd abandoned her purse, too?" he says, heavy, like he's interrogating a drug runner.

"I didn't see her purse," I repeat.

"I got that cart from the front." The old lady still points, still flutters, still avoids imaginary flames. "He couldn't get one loose."

This, I feel, is entirely unnecessary. The old lady is showboating for the cop, the real one. And the security guard backs her. "I saw him. He couldn't even get his own cart."

"Detective Goss," he introduces himself, then asks. "Did either of you see the purse actually being taken?"

Suddenly, it's like I'm not there, and for a quick second, I wasn't sure either. I check to confirm that I am.

"Look, I'm sorry. I didn't do it on purpose. It was purely accidental, I swear. I've had a very accidental day. Most of my life, lacking the purposeful. You have your purse, and nothing's missing. Let me get this stuff out of my cart—"

"It's my cart," she says, solemnly pressing her hand on her chest. The deaf security guard grabs her arm like she's going to pass over right there by the cereal.

It's best to start loading my items into the cheap little basket. The detective hands the rolls of tape to me one by one. Very helpful and creepy, this guy. I manage the tape, the notebooks, the protein bars into the basket, but not all the jerky would fit. Not stuffing things in my pockets seems wise. I set the basket on the floor, bend over it, and pack in what I can.

"Excuse me," the detective says.

He hovers over me, and he must Old Spice his socks, it's that strong on him.

"Do you mind if I ask your name?"

"Actually, I do kind of mind," I say, staring at his shiny black shoes.

"Excuse me?" he says. And he's not asking this time; he's threatening.

"Look, I'm not a thief, okay? I didn't mean to take the lady's purse. I just want to go, if that's all right with you."

No answer, so I ignore him and keep piling stuff in my basket. I watch the shoes turn and go, and finally, Detective Goss walks away.

It's the way he walks away that unnerves me. Not like a guy shopping. His back is alert, if you know what I mean. He's on duty now, and I can tell from his shoulders that he's aware of me, what I'm doing. He walks to the end of the aisle, stops, pretends to be looking at a box of Fruity O's. No way this guy eats Fruity O's. He's watching.

I keep packing my basket. It takes awhile, but that's good.

So I'm fine, right? Items in basket, fine. I stand, and doing some fine standing. In a few minutes, I'll be in the Volvo on the way to my apartment for a fine evening of self-induced solitary confinement. Fine. I heave my hands up near my chest and lean back just to carry the heavy basket—even this is fine. I slip to the next aisle, an empty aisle. Finely done. I can see the registers up ahead, and there's hardly a line. Very fine. I just have to make it down this one empty aisle, and I'm as good as free.

Dear God, just let me make it to the Volvo...

I huff and shift the basket.

As if an answer to prayer, Detective Goss appears at the register-end of my aisle. He waves at me, signaling me to come to him.

Of course, I turn and walk back the way I came.

"Hey, buddy," he calls out.

I don't feel like his buddy, so I keep walking. I'm almost around the corner of the aisle when I hear sharp shoe squeaks, like he's running to catch up me with.

"Hey, guy!"

I stop. I'm hyperventilating. No, I'm definitely not ventilating, hyper or otherwise. I don't turn, but I hear Goss come up behind me. I look at my hands—the basket's wire handle cuts whitely into my fingers, and they're numb. I look at the heaping basket, the duct tape, the jerky, the protein bars and their shiny silver wrappers, and I feel like I might black out. My eyes blur.

A heavy hand lands on my shoulder.

"Hey, listen. I'm sorry you're having a bad day. Everybody thinks because of who I am, I mean them trouble. But I'm sorry if you felt leaned on—"

It's too late. I'm so dizzy my eyes blur on the shiny wrappers like I can see through them. I rush around the corner to get away from the detective. *Please, God, not right now!* But I pray way too late. It's got me, I feel it happening, feel like that bird flying from aisle to aisle not knowing where a door is…

I'm blinking.

I stand there, staring and blinking. The amber reflection of my face on the Volvo's windshield, the way the parking lot's lights directly above me make the Volvo's dirty windshield an amber mirror, my face in a dirty amber mirror, and perched on the wiper in the amber, artificial light…a bird.

A brown-and-white sparrow.

A car horn blows. A minivan pulls into the empty space beside me, and I step closer to my Volvo so as not to be hit.

Third time's a charm, right? The bird flies away.

I open the Volvo's door and heave the basket onto the passenger seat. I stop because I should go back and tell them what I have, to pay for it. But when I look back at the glass front to the bright grocery, I see a dark, authoritative silhouette—Detective Goss stepping on the electric mat that opens the sliding doors. I've parked far from the entrance, but I see the guy, all backlit and angry. His head shoots left then right, scanning the parking lot.

I duck.

Even the least paranoid of us need to duck now and again. I crawl into my car. I'm not sure if he's seen me or not, but I'm not about to trot out a second crazy explanation for Supercop. The Volvo actually starts again, so there are still miracles available to the ordinary man. I back out, slip it into first, and start to drive away. I'm thirty, and this is my very first getaway.

I don't turn on my lights. I adjust the rearview mirror only to see Detective Goss, his silhouette against the Shoppy Mart doors. I can't tell if he's looking my way or not.

Maybe he wasn't close enough, I think. No worries. *Maybe he didn't see me? Maybe, in his surprise, he didn't even think to look at my license plate number?* No worries. *Maybe I'm completely forgettable?* All fine.

Dear God, please...

I think this despite how stunningly my prayers have been answered of late.

Make me forgettable...

5

The crazies don't set in till later that night.

Looking back on all I've written so far about my first day—none of it could happen, right? How could any of it be true…but I remember all of it so clearly. And if it's true, and it can't be true, then what's gone wrong in my mind?

As an answer to that, I can see my barricades, the duct tape everywhere, on the door, the windows, the walls, stuck to my arms, my fingers, in my hair. I feel very stupid or exposed, like I've yelled out, "Surprise!" in a room full of people waiting for the guest of honor to arrive. Like I yelled too early and all those staring faces become frowningly uncertain, as if it's even a party, if any guest is coming at all.

That's what I mean by the crazies.

When something happens to you, something unworldly and inexplicable, a thing that cleanly surpasses your ability to categorize it—you don't doubt it in the moment.

During the crisis, you simply react and respond as best you can. You have to stay afloat, no doubts then because you're inside it. But later, when the crisis has passed, when you're trying to remember exactly how it happened, it all seems unreal. Make believe. 'Cause you're fine now, you know?

Or so you think.

If you've ever slipped and cut yourself with a knife, afterward you don't remember the sequence of ordinary events that led right up to it, just that dizzying recollection of strange pain, the creepy sensation of blade opening flesh, of the senses screaming that something is very wrong before the brain translates the message for pain, you know?

I know I should sleep. But deep inside, I feel…

It's like this: Meg's an ice-cube user. Not excessively; in fact, rarely. But when she wants a cube or two for a beverage, she expects ice to be there. She used to become enraged and yell at me for using up the ice cubes, then putting the empty trays back in the freezer. She'd get chin-cocked, eye-fluttering furious. She couldn't fathom why some idiot would go to the trouble of putting the trays back in the freezer but wouldn't take the three seconds to fill them with tap water. Somehow, it just bent her mind the wrong shape. Meanwhile, I always eyed her suspiciously, as if she'd popped her last emergency mental bobby pin, because I don't use ice. I chill a beverage beforehand. Meg was the only other being with opposable thumbs in the house using ice, and then she'd deliriously, foggily forget she had done so.

And just try telling her that. She'd get this tilted-back, wild-eyed Vivien Leigh sort of crazy face when I'd tell her she must've used the ice, because this woman fills an ice tray, if you know what I mean. She'd yell and chase me through the house, clapping trays together.

We found out after we were divorced.

Left too long in a freezer, ice evaporates.

All that is to say: tonight my head's the freezer. Something's evaporating. I can feel it. Something I didn't know could do that. How do you check on that if you're the freezer? How do you become certain of something outside your own head? How do you verify something outside your own mind when verification is an act of the mind? There's a piece missing.

I believe I leapt through space. I remember it; it happened. But that can't happen, can it? If it can, it sort of madly rattles my known universe.

I'm not sure I believe any of it. But I'm not sure if I can simply *not* believe.

How do you believe? I mean, something completely impossible, some strange thing that happens only to you, the one thing that changes everything? Isn't that madness?

How do you believe something with your whole life?

6

The next morning, I feel fine.

I don't mean, *Gee, what a great day to have an inexplicable power!* More like, *Maybe nothing happened at all.*

Nothing to worry about, maybe none of yesterday was real. *My dear James, you do have a penchant for imagining things,* I tell myself. After crazy days, that's the way next mornings go.

You've finally managed sleep; you wake up late. You put on coffee, and that smells homey and normal. You eat some beef jerky, brush your teeth, get another cup of coffee, clean your glasses, slap on your baseball cap, and everything's fine. Yesterday was somebody else's day, somewhere else, and it doesn't touch you.

I'm safe.

I've been here before, you see. Whole days of worried stuff, only to talk myself down the next morning, and usually, events turn out fine. Maybe not one hundred percent fine, but not gruesomely tragic.

I'll confess:

I have spent an entire day spinning myself around, thinking that my identity had been stolen by our mailman.

Then a day when I have skewered myself onto the imagined prong of accidental but nonetheless punishable tax evasion.

I have suffered twenty-four hours basting my well-being with juicy worries over contracting a not-so-real case of consumption.

I've spent more time bordering on nervous collapse than the average coffee drinker, overcooked by my own horrified imagination, too often wakened bewildered by my fearful, turning mind, the sheer rotisserie of it.

This morning's hopeful turnabout is more than possible—it's right on schedule. I smile warmly at my slept-in clothes, chuckle nostalgically at the duct-taped mess, and chew another wad of beef jerky while sitting, smiling, on an unpacked box in a sunny spot by the window. Home sweet home. I thumb through my notebook like it's a fashion magazine, read a snip here and there, and laugh at what I find. I stretch and consider bathing.

A knock at my apartment door stops me.

"James?" Meg's voice.

"Coming, Meg!"

To give you a read on how deep my denial runs, I walk over to the door, unlock the chain, turn the key, and only then realize it's going to be much harder to open the door. I'd just been admiring all of it a moment before: the duct tape, the chairs, the stacks of books, the wedged coatrack. Now I'm confused as to why the door won't open. Deep, I tell you.

"Hey, Meg," I call through the door. "What's up?"

There's an awkward pause.

I hear Meg's voice. "Would you mind opening this for a minute?"

"Well…"

I don't know what to say. I don't want to tell her about the barricade, don't want to explain it. I relock the door so she won't try to push her way in.

Another pause. This one, also, very awkward.

"James, did you just unlock then lock the door?"

I don't answer.

"James? Are you still there?"

"Yeah, Meg, I'm here… You still there?"

"If you could please open this door, then we could stop calling roll and actually speak."

This is reasonable. Barricades are less reasonable. I sigh.

"It's going to take a minute."

"I've seen you naked, so just throw on anything and open the door."

"I have a lot of clothes on." This is my thoughtful response.

"Way to go, James, dressing yourself like a big boy. I'm proud for you…and tired of standing in this hallway."

"Just a minute!"

I call this out, singsonging, like a prairie mother yodeling "Supper's ready!" to her eight kids.

"James, is somebody else in there?"

It takes me a moment, but I realize she means another woman.

"No, Meg." This almost as flattering as her suggesting that I can pick locks. "I'm all alone, it's just that—"

"James, it's fine if someone's there. It's none of my business. I was just a little concerned about you yesterday, that's all. You were acting a bit crazy even for you, and I need to get Doug's shirt back."

I stop moving books.

I ask her, "Did I sound crazier than normal…or more normal than crazy?"

"That's a hair I hope I never have to split," she answers through the door. "Look, I'm glad you're fine, and that you've found someone. I'm sure she's lovely, but I need that shirt."

Now it seems even trickier. I don't want Meg to think I've found someone, although I'm not sure why. I would rather she thought I was just lonely instead of jumping headlong into another relationship. Maybe it's because I'm a little tweaked at how quickly she's taken up with Dougie, how she's up early on a Saturday for poor Dougie's shirt. But I'm also thinking I hear a twinge of resentment behind that "lovely" comment. She's usually not openly rude to people unless she knows them. Can a person exhibit animosity toward you and jealously about you simultaneously? I'm genuinely intrigued, and I want the door open.

"There's nobody here, Meg." I start throwing boxes whichever way they'll go. "Just boxes piled up against the door."

She doesn't say anything for a few seconds. "Are you piling them up now that I've knocked, or are you moving them away?"

"Meg, just hold on."

She tries the knob. "You've locked the door on me, and now you're piling stuff against it."

"One minute."

"Look, I'm sorry I bothered you!"

I can hear it. She's mad now, shoe-throwing mad.

"Meg—"

"I didn't mean to interrupt your…whatever. I don't know why we can't ever seem to talk like two normal people using normal-people words in normal-people situations."

I just stand there, hoping she can't hear my blinking.

"If you don't want to talk to me, then just say you don't. You can not talk to me as much as you'd like. I don't even have to see you, but open the door three inches and stick your naked arm out here with Doug's shirt. Stick your girlfriend's naked arm out here…I don't care. Why do I have to yell through a door, James? Just say, 'I don't feel like talking.' Or say, 'I've given up conversation till Christmas.' It matters not to this ex-spouse, but don't make me stand in this spooky hallway while you make up excuses and slide furniture around."

"I'm not sliding furniture around. I don't have furniture."

The slam that followed that remark sounded like a fist punching my door.

"Put Doug's shirt in a plastic bag, and leave it in my mailbox. Today!"

"Meg—wait!"

So diligently had I crammed a chair beneath the doorknob last night, it's stuck.

"Here's the shirt." I yell this, hoping Meg will hear and that she'll wait. I realize I have no idea where I put Dougie's shirt.

You'd think it would be easy to find things in a desolate apartment until you've actually lived in one. Nothing is anywhere specific, so there's nowhere to start looking for anything but everywhere.

I run to the bedroom, throw the sheets to the floor, rummage in them because they are white like a shirt. No luck. I drop to the floor, look under the bed, and remember never to look for something under a bed. You'll only be distracted by what you do find.

I check the bathroom: the floor, the towel rack, the hook on the back of the door. Nope. I run to the kitchen: not on the counter, not in the garbage, not on the card table, but hanging on the refrigerator handle is a very wrinkled shirt with obvious coffee stains.

I grab the shirt and run to the window. It's a second-floor apartment with a great view of the parking lot. I yank at the duct-taped curtains, only serving to bring the curtains and rod crashing down in a heap on my head. I throw them off and see Meg walking toward her Jeep.

"Meg!" I call out.

She can't hear me—or won't. She's got her keys out. I want her to know I didn't break in her house. I want her to understand. I don't want to slink over to her mailbox later with a bag o' shirt. I want her to come in, have a cup of coffee, and for us to talk like the normal people she mentioned. I'm tired of everything going badly between us.

I pound on the windowpane. "Hey, Meg!"

I'm really close to the window, so close I see my breath fog a quick patch on the pane. As quickly as my breath fogs the window, it clears. And just as quickly…

Her Jeep's dashboard. She's waxed inside her Jeep, the dashboard is shiny.

When she opens the driver's door, I say, "Hey, Meg," from the passenger seat.

I wince as her keys fly past my face and hit the window. She jumps back out of her Jeep.

"Holy...how'd the...don't...freak...freak...freak...James!"

Meg's doing her scared dance. She squints her eyes shut, lifts one leg, then the other up slow, like an injured horse, and shakes her hands till her fingers loosen. I used to hide in closets and scare her just to see this. After the dance, she takes a slow lap around her Jeep with both her hands on top of her head. She gets back in, grips the steering wheel, and stares forward.

"Hand me my keys, please."

Sitting in the passenger seat, I reach down and feel for them.

"Here you go, dear."

She leans toward me.

"How'd you get down here so quickly?"

"Here's the shirt...sorry." I say.

"James!"

"I don't want to talk about it."

"How did you—"

"You don't believe me when I tell you anything, so I don't want to talk about it. Will you believe me?"

"Is there a fire escape?" She cranes her head out her window and looks back at my apartment building.

"Actually, there really should be a fire escape. I could probably get out, but everybody else—"

"James, stop it."

Truly, I don't know how to talk to her anymore. Not about anything. Especially not this.

So I ask, "Do you want to come in for coffee?" She always liked the way I made her coffee.

"Do not scare me like that ever again!"

"I didn't mean to scare you." We both stare forward like we're driving through a tunnel and watching for the end. Silently staring, but not going anywhere.

"Do you want coffee?"

"No, James," she answers. "Thank you, but I need to go."

"Sure," I say. I open my door and pull myself out.

"James?"

I lean back inside. "Yeah, Meg?"

"How did you get down here so fast?"

After a few years of marriage, a couple develops the means to simply leave a conversation unfinished by staring at each other quietly, patiently until one or the other looks away. Sometimes it's all you got.

"See you later, Meg." I shut the door.

She peels away.

Good thing Meg didn't stay for coffee.

Walking up the stairs to my apartment, I realize my door is still locked and my keys are hanging in the lock on the inside—not to mention the tape, the chair, the coatrack. I lean back against my apartment door. I could check into a hotel maybe, but I'd left my wallet inside. Note to self: duct tape wallet securely to face.

Leaning there, I want inside that room, so I think about trying it. A leap. What are the similarities of the leaping occurrences? Something too close to my eyes, too close to properly focus on and usually reflective: a watch face, the lenses on my glasses, silver protein bar wrappers. Each time my eyes tried to focus on what was impossible to focus on, until my eyes flitted back and forth between surface and reflection. Transparency and reflection.

And each time, I had an intense desire to be somewhere else. The image of elsewhere appeared in my mind because I desired it. And the moment my desire pulled my focus away from what couldn't be seen, I leapt.

Proud to say, I'm thinking all this with only three cups of coffee in me.

I look down the hall. Coast is clear.

I take off my glasses, close my left eye, and press my right eye, my good one, up to the peephole. For reference's sake, peepholes are ingenious little things—they only peep one way, but the other way, not so good. In this case, seeing didn't matter, and I stood there up against my door, shifting focus between what I *couldn't* see inside my apartment and back to the actual glass of the peephole.

Once I feel this is going pretty well, I try to think, suddenly, of being inside.

Regarding sudden thinking: try this sometime. Try thinking of a thing, but suddenly. Either you screw it up 'cause you realize you're *already* thinking of it when the moment for suddenness passes right by, or you make yourself *not* think of it too fast and basically consciously forget to think about the thing when the moment of sudden thinking is called upon. I'm not crazy. This is difficult.

I give up, and start shoving, hitting, and kicking at my door.

I don't leap anywhere. I do, however, hop around the hall with my foot basically broken from poor door-kicking form. I hop, I sing, I swear, I sing swearingly.

"Need some help?"

The question comes from the guy I told you about, the one in my building who nobody talks to. The only one who talks to me. He walks up in ripped jeans and a "Mind, Spirit, Body" T-shirt; it's in quotes on the shirt—I think it's an ad for moisturizing lotion.

When I see him, I sort of pity him because everyone thinks he's a drunk or crazy, at least smelly, and then I realize, as I hop and sing in front of him, that he's definitely thinking the exact same thing about me.

"No, I'm great," I say. I sort of sing it, with the pain.

"No, you're not," he says.

"Who are you, by the way?"

"Nelson. What's yours?"

"James," I say and immediately regret telling him my real name. My toe's throbbing, so I sort of lean over, hum my name to myself, and ignore Nelson.

"Let me help."

I look up at him. He's not a small guy; he's got a little weight and muscle on him.

"Sure," I say. "Thanks."

Then Nelson starts to sing. He's helping me sing, looking at me to try to match the pitch. I squint at him, to show him how very far he is from the rest of us.

"Sorry, no," I correct him. "Could you help me bust down my door?"

"We're not singing?"

"I'm not singing, no. I think I broke my foot."

"You're not broken yet."

"Thanks, Doc." I try to lean my weight into the door.

"We trying to break this down?"

"Good idea, yeah." I bump my toe again. "Oh!"

"Go on, sing out. It'll help us push, like pulling oars. What are we singing?"

"We're not really. I'm just giving voice to my pain, thanks! But I think if we lift on the knob and then both shove—"

"Sure. Go on. Sing out!"

"No, but thank you…"

He stares at me, considers me sadly. "You know, people who have to drink before they'll sing out depress me."

And I think, *Oh, is that all?* but I say, "Who said anything about drinking?"

"Well, it really is too early for it."

"I haven't been drinking," I protest.

"Your drinking doesn't bother me. Just your fear of singing out while sober."

"Look, even if we get inside, you'll see I don't own a drop of booze."

"Oh, I wouldn't care for any." Nelson sniffs.

"Good, 'cause I wasn't offering."

"Good, because I never touch the stuff."

We stare at each other, he tucks in his T-shirt with the lotion ad, so now it just reads "Mind, Body."

"I haven't been drinking," I say.

"I thought you were Catholic?" he asks.

We take a lingering, second round of staring at each other in the hall.

"How do you—no, *what* is that supposed to mean?" I say.

"Wait…," he says. "You admit you're Catholic?"

"Yes, of course," I answer. "Sort of—"

"And you haven't been drinking?"

"Absolutely not!"

"Then why are we breaking down a door?"

Staring at this guy, I fear I'm looking at myself after a few more hard years.

"Okay, focus, Nelson. You should either go away right now and never come back here, or help me shove down this door, please."

"Sure." And he starts ramming his shoulder into the door with great fervor, like he'll do it all by himself. I join him, and we shove, grunt, and take turns hurtling ourselves against my well-made door. This is painful, and after a while, we stop to catch our breath.

"This door breaking sure makes a man thirsty," he says to me.

"If we get inside, I've got a sink with tap water just like your apartment, Nelson."

"Mmm-hmm," he says. "I'd enjoy some tap-tap-tap water." He shoves his shoulder into the door three times, on the taps. "Get it?" he asks, pointing at his shoulder. "Tap-tap?"

Then he shoves his shoulder again, until it seems he's forgotten his own joke. He's just strangely taken up with shoving at the door because he doesn't wait for me to laugh, but frowns and starts banging furiously into my door, which doesn't budge in the slightest.

"Nelson, Nelson…stop it!" I have to slap his kidneys to get him to hear me.

"Ow…what's the problem, Johnny?" he says.

"It's James."

He looks around confused, as if I've seen a third guy coming down the hall.

I look down the hallway too, but now I see a potted plant. I leave Nelson, fetch it, and with several cavemanlike swipes, I bust off the doorknob to my own apartment.

Nelson and I still have to throw our collective weight into the door several times to break the tape and topple the junk leaning on the other side.

"This place is a wreck, Junior."

"Thank you, Nelson," I say. "Did you want some water before you promptly go?"

Nelson looks at me strangely, like he doesn't understand why I'm so angry with him, like he doesn't understand why anyone would be angry at all or why people look harshly at each other. He nods, so I fetch him a glass of water. He takes a sip, but it seems he doesn't really want it. Just sipping like he's fulfilling some promise he made, and then he looks for a table to set the glass on, finally setting it on the floor.

"When I was thirsty, you gave me..." he starts, then says. "Thanks."

"You're welcome," I say. "Thanks for—"

But he's gone.

After I get my wallet, I fill my backpack with my notebook, my recorder, a roll of duct tape, protein bars, and jerky. I pile my television, my CD player, and anything else valuable in the bathtub and close the shower curtain. My thinking: if someone breaks into my already-broken-into apartment, maybe they won't look in the bathtub for valuables. Heading out for the coffee shop, I take the useless keys out of the lock and shut the door. I duct tape the doorknob vaguely where it should have been. The doorknob sags stupidly, but hopefully no one will notice.

Besides, who'd sneak into my apartment?

7

About time you showed up."

This is how I'm greeted when I walk into my workplace.

"Glad to see you, too, Mike," I say.

I wasn't. I've never liked Mike, and Mike, he's not pleased either. He's a tough guy, or thinks he is. He likes to terrorize everyone with the way he bumps into them as he squeezes past to his register. Thinks it's funny to trip people. Stumbling's funny to Mike. And he ties his apron real tight, like he's showing off his stomach muscles.

"You're forty minutes late, Jimbo. We've been running crazy all morning," Mike says.

I turn to him and say, "First of all, we've spoken about that Jimbo thing, haven't we, Nancy? Secondly, it's not that busy on Saturdays. Thirdly, I've been running crazy for days; try to catch up."

I'm decent at the quick bluster. Meg and I practiced on a regular basis. Truthfully, however, I had no idea I was supposed to be at work.

"I stayed over a little, James. It's all right." This from Monica, and she smiles at me. She stayed to pick up my slack. She never seems to go home. I don't know if she has a home, but I've always thought that if she does, it must be a happy, warm one where people sing and sway like some animated movie. Birds clean up crumbs in Monica's home.

"Thank you, Monica."

She blushes. "Thank you for the tickets, James."

"Did you go?" I ask.

"No, I had to work." She shakes her head.

This makes sudden sense to me. How could she use tickets for last night when I gave them to her last night while she was working? I'm a crown jewel, a real peach.

"But thank you, James," she says.

"Sorry, I do everything too late—"

"No, it was sweet. And…I kept them." She blushes again.

I remember then that I sort of professed my love for her, and well—we're all less than comfortable.

"I'm taking a break." Mike scowls and throws his apron to me.

"I'm not staying," I say and throw it back to him.

Mike says, "You going to call and tell Charlene?" Charlene's the manager.

"No, you call her. Tell her I called in sick."

I'm not sick, of course, not normal sick. But if I haven't mastered this leaping ability, what's to say I won't just blip out during the middle of a mocha? What if I zip-zap away while I'm holding someone's twenty? I've already added shoplifting to the rap sheet this week; I'd probably get fired. If I'm going to wreck a thing, I'd like it wrecked on my own terms. I need a little more time to straighten me out, and I would rather disappear the old-fashioned way just now.

"Are you not feeling well, James?" Monica asks.

She's incredibly sweet. She hands me my twelve shots of espresso in a big paper cup.

"Thanks," I say. And I think, *I should ask Monica how she pulls off so much kindness amidst insanity on a daily basis.* Maybe I really should ask her out, maybe proximity to her kindness would negate some of my hyperneurotic, terminally paranoid, overcompensation.

But it wouldn't work, she and I.

I'm not used to nice, and she'd nice me straight into apoplectic shock. Besides, I got metaphysical issues to straighten out and don't have time for a relationship. But she's standing there, calmly concerned if my coffee tastes right. Kind and coffee-conscious when I'm most insane.

It's not fair.

"I'm not sick," I say, "I'm just losing my grip on which things are the real ones, Monica. Thank you so much for asking."

I've never seen someone blush three times in a row. I didn't think that was possible.

Then I spot Kevin, and he knows about his tickets. I don't know how he knows, maybe Mike told him. He knows I gave Monica his tickets and didn't go with my ex-wife. He wears a limp, the-world's-too-large-but-I'll-be-fine look. He knows that I was avoiding him.

So I say, "Hey, Kev!" Now it seems I'm going to call him that the rest of his life even though I truly want to stop.

"Hey, James." He turns away as if that's all for him, then remembers. "Oh yeah, some police guy called here for you this morning."

"What did he want?"

"He didn't say, just asked for you. He acted like he knew you. Knew your name."

"When?"

"I guess around nine," Kevin shrugs. "I told him you'd be in at eleven."

It's almost noon. My grocery cop? I'm crazy enough without this.

How did he find out where I work? Did he see my license plate? For the love of coffee, it was beef jerky! No, it can't be Goss. Even my paranoid mind can't believe the police are that efficient, but I'm not sticking around to wait for whatever.

Kevin turns to go.

"Hey, Kev…I'm truly sorry about yesterday," I say. "The truth is, I am a little out of my head right now, and I was no good person to know last night. That's why I cancelled, not because I was avoiding you. It's nothing personal."

"I understand," says Kevin. The guy looks right through me. Like he really understood. Like I'm transparent. How could he know? He says, "It's good to talk to someone when you feel out of your head."

And almost. Right then and there, I almost sit them both down, hold Monica's hand and tell Kevin everything. Get it all off my chest. I don't have that big a chest. Wouldn't it feel so much better to tell someone what's making me crazy?

But who'd believe me? It's not believable. Plus I'm supposed to be leaving—my detective knows where I work, and I am supposed to be working a shift. With Mike, no less. Mike's throwing ice against the back wall. He does this. Mike is somewhere between Pre- and Cambrian. When he gets angry, he likes watching ice shatter and fly into a million pieces all over the back room.

The phone rings.

Monica answers. "Hello. Oh, hi…Charlene. Did *who* ever show up? Oh, you mean…James?"

Her eyes grow huge when she says my name. She stretches out my name like I'm supposed to hide from the voice on the phone before she gets to the end of it. She looks at me, pulls at her apron. She's anguished, caught between truth and loyalty.

She blushes again.

I give her a finger-across-the-throat slashing signal, shaking my head no. But I don't want to listen to Monica trying to lie, so I try to make her honest by leaving. I knew she'd think that inbounds.

I grab my espresso and head out the front.

"Later, James," Kevin calls out.

I wince. Kevin kills me, I swear. I give Kevin the finger-throat-head slash and shake. It's not personal—I just don't want Charlene hearing him, but Kevin turns away like I've killed him. He helps a customer. I should stay and explain. I should give someone a believable explanation for my behavior. I should be nicer, less blustery. I should bring a big box of doughnuts to grease interemployee relations.

And I should've let Monica and Kevin tell Charlene whatever they want, because Mike will rat me out regardless.

I think of all the good *shoulds* too late.

I drive to the bookstore.

It doesn't take long, being directly across the street from the coffee shop. I drive a block though, park on the back side so nobody at my store can see where I went. I don't want my manager to know I ditched work only to go to the bookstore across the street. Ditching that close to the ditched shift—that's just impolite.

My plan is to isolate and repeat leaping similarities. I can't deny this is happening to me, not now. It wasn't just yesterday's superproblem. It happened again this morning.

But then I couldn't make it happen, and I had to bust my own door down. There must be some trick, some gimmick, some missing piece. If I can make it happen consciously and not accidentally, then I can show somebody. I can prove I'm not crazy. I've always longed to prove that.

I go for the bookstore's handy customer-reference computer. It's one of those big chain bookstores, the Book Barn, a barn for the slick, new, and shiny. I navigate the options on the dirty touchscreen, trying to find any help I can, search all the "leaping" literature. Odd as this may seem, I find nothing.

Seems the bookstore doesn't get a lot of requests for superhuman how-to books. All searches lead nowhere. If there are books, even fictional ones, about leaping through space, I don't find a section for them. I don't think the graphic novels will help, being a short step above comics. And it doesn't feel smart to ask a clerk, "Excuse me, Miss, but I'm having a little trouble controlling my superpowers. I was wondering if you could point me in the direction of the super-hero reference section?"

Besides, I know these people—I serve them coffee every morning. They might talk.

I put my hopes into wandering the self-help section.

Ah, bliss in pocket-size paperback. Happiness in a helpful, step-by-step format. Besides weight loss, I locate two key sections: two-minute meditation guides and mental yoga exercises for making more money. I go more for the former, grab a thin book with a cartoon picture of a Buddha wearing a jogging suit and earphones.

Yes, it's promising that he's sitting in the lotus position, but much less promising that he's making a sort of rap gesture and that the bubble caption reads "Peace Out." But it's all they've got, so I take the book over to a comfy chair by a window in the far back corner of the store.

I try to arrange my legs into the lotus position in the chair, but with the armrests, my work boots, and general inflexibility, this proves impossible. I can send my body across untold distances, but managing both ankles on top of my knees—ridiculous.

I thumb the table of contents. No references to my predicament, but I do find a chapter about "Visualizing Your Dream Day." Chapter 8. After a glance at this chapter, it seems to be about imagining yourself in a job you don't hate. Not getting a different job, but just not hating the one you've got.

This book is written as a dialogue. Someone asks the Hip Buddha questions—I guess that would be me, the reader. And Hip Buddha, he's all down with answering my annoying questions. He's like Socrates, except using cool slang and never actually making an argument for anything. He just pops out these non sequiturs like he's misheard the question.

Or maybe Buddha's not listening so good. But the guy who's asking the questions—and again, I'm assuming that's me—this guy's thrilled at the swerving conversation of Hip Buddha. I think, *Who publishes a book of insane rantings?*

I riffle back through the earlier chapters, thinking I probably missed something stunningly important. I land for a while in a chapter called "Clearing Your Mind for *What's Important.*"

It scares me that *What's Important* is in italics. It seems tricky, disingenuous, and underhanded. A sneaky-but-upbeat way of telling you you've been doing it wrong, wasting your time on all the unimportant things.

I'm suspicious. Seems Hip Buddha's up to something.

"But, Hip Buddha, I don't understand. What are the *important* things?"

"The important are the only—" saith the Hip Buddha.

"I'm sorry. I don't follow. What did you say?"

"The only thoughts we must have are the *important* thoughts," saith the Hip Buddha. A cartoon picture of Hip Buddha bumping his heart with a cool fist accompanies his answer.

"The conscious being must take out the garbage," he purrs. "Garbage gone, the truth appears."

Despite the fact that "we" muddle up my brain with a trash truck full of thoughts, it seems I really have precisely nothing that matters to think about.

On the next page, Hip Buddha is nodding; he agrees. There's little shaky movement lines around his bald head so we know this. No words on this page, but it seems I was right; I already knew the right answer.

I check. This book costs $13.99. And a whole page for a bald cartoon to nod, but wait, the next page is better. Here, Hip Buddha stretches his arms and yawns.

Me too, Buddha.

The point, I find out, is that we need to let the *important* thoughts sort of yawn, stretch, and knock around in all that empty brain space we've managed to make by taking out the worthless mental trash.

The yoga-ankle-meditation thing would be easier.

"Excuse me, Hip, but I've been having this problem leaping through space."

"Find the inner question, you must."

"No, Hip Yoda, listen…please. First, my eyes focus on a reflection, then they go blurry, and then I—"

"Release your garbage from the orbit that is not you."

"Whoa, Buddha man. What I need here is—"

"There are no needs."

At this point, I realize, I hate Hip Buddha. Animosity toward cartoons has to classify as garbage. So, in a way, the cartoon I hate is right. I can't read this.

I find I'm staring out the window at a tree, at the wind. Very Easternlike, I encourage myself, back to nature, staring at a tree. Of course,

I'm sipping espresso inside an air-conditioned bookstore, sitting in a comfy chair, but hey, one step at a time.

I close my eyes.

Eye closing is the entirety of Hip Buddha's chapter 1. Apparently, I've never closed my eyes right either. You don't just shut them like you're playing hide-and-seek. No, you relax your eyes, your sight, until you're not actually seeing anything although the eyes remain open. Once one reaches this state of unseeing sight, saith Hip Buddha, the eyes will mystically close of their own accord.

My eyes, however, are wide open, and uncomfortably dry. I've got a backpack to watch out for, my stuff, my coffee. It's good coffee. Someone might take that while my eyes are mystically closed. Maybe a sixteen-year-old bookstore employee will think I'm done, in my clearly catatonic state, and throw good espresso in the trash.

Frankly, I don't trust sitting with my eyes closed. I don't trust book shoppers not to do me harm. I don't trust myself to not fall out of the comfy chair. Why does my sitting involve so much trust? Do other people have this much trouble sitting?

Don't Buddhists worry about their backpacks, at least a little?

Why does closing my eyes feel like I'm slipping away?

"Forgive me, Mr. Buddha, but I need to—"

"There are no needs to forgive."

Now I'm mad at Hip Buddha. He's just wrong. I'm not supposed to close my eyes at all. I should be focusing on something, not on nothing. In fact, that's all I got, the focusing. Why am I working so hard on making myself black out in a chair?

So I leap up and begin pacing the book aisles. I don't go far, never out of sight of my backpack. You have to leave something as collateral, a claim, or some person will think the chair's free if it's left unattended too long. Like a shopping cart. I'm picking up books I don't really want, feigning interest so as not to draw attention to myself, all the while periodically spinning around to stare at an empty comfy chair.

The good news is that this behavior is exhausting. I return to the chair, plop down, toss the meditation guide on the table next to my coffee, and put my feet up. I wonder what time it is, wonder if the shift I've ditched at the coffee shop is over so I can go get another coffee.

12:34 p.m.

As I stare at the time, my watch face catches an image of the tree outside the window. Everything's upside down, and it's windy outside. I just look at the reflection of the tree, its branches playing in the wind. It feels odd and quiet to see a gusty wind without hearing it or feeling it on your skin. It would be good to feel it. A soundless wind making branches bend and wave, reflected atop the snick-snick of the second hand on my watch face. I lean in close, but too close. The tree's harder to see now, the time easier. I focus. I want to see it, so I do: flapping yellow leaves on branches, inverted in a soundless wind...

Like sand.

When a leap happens, it feels like you're sand.

For a quick second, your whole body is sand sifting through an hourglass, but pouring upward, filling the top bulb and pushing into it from below. Everything sifts upward into your head, through it, up, and out the top. That's all. A few seconds like that, or maybe a second. For that second, you feel like you're falling upward, outside yourself. It's that brief, that quick.

But for a moment, you're outside of you.

Standing outside, I'm looking straight up into the tree; the rustling branches seem upside down; the leaves seem to dangle awkwardly. I touch the rough bark of the tree trunk, feel the wind on my face.

I look back into the bookstore through the window. I see some kid by the comfy chair. He's messing with my backpack, looking around to see if he can find its owner. He picks up my coffee cup by two fingers like it's trash.

I check the time. 12:35 p.m.

It's real now. I can make it happen.

8

Back in the Volvo, I get jittery.

More than the espresso, I mean, I'm all excited and giggly that I'm able to control it. I mean, it's amazing. And the implications are tremendous! I can work a shift at the coffee shop, then spend the afternoon in Paris or Rome, instantaneously arriving free of charge. I can save a bundle on gas as long as no one catches me appearing. I'll say I walked, or I've taken up running. Buy a sweatband and act all out of breath, that sort of thing.

What if I can take someone with me? What if I grab Monica by the hand, like Peter Pan, and we can both go to Paris or Rome? I could charge for it. Not Monica, of course, but other people. Charge just slightly less than the airlines. No, I could charge slightly more because it's instantaneous—no stale food, no delays, no cramped, germy airplane bathrooms, just whoosh and you're there. Or I could work for the CIA. This deal is perfect for the espionage circuit.

What if I can teach it? Or maybe just impart it to someone else? Just one touch, and bam! Like Midas? Okay, bad example. But think: a whole squad of leapers out there in the world, doing good. We could have weekly meetings in a remote castle. A thousand leapers…or maybe not. It kills the "super" in my superpower if everyone else can do it.

But a superhero, he has to think about these things.

As I drive, I look at the people. People in their less-than-instantaneous cars; people bunched on the sidewalk, waiting forever for the signal to change; people huffing away on their slow, ordinary bikes. And I think of the live coverage: me, leaping atop tall buildings with a single bound. I'll need a mask, a suit, huge odd gloves. I could get sponsors, like NASCAR, put endorsements on my cape.

And I think: *Meg.* I want to call Meg right now. She's got to *see* this happen, then she'll believe me. Good ol' Meg. Who cares if we're divorced, this is a kick in the gut! Blow her angry lawyer mind. Knock her affidavits off. I drive there, to my good ol' home. Meg's, but that doesn't matter now. Once she sees this, perhaps…

But I get a firm reminder of whose house it is when I pull up. In the form of a Lexus. Dougie's car. Doug's Lexus takes up most of the drive; he parks squarely in the middle. He's a middle-of-the-driveway parker.

The espresso in me turns a little mean.

I park across the street, sit in the Volvo, and stew for a minute. I wish I had my phone, but it's back at the apartment, hopefully safe in the bathtub. I'd call Meg and tell her to come outside. I don't want to knock or to talk to Dougie. He can sit inside in his starched shirts and miss the whole show. Maybe I can leap home and get my phone, then leap back? But as I sit there, the front door opens, and Meg comes out. Of course, she spots me.

Politely put, my Volvo is unmissable, and I'm parked directly in view of the house. Meg's already headed my way. I don't like the tone of her walking.

I roll down my window.

"Ah, what a surprise." She leans on my door.

"Hey, Meg. Can we talk for a minute?"

"I see you more now that we're divorced than I ever did during our marriage. Why is that, James?"

"Maybe I miss you?" I smile.

She doesn't.

"No, really. I've got to show you something." I start to open my door.

She slams it closed. "You're not staying. Thank you for not washing the shirt, by the way. What do you need to show me?"

"I have to explain, and it might take a minute. Get in."

I lean across and unlock the passenger door.

"James, why do we have to—"

"Get in, Meg, please. Five minutes…I swear it'll be worth it."

She puts her hands on her hips. She walks around reluctantly, opens the door, leans down.

"We're not driving anywhere, are we?" she asks.

"No, Meg. I promise." I take the keys out of the ignition, toss them on the dash, and hold my hands up safely.

She climbs into the Volvo, grunting. Volvo doors are bulky, heavy, and prone to shutting on your leg. She's always hated my car. She could never even start it. And she refused to drive a car without a knob on the gearshift. She claimed she always broke a nail shifting without the knob, and she hated the smell. There's this sour coffee smell in the floor mats, which she never fully appreciated. She always slammed the doors—she slams it now. An old heavy Volvo door slamming sounds like someone dropped a toolbox. She shakes her head.

"Okay…so…"

"Hi, Meg," I try.

"You know the jail time is serious for kidnapping, right?"

"We'll sit right here, dear."

"Please stop calling me *dear*."

"Sorry, hon."

She looks over at me, then looks away. She drops her head back against the headrest.

I didn't mean to do that, to make her mad. It seems it's all I do these days. This isn't going well so far, but in a minute, she'll forget all about that. I hope.

"How's Dougie?" I never know how to start.

"How's Dougie?" she mimics. "Well, right about now, Dougie's wondering where Meggie went. Meggie went outside because the kids thought they heard the ice-cream truck. Dougie said, 'No, children. I, your father, did not hear the ice-cream truck.' But Meggie, being the good Meggie she is, said, 'I'll go outside and check. Wait here, kids, Meggie will be right back. Don't worry, I won't be gone long at all.' That's what good Meggie promised the children—her last words before being abducted by her crazy ex-husband."

"Do you two really talk like that?"

She opens the door to get out.

"Wait! Wait, Meg." I stop her. Besides, she can't manage the door. "I'm sorry. Just listen, okay?"

"James, every time you start with, 'Just listen, okay,' it's never okay. It gets weird quick. Don't get weird this time, okay?"

"Okay, Meg."

"You promise? No weird? Absolutely none?"

I don't want to lie to Meg. I never have. So I don't want to promise absolutely no weirdness when technically it's going to get weird. Leaping is weird, without doubt. If I show her I can leap, though, the amazingness of that, the spectacular nature of my new weirdness and the sheer possibility of the formerly impossible—that'll outweigh weird, right?

I hold up three fingers like a Boy Scout. That used to mean "honest" or "Scout's honor," but neither of us has any idea what it means now. It seems I've broken the Boy Scout finger thing. So many things broken between us.

"What do you want to show me?" she asks.

"You know this morning?"

Meg blinks. "We've met, yes, this morning."

"Right. This morning. When I popped into your car. Suddenly and without logical explanation. I was up in my apartment, which you left, and you walked directly to your car without pause, you walked quickly to your car—"

"I fled to my car."

"Exactly, fleeing toward your car by the most direct route to get away from me. Me locked away, back in the apartment from which you were fleeing."

"See, you're getting weird." She reaches for the door handle.

I grab her arm. "Meg, I can do it."

She looks at me and waits. She opens her hands slowly, like a flower blooming.

"Do what, James?"

"Leap," I say.

She just stares. She doesn't know what to say. She doesn't know what I mean.

"Yea for James!"

"No, really," I say. "I can do that—leap! Across space, without time, without walking, without cars or steps or feet or anything. I can leap from place to place. From my apartment to your Jeep. From my acupuncturist's to my…I mean, to a…I mean, to *that* garage!"

I point at the garage in question. No response.

"How do you think I got into the garage yesterday? How did I get in your house? Come on, Meg! I don't have a key. You took all my keys. You took the spare key out of the little smiling-dwarf flowerpot. So how'd I do it? How did I get in your Jeep today when I was upstairs, locked in my apartment? And I just did it again at the bookstore, a half hour ago. I leapt outside beneath a tree. I leapt last night, leapt out of a grocery store into the parking lot."

She folds her hands in her lap, checks her lipstick in the passenger-side mirror.

"Well?" I say.

No response.

"Meg?" I plead. "Say something."

"I'm just glad this didn't get weird." She starts to get out.

"Wait! I'll leap right now."

And it's her face that gets me. She stays in the car, she shuts her door again, but her face. Her look is somewhere between sheer disgust of having ever married me and complete pity.

Honestly, the pity griped me more. This woman who used to make up the bed every night before she went to sleep so that the covers would "stay right" all night; this woman who used to lecture me as to how dishes "liked to go" in a dishwasher, used to lecture and demonstrate the dishes' preference, then remove these sentient dishes so I'd get my turn at putting them in pleasingly; this woman who would wander through the house having conversations with imaginary people, begging them to tell her why toilet-paper rolls were hard to replace. This woman thinks I'm the crazy one.

Meg folds her hands and relaxes, waiting to watch me make an idiot of myself.

Now I'm brimming mad.

I look at my watch, move it too close to my face. I stare at it intently, spitefully. Look at it from an angle through my glasses. I'm going to leap like she's never seen.

I see the hands on my watch, see my own eye on the watch face. It's an angry eye. Where am I going to leap? I have an intense desire to leap onto the hood of Dougie's Lexus. I focus on my own eye on the watch face. An intense desire to leap, stand, and stomp on Dougie's hood, until Meg gets over the shock of my disappearance from the Volvo and runs over to slap me. It's not working, so I use my other eye, stare at it for a minute. I move the watch back and forth, closer and farther from my eye, thinking about how the surprise will take Meg a minute to recover from and I'll be stomping the guy's hood.

Meg whispers. "Did you do it yet?"

"Shh."

"Well, did you?"

"Be quiet!"

"I mean, you might have left and come back, and I missed it, right?"

"Shut up, Meg."

"Tell me when you're gone, so I'll know."

"Can you be quiet, please?"

"Oh! It's like golf."

"Have you always talked this much?"

"Was I talking?"

"There's no way to concentrate with you talking—"

"Sorry, Houdini," she says. "And yes. Yes, I have always talked this much."

I'm so hacked off! But I sit there focusing and unfocusing and trying to suddenly think of Dougie's smashed-up hood.

Nothing. I don't leap anywhere. I'm sitting there, cross-eyed and out of breath, next to my ex-wife who's just waiting to completely ridicule me.

I don't want to give up. Not in front of her. Not again. I keep staring at my watch, but it's not working, and I can hear her pity bubbling into sarcasm.

"Tell you what, James. I'm going to go back inside," she says. "When you get your magic-bean-double-agent watch working, leap on into the den, and we'll show the kids. They love a good leaper on a Saturday afternoon."

"Meg—"

"Can you fly, too?" she asks.

"I really can do this."

"Oh, I have no doubt," she says.

"It's just that this is my first day of leaping—"

"Everyone has to start somewhere," she says.

"I'm just now learning how to leap, to leap when I—"

"Fa-la-la-la-la, la-la-la-la, James!"

"Okay, I know it sounds crazy, but—"

I try to speak, but she's in full song now. "Meg, please, don't."

But she can't stop. She keeps singing while I get out, walk around to her side, open her door for her.

"On the first day of crazy, my ex-spouse gave to me: eleven wives a-sniping, ten James a-leaping, nine counselors counseling—"

"Stop it!" I yell.

I didn't mean to yell, but she stops. "I'm sorry I bothered you, Meg."

She was being a jerk, but she could often be a jerk to cover a sadder thing. She sighs, pushes back her bangs.

"James?" she says softly. She looks up at me, but I can't look at her eyes. "James, have you thought of talking to somebody about what's going on with you?"

"Doug's waiting, Meg. Let's go."

She gets out. She realizes she's gone too far, but she thinks I've gone too far as well. In her mind, it's a tie ball game.

I say nothing, just shut her door, walk around to the driver's side, and get in. She steps up to my window.

"I'm sorry," she says, "but, James, I can't keep doing this. I'm sorry things between us didn't work out. Married things. That's over now. I have a life, a different one, one with people who don't break into garages and steal shirts. Don't make what we do have left go bad, James, okay? Let's try to get through this adjustment period. Can we try that…please?"

I look at Meg, and she means it. She doesn't want to completely shelve me somewhere. She wants us to be an amiable, divorced couple. And it appears I'm wrecking that.

I mean, five years, right? We knew each other another three before that. That's a long time to know a person. I like knowing Meg. She probably knows me better than anybody. And I'm trashing all that *knowing* by convincing her I've swallowed my last marble whole.

I watch as she walks back across her yard—what used to be our yard—and goes inside.

"Sure, Meg," I say.

I sit there.

I don't have anyplace to go. I'm still reluctant to go back to the coffee shop. It's probably still a hostile environment with me ditching my shift. A visit to Meg isn't without its own hostilities.

I don't feel like going back to my apartment. Boxes of fun, there. I think that I should get in some practice time on leaping, work out all the kinks. Maybe if I got it down, I could still show Meg how it worked.

That's when I hear music. Electronic music.

Like a circus, a jewelry box, or maybe a calliope. It's the ice-cream truck coming down the street. Playing a ragtime version of "It's a Small World" or some such song. It passes right by my Volvo, and I watch the driver ringing the little bell. All the delicious frozen treats have their pictures pasted on the side of his van. A red stop sign is painted on the back, but with an exclamation mark: "Stop!"

Not seeing any children, the driver speeds up, takes the next right, and disappears around the corner, trailing that music. Meg comes out her front door with Doug's children. Meg, she's got a wad of dollars in her fist, and she's hurrying to catch the truck, see which way it went, but she stops at the curb.

With the wind, it doesn't seem she can figure out which way the echo of music leads, this street or that. Her hair blows in the wind. That hair that she's always tending to, just blown across her face. She doesn't seem to care. The kiddies each seem to think it's gone a different direction, and although they're serious about getting ice cream, they're shouting and laughing. But Meg's so serious. She's standing with the wind tossing her long hair, completely serious. She wants to do this for the kiddies, to be the one who catches the truck for them.

Meg always wanted kids. She'll make a great mother.

"It went up that street," I call out the car window, pointing.

The kids seem a little scared once they recognize me. Meg doesn't seem exactly pleased that I'm still hanging around, but she waves anyway.

"Thanks," she says and waves for me to go, to let me know she doesn't need my help or want it. And she starts to cross the street.

"You'll never catch him," I say.

She doesn't even turn around.

I dig out my wallet—feels good to know where it is. I've got a twenty-dollar bill, and I hope that's enough. It's been awhile since I bought anything from a truck that roves around the neighborhood.

I'll go catch the ice-cream truck, I decide. For Meg and the kiddies. I try to start the Volvo, but it just cranks and sputters. I'd been waiting for this. Often I only get so many starts per day, then I have to wait for sunrise again. It's just the way a Volvo this age works.

I see Meg walking and remember how the ice-cream truck sped up at that corner. I know she'll never catch him. Meg, she's not a runner. Not built for it, she's too thin, too dressed up, too heavy in the hair, never wearing the right shoes. I try the car again. Nothing.

I look in the side mirror. I see my own face, and that's the last thing I want to see. So I lean toward the mirror till it's just me and my own eyes. Just eyes to eyes, and I think of how much I miss Meg and how stupid I must seem to her. I think of how much Meg wants to please those kids and her hair blowing in her face while she looks for the truck. I see the ice-cream truck in my mind. The little silver bell on the outside of the cab, but somehow, inexplicably, the chain to ring it inside the cab.

I can see it: the little bell, the chain, the guy pulling that chain, his stubbly beard, I hear the tinkling music, the electronic ragtime playing louder and louder then louder until I'm looking straight at the unshaven driver through his windshield...

Wide eyes.

The driver's eyes go wide as he stomps his brakes.

I look down. The front bumper of the ice-cream truck stops about two inches from my knees.

"Whoa, fella!" The driver sticks his head out the truck's window. "Most people just wave from the curb when they want me to stop."

"Sorry," I say.

"I didn't even see you," he says, getting out to make his sale. "Where'd you come from?"

"My family's from east of here," I say. He allows this evasion because my wallet's out.

I have no idea what the kids will want. But what kid would refuse a Bomb Pop? And if I only buy one, there could be a fight. If not a Bomb Pop, then the next best is the Fudgsicle. Meg likes the Fudgsicles.

"Three Bomb Pops and three Fudgsicles." I order to cover all the statistical bases. Besides, I want one.

"Nineteen-fifty," the driver says. I can't possibly divide nineteen dollars and fifty cents by six quickly enough to challenge this insane price, so I pay the man. Gas costs a million dollars these days, so I'm sure I'm paying for this guy's gas.

"Whew! I didn't think I'd catch you." Meg says, coming around the back of the truck. She stops cold as a Bomb Pop when she sees me.

"How'd you…"

"Here." I hand Meg the Popsicles. "I had no idea what they'd want, but these are good. Tell them they were out of everything else if they complain."

I keep one of the Bomb Pops for myself.

"James? How did you—"

"You know how I got here," I say. We just stare at each other.

"Go on, they're melting," I say. "Nothing's as bad as a mushy Fudgsicle."

She looks at me with her mouth open, then turns to the ice-cream truck driver, but he's already climbing back into his truck. She looks at me again, closes her mouth.

"Thanks," she says. "I…they'll be…the kids will like these."

With Popsicles crammed in one arm, she uses her free hand to loop her hair behind each ear, finger swoop by finger swoop. She turns and walks back up the street toward her house.

It was good. It was a good thing to do. Meg would get the credit in the kiddies' eyes for chasing down the speeding ice-cream guy and bringing back the goods. They'd think she was Supermom. A hero.

And I was glad I did it for her.

I take the long way around the block back to my Volvo, eating my Bomb Pop.

Sure, I could have leapt, but I needed a walk just then.

9

I t was the good thing to do.

That leap for Meg, for the kids. And I realize what's missing.

I drive around most of the afternoon. Just driving till dark and piecing it together. I'm no longer worried that I will leap uncontrollably, leaving the Volvo to crash into an innocent pedestrian or some unsuspecting light pole. I know the missing piece now. Transparency and reflection? We know that part. A sudden intense desire to be elsewhere? Check.

So why couldn't I leap on top of Doug's Lexus and smash his windshield? What's wrong with that desire?

Yes, partly obvious, but look—with the cutting board, even though it was mine, it was a good thing to let Meg have it. With Dougie's shirt, Meg needed that back, and it was good, for Meg's sake, for me to give her the shirt back. With the yellow slip of ribbon at the church, I prayed. Praying's good, right? Talking to Father Chavez, a priest, is good, right? I leapt back near where the priests are. Good, good, good.

Leaping out of the grocery store? This one's harder 'cause it did make me steal groceries, but the theft was unintentional. I plan to go back and pay for that stuff. That's good, right? The impulse of the moment was, at worst, self-preservation. Officer Goss wouldn't have shot me, but he was clearly a threat, or could have been a threat, right?

The desire was simply to protect myself, and that's fairly good.

However, albeit intense, the desire to pummel to pieces my ex-wife's new boyfriend's Lexus's windshield, well…not so nice. See? That's the connecting thread. I'd never thought I'd say this, but super-heroic clichés are clichés for very practical reasons.

I must use my powers for good.

Actual good. Verifiable good. Usually, a guy gets sloshed with radioactive la-la and then events, personality, digestion, temperament, and perhaps childhood traumas dictate whether he becomes a super-hero or a supervillain. It doesn't seem I've been given the choice.

It's doing good or bust.

Then there's this: doing good feels, well, good. I realize that's like saying green looks greenish. What I mean is that to do something wholly for the betterment of someone else, strictly for what that person will get out of it, makes you feel wider, taller, or like caffeine addiction without the jitters or the eye aches.

It makes you want to hug babies. You're on the ground but something's soaring. Makes you want to poke everybody like a kid, saying, "Do it again! Do it again!" because it's its own strongest desire.

That isn't enough to make you good, but it's a start, isn't it? The beginning of an actual desire to be better, to do good…at least the train's pointed in the right direction. It makes me believe, just for a moment, that maybe I could be good. Maybe I'll feel the right things and I'll want to feel them. Maybe I'll want to believe.

How do you know what you believe when you're afraid to feel?

I believe, for that moment, I did Meg some good. I can see her, the crooked corner of her smile, her hair flapping in the wind. For a moment, for Meg and I, no wants were shoving past each other. We could see each other, and for just that moment, we were good.

Good should always feel as messy and surprising and gusty as hair blown across your face.

I stop for a burger, fries, and a Pepsi from a drive-through because I don't remember having eaten today except the Bomb Pop. I'm starved. Being a hero is demanding work and deserving of a hot meal.

I push my way inside my apartment, past the fallen barricade, shut the door, and secure it with a piece of duct tape. Everything is as I'd left it: miserable, wrecked, pitiful. I check the bathtub to be sure, and the valuables are unmoved. I need to watch some television, but not for bumming, not tonight. No, I plan to channel-surf the news for heroic opportunities. I've caught the do-gooder bug, and television is a perfect smorgasbord of calamities, disasters, and people in distress.

TV is still in the bathtub. I can lug it out to the living room, but I haven't fixed the door, so I know I'll just end up lugging it back tomorrow morning. I drag the card table over to the bathroom door and open the shower curtain. I plug the TV in at the sink outlet and turn on the news.

I sit down to my meal.

The news is very depressing, especially when you think of the people in tough spots as people you might actually help. You forget that when you're just watching. World news comes on first. The hurricanes. Military coups. A bomb threat on a Paris subway.

I don't see how I could help any of that. I can't leap to where a bomb is because no one knows where the bomb is. I could leap into the middle of a military coup only to be shot seconds later like anybody else. This doesn't sound very promising.

The hurricane looks a bit more possible. Pictures of people standing on their rooftops trying to escape the rising floodwaters flicker on the screen, but I'm not certain I can leap someone else away from a predicament like that. Basically, I'd be one more guy trapped on a roof. Rescuers probably hate leapers leaping in who then need rescue as well.

It's not easy. Just imagine a superpower for yourself, and you'll see. Don't pick the best one either—pick a sort of middle-of-the-road superability. Only one. Then go watch the news for heroic opportunities. It's not all secret high-tech caves and emergency signals.

This is more like horseshoes or homework, like a job interview for a job that doesn't exist. It's like trying to think good thoughts all day. You can try, but it takes effort. Maybe after a few successful super-rescues I'll get the hang of this, but right now I can't find a single good deed on the news that won't end in my own peril. Besides, I can't go saving folks on an empty stomach. The swimming-pool rules should apply: no leaping for thirty minutes after a meal. Don't leap in where you can crack your own neck.

The burger is fine, very greasy, and this food is warm. The Pepsi's fine, very drinkable and far superior to a lumpy protein shake. I couldn't imagine eating another stick of dried beef. Actually, the beef on the burger is almost identical to the jerky, but the fries are salty and good.

Finally, the local news comes on. The lead story is an apartment building on fire. I sit up, put my Pepsi down. This looks like it—complete with live coverage.

They're filming a fire that's burning up a building in town right now. Fire trucks have arrived, but the blaze isn't under control yet. Hoses and water and firemen with ladders and bullhorns. The camera shakes a little as we watch. It must be dangerous for the camera guy.

I stand and reach, turn on the bathroom light, the one above the mirror. I figure that will give me the best glare on my watch face. I tie my shoestrings securely. Maybe I need a coat. Leaping into a fire might be dangerous. I have no idea where the coats are packed, I'm only sure they're not in the box marked "Coats." That's full of pans. Maybe my coats are still in Meg's garage. That fire looks hot, an inferno.

I set down my burger and stare at the screen. The reporter keeps on looking over her shoulder at the blaze and pointing up at the windows. A couple of firemen rush out the front of the building with victims that were trapped inside. They're safe now. A few more people scurry down the fire escape. They look safe too, but the reporter keeps pointing up at a window on the third, maybe fourth floor, where the flames seem to be at their worst.

She's pointing because a lady is hanging out a window, waving her arms. She's definitely trapped, definitely in need of some help…maybe superhelp? How do you start? I figure my angle. Where to leap? I'm not so sure about where I'd come out. Would I just appear hanging from that lady's window? Would I appear inside the apartment with her, just as trapped as she is?

It's terrifying, really. Try it. I want to help her, but I don't feel qualified. I haven't practiced enough. I haven't practiced at all. This is a new shirt. I've just eaten a full meal. I feel more flammable than I ever have. How do I help if I don't know anymore about the inside of that building than the people who are trapped?

I admit it, okay? I do no more than anyone else watching the news that night. Like everybody else, I just watch. It's like I'm standing on the edge of the pool with my arms out, but I'm too scared to dive in. I admit this isn't necessarily heroic, let alone superheroic, but I'm in training.

Batman trained for years. Superman grew up like a regular kid in some small town before his human mother made him the cape. It usually takes a personal crisis to bust the super out of the hero, right?

Besides, right then the news cuts away from the fire. They promise updates, but they've only got so much time to get in all the bad news.

The next story is a gas-station robbery. It's not happening live like the fire, but we see a fuzzy black-and-white video clip of a man in a stocking cap pull a handgun on the station attendant. The lady backs up, afraid, and holds her hands up as the guy reaches across the counter and grabs all the cash out of her register. He waves the gun around, points it, shoves the cash in his coat pocket, and runs out of the store. I watch, sip my soda, and I'm entertained, but I wonder: if I leap there, do I leap into the gas station currently, or would I leap into the scene I just saw? Would I just be another customer tonight because this robbery happened late last night?

I've polished off all my fries, and I wonder if news research is the way to do this. By now, that feeling, the good rush from helping Meg, has completely worn off. I don't even want to leave the house tonight. It's already late, and the burger's made me sleepy. Where did it go? The will to do good? The news report about the gas station concludes. Luckily, no one was hurt.

We're all safe.

They cut back to the fire, but I can't watch.

I turn off the television and walk into the hall.

"Hey, Jack!"

It's Nelson. He comes down the hall, same old jeans and T-shirt, but this time the shirt's inside out so the words read backward, like in a mirror.

"Hey, Jackson," he says. "You got a pair of scissors? My toilet won't shut off."

I'm pretty sure I don't like Nelson, but what with my recent, complete lack of bravery, I'm just not feeling up to contempt. "What's up, Nelson?"

He stops and stares at me like this is precisely the problem he's always having with me. "Perhaps you heard? My toilet won't shut off."

"If I asked you why you need a pair of scissors for that, you'd actually explain, wouldn't you?"

"Do we have time for that?" he says.

I don't know what that means, so I can't be sure about the time requirements. "I don't believe I have any scissors, Nelson."

He makes a disgusted grunt, walks a little circle in front of me like he might leave, *please let him leave,* but no, it's just a thinking circle.

"You know what? If you don't like me, just say so."

"Haven't I?"

"If you don't want to help me out, even after I helped you out, just say you're a lopsided helper, but don't talk nonsense."

I pause to savor that irony. "I would be glad to help you," I say. "Okay, glad is way out of proportion to what I feel, but I'd do it, but I don't have any scissors."

"Then why didn't you say that?"

I lean cautiously toward him, smell his breath.

"Old Spice," he says, proudly. I can honestly say there's too much of that product being used in this world.

"I did, Nelson." I don't really want to have this conversation, but it's better than watching the news and doing nothing about it. "I told you I didn't have any scissors."

"No, Jack, you didn't."

"James," I say.

Again, he checks to see who's coming. After a thorough look down the hall, he turns a concerned face at me and takes a step back.

I sigh. "That's my name. I'm James. And James doesn't have any scissors either."

"Oh," he says. "I thought you said you didn't *believe* you had any."

"That's the same thing," I say.

"No, a person can believe all the wrong things and still have scissors somewhere."

"Right," I say. "You're absolutely right, Nelson." I just want him to go.

"No worries," he says, and he slaps me on the shoulder, it's all forgiven. He turns to go.

"Hey, Nelson."

"Yes, Jim?"

"What are the scissors for?"

"All my tools are tied up in a pillow case, and I can't work the knot loose. Gotta do the little things before you get to the main one. And all the time, she's arunning."

He walks away.

I go inside my apartment, shut the door. I walk over to my card table, stare at the remnants of my food—a hamburger wrapper, the empty fry carton. I don't have the heart to turn the television back on, but I want to find something, one little thing to do. I take another sip of soda. There, on the side of the cup, a boy's face stares at me. A missing kid, last seen two weeks ago with his father. They think his father nabbed him after school. His mother has sole custody. Chapman Collins is this boy's name, and it's some kind of school picture. He's only six. He's smiling as big as day, and his hair looks freshly combed.

"Chapman Collins," I say to no one particular.

Gotta do the little things before you get to the main one...

I twist my wrist so my watch catches a glare, and it flashes. I move my watch closer to my face. I squint hard and focus till my eyes go hazy.

The eyes flit between sight and that moment between, fleeting. Where you lose sight of yourself for a moment, long enough to see through, to see yourself reflected in the other, more than just you. Until you can't see either properly, till what you truly desire shows up...

A missing tooth.

The boy's missing a front tooth, but he has the widest smile.

"How'd you do that?" asks Chapman.

I'm sitting on the end of a bed in a small room. The boy leans against the headboard with his legs sprawled out on the bed. He's eating dry Cheerios from a coffee mug and looking straight at me, still smiling. I hear laughter behind me. It seems I appeared between the boy and his television.

"How'd you get in here?"

"Get up," I say. "We have to go."

"Who are you?"

"Chapman Collins!" I say, trying to sound as official as possible. "I'm here to rescue you."

"Cool!" he says.

"Put your shoes on, Chapman."

I stand up. It's a small little bedroom. The TV's clearly been pulled into this room from another, because it takes up way too much room. It's plopped on a set of drawers, covered with months of dust, dust that the TV seems absent of. Clearly, a man has moved this TV in here for the kid, the potentially dangerous, kidnapping father. Suddenly it hits me, I don't know if the father is in the next room…and I don't know just how unpredictable he might be.

"How are we going to get out?" Chapman asks.

"Shh!" I say. I move over to the door, listening for what's happening on the other side.

Chapman whispers, "Hey, Mister, is there something in my closet?"

"Oh." I shush Chapman again, step over to the other door, and put my ear against it.

"What are you listening for?"

I turn on the boy, grab him by the shoulders, surprising him. "Look, I'm here to rescue you, but you'll have to do exactly as I say, okay?" I heard that in a movie once. He just nods.

"Now, quietly, get up and follow me."

Chapman doesn't move. His shoes are on, untied, but he's sitting on the bed, kicking his legs.

I put one hand on the doorknob and take a deep breath. I hold out my other hand toward Chapman. "Okay, on three…" I say.

"One-two-three!" Chapman counts quickly.

He's seen that movie, it seems, but he's still sitting there eating his Cheerios.

"Come on," I scold him. "We're getting out of here."

"Mister, how are you going to unlock the door?"

I stand up straight and stare at him. Reach over and try the knob. "We're locked in," I say.

"My dad locks me in here when he goes to work."

"Your dad's not here?" I ask.

"He works nights, till three," he says.

He's really enjoying the Cheerios, shoving in handfuls like he's watching a movie, but he's watching me instead.

"What's your name, Mister?"

"My name? Oh, James."

"Mine's Chapman. You going to break down the door, James?"

"I hadn't thought of that," I confess.

I should think these things through better than I do. The door looks very solid and well made, this door.

"What about that window?" I ask him.

Chapman shrugs. I step over to the window and see why he's not moving. The window overlooks a parking lot, about four stories below. We're trapped.

"I think you should bust the door down," says Chapman, confidently.

I go back to the door, tap on it to see how thick it sounds.

"You sure your father isn't here, right?" I ask.

"You're kind of skittish."

"What?" I say.

"Skittish. That's what my dad calls my mom. It means antsy or jumpy, like you're afraid someone's going to jump out at you, and maybe hit you. I think you look jumpy."

"You mean I look too jumpy for a superhero?"

"No, for an adult. Are you okay?"

"I don't think I can break this door down, Chapman."

"Are you a superhero?" he asks.

"Kind of."

"Where's your stuff?"

"Excuse me?"

"Stuff. Don't you have a machine gun or a laser or a belt with tools? You know, stuff. Superstuff. Anything?"

"I've just started this superhero business, Chapman."

"You gotta have stuff."

"What do you recommend?"

"We could use a rope, for that window. You got a rope?"

"I don't have rope."

"You need rope. At least carry that. Can you fly?"

Why is that everybody's favorite? What's with the flying? Super-man's ruined it for the rest of us.

"I don't fly, and I didn't bring any stuff, Chapman."

"Oh."

His nose is running, and he keeps wiping it on his sleeve. He munches on the cereal like he hasn't eaten in days. He notices me watching him eat.

"My mom makes me eat fruit, but Dad says I can have all the Cheerios I want."

"Fruit is good for you," I say.

And I think, *That's it—I'm Nutrition Man.* I could paste the food-groups chart across my chest. Enforce good eating habits to all the kidnapped children in the world.

"You could loop it to your belt," he suggests.

"What?"

"A rope…they're not heavy."

"Sorry, no rope."

"A gold rope. That'd be cool. Or a helmet that shoots rope!"

"Drop the rope bit, kid."

"Are you going to buy a mask or something?"

"I was thinking about the cape."

"But you can't fly."

I stare at the locked door.

"I have a cape," he offers. "A green one. It's at my mom's house."

At this point, I'm not sure this boy knows he's been kidnapped. In fact, I'm beginning to wonder what I know. "Chapman, do you know where you are?"

"I'm in my room," he says.

"Yes, but do you know what's happened to you?"

"Oh, that. Sure," he answers. "I've seen my picture on the news. I'm a 'napped kid."

"Did your father kidnap you?"

"Sure. Then we moved in here, and he grew a mustache. His hair's blond now, but I think it looks funny. He works nights, and I know he has a different name 'cause of I've seen his nametag. And when he gets enough money, we're moving to Philadelphia. You got any weapons?"

"Why?" I ask. "Does your dad have weapons?"

"Yeah!" says Chapman, his eyes lighting up.

"My dad has the coolest knife. A Swiss army knife, and it's got a can opener and a toenail clipper and a—"

"No…I mean does your dad own a gun?"

"You're super jumpy."

"Is your dad a big man?"

"Medium."

"Just medium?"

"Yeah, but he's real tough. He could probably take you."

"You want me to stay or go?" I ask.

Chapman puts his coffee mug with his cereal on the nightstand, then hops off the bed. "You're scared, too, huh?"

"I just want to prepare, okay, kid? You got a baseball bat?"

"Are you going to hit my dad with a bat?"

"I hope not to meet your father," I say.

"You should get a gun before you get the cape," he says.

"Why don't you think I deserve a cape?"

"You don't fly or bust down doors. You need a laser gun, or some-one's going to pound you."

"Help me get us out of here, okay, kid?"

"Hey! That's not nice!"

And it wasn't, so I apologize to Chapman. I sit down on the bed, and he sits beside me.

"We're kind of trapped in here together, huh?"

"Looks that way."

"Want some Cheerios?"

I shake my head.

"It's cool you came to rescue me, James."

"Well, we're not out yet."

"You're trying. That's what is important," he says.

I just chuckle.

"What do you do, James?" he asks.

"You saying I shouldn't quit my day job, that it?" I say. "I work in coffee, Chapman."

"My dad likes coffee," he says.

"Other than that, I don't get out much."

"Me too."

This is crazy. There's got to be a way out. Surely a grown, caffeinated man can find a way out of a locked bedroom. I wonder if I can leap with the boy if I'm carrying him, but I have no idea how that'd work out. What if Chapman gets hurt? I'd definitely get sued, and I've lost my lawyer. Maybe I can help him escape later.

"Does your dad unlock this door when he's home?"

"When he's here, sure. But he locks the front door. He's smart. I thought about running and calling my mom, but he's too smart. He locks me in here when he goes to sleep, too."

I look at him. "You miss your mom?"

Chapman shrugs. "Yeah, but she's pretty much same as my dad, except she doesn't lock me in when she's asleep."

"Right," I say.

Chapman looks at me. "You married, James?"

"Have a Cheerio, Chapman."

"Divorced, huh?" he asks.

I stare at him. "Yeah."

"Oh," he seems sad. "I don't know any grownups who are married anymore."

"Well, we're sorry about that, kid. All of us."

"Mister, I'm sorry about that cape thing. You can get one if you want."

"Thanks," I say. And it's really ridiculous. Me and the six-year-old trapped, so I'm trying to think of options.

"Hey, you can call me Chap, okay?" he says.

"Can I call you Chappy?"

"Okay. Can I call you Jimmy?" he asks.

"Okay. Chappy, listen. My superpower is leaping. I leap from place to place. So what if I leap out of here and go get help?"

"I thought you were the help…"

"I did too, but it seems I need help being the help, okay?"

He shrugs. I stand up and hold my watch up to the light.

"Hey, Jimmy." He stops chewing. "Don't go yet. Please."

I realize I couldn't if I tried. There's no way I can focus on something else with the poor kid staring at me like that.

"If I don't go, what are we going to do?"

"Well, you can go in a minute, okay? My dad won't come back till three."

He's almost whining. What do I do if he cries? I sit down with him to wait and try to think.

Chapman picks up his Cheerios. He's perfectly content to wait for his father to come home and pound me. He asks, "Why'd you come?"

"What?"

"Why'd you pick me to rescue?"

I didn't feel it appropriate to tell him I was too afraid of a burning building.

"I saw your picture on a cup. I figured you needed help."

"Yeah, but just because you see my picture doesn't mean you gotta help me. I mean, lots of people know I'm missing. No one else has helped."

"I guess…well…" I stall. "If I went missing, I hope somebody would come for me."

"Oh," he says. He digs an entire Cheerio out of the gap from his missing front tooth.

"I bet my mom misses me," he says and eats the Cheerio.

"Do you miss her?" I ask.

"Yeah."

"Your mother must love you a lot."

"My dad loves me too."

"Yeah, but he's sort of a felon now."

"Yeah, Mom says he's crazy."

"Do you think he's crazy?"

"He's my dad."

"Right. He's probably crazy, and he loves you."

"Yeah," Chapman rubs his nose. "Why'd you get divorced?"

"Me? Things didn't work out."

"My family didn't work out either," he says.

"Why'd they get divorced?"

"They stopped trying to trust each other. That's what Mom says."

"That's why, huh?"

"Yeah, and she thinks he's crazy."

"Right."

"I couldn't help them either."

"Yeah."

"What about your mom and dad?" Chapman asks.

"They're dead."

"Married dead?"

"No, divorced dead."

"See, nobody's married anymore. Not even dead people. Mine are still alive though, huh?"

"Right. Your chances are still kicking, kid."

"Maybe they'll help each other later."

"Well, maybe, but your dad's in a heap of trouble for kidnapping you."

"I could say I ran away and he found me."

"But he didn't call your mom or anyone, Chappy, and it's been over a week. The police aren't going to buy that."

"I could say I forgot my mom's phone number."

"Too many phone books in the world for that to work, I'm afraid."

"Are you afraid, Jimmy?"

"No, I just drink too much coffee at work."

I could use a cup of coffee just then, a cup of something. This kid, my chosen superdeed, my act of goodness—none of it seems to work easily. How do television shows always wrap up so cleanly, right on the hour? This kid's alive, he's real, he talks, thinks, and eats Cheerios and asks too many questions. I just wanted to leap in and leap out. Now I'm sitting on the edge of a bed with a real kid who needs a real tissue. His little room is too hot, and his felon of a father probably turns off the air when he goes to work. I can't cool the room off, let alone un-nap this kid.

"Jimmy…are you a little afraid?" he repeats.

I stare at him. "I'm always a little afraid, Chappy."

We sit together listening to Chappy chew. It's louder because his mouth's open.

"Are you going to turn my dad in to the cops?"

"No, Chapman. I just want to see you back with your mom. She's probably worried sick, and I'm trying to help her out. Frankly, I hope I never run into your dad."

"You'd like him. He knows all kinds of stuff."

"Like what?"

"He can bend pennies with his teeth."

"Dear Lord in heaven—"

"I'll show you one. I've got one in my backpack."

"Never mind that, right now. We've got to find a way out of here."

Just then my cell phone buzzes in my pocket. I pull it out and see the number; it's Meg. Being in a situation that I cannot explain to her, I just let her leave a message.

Chapman looks at me, surprised. "All this time, you got a phone?"

It dawns on me. I may not be hero material.

"Why don't we call the police?" he suggests.

"Right." I dial 911. "Uh, yes, I have information about a missing child, Chapman Collins."

"Let me transfer you to the detective in charge of that case. Please hold."

I cover the phone. "Good idea, Chappy."

"Yeah," he says. He's smiling again.

It takes a minute, but finally, I hear, "This is Detective Goss. With whom am I speaking?"

I freeze and cover the phone, hoping my whole hand will cover the little speak hole. I hold it out to Chapman and mime for him to talk to them.

"Hello...Hello?" I can hear the detective talking. He's basically shouting.

Chapman takes my phone. "Hello?"

Chapman listens for a second. "Yeah, it's me. Chapman Collins... I'm the 'napped kid, right. Yeah, I'm okay, but we're trying to get out of here...yeah, me and James."

I shake my head at him and mouth, "I'm not here."

"James can't talk 'cause he's jumpy. He drinks too much coffee at work."

I fall off the bed. Fascinated, Chapman watches me but keeps talking.

"Yeah, James doesn't want me to tell you he's here... No, I just met him. No, my dad 'napped me... My dad? He's at work...yeah, me and James are locked in here... No, I don't know the address. Uh-huh...uh-huh...okay."

Chapman offers me the phone.

"He wants to speak to you."

Shaking my head vehemently, I whisper, "Tell him the address."

Chapman shrugs. "I don't know the address, Jimmy."

My detective is hearing the boy call me Jimmy. The kid doesn't know where we are.

"Jimmy can't come to the phone right now," he says.

I lean weakly on the television. That's when I see the old mail. I grab a letter and hand it to Chapman, pointing at the address.

"Oh, here it is," he says, then reads the address to the detective.

"Uh-huh. It says apartment 409…that's right… No, no. My dad 'napped me, but he's at work. He won't be back for a while. You guys can come anytime…right. No, no…James wants you to come. He's rescuing me… Nope, I checked, he's got no weapons, not even a rope, but he's a superhero."

Chapman looks over, smiles at me with that wide little-kid smile. He thinks he's doing me a favor. He gives me the thumbs-up.

"Uh-huh… Hold on, I'll ask."

Chapman covers the phone. "The policeman wants to know if you'll wait until they get here?"

I nod that I will.

"Yeah, James can stay till you get here… What?… No sir. James is real cool. He's a superhero… No, I've never met him before; he just appeared in my room to rescue me. That was the cool part. Otherwise, he's just a guy. Then he let me use his phone… Nope, the door's locked. We can't get out. That's why we called you… Yeah, you're going to have to bust the door. James, he couldn't bust it… Hey, sir? Can you call my mom and tell her I'm okay?"

I take the phone from him, cover the receiver, whisper, "Tell the police I'm really a good guy, okay?"

Chapman nods as if he understands, reaches out for the phone. "Hey, you still there? It's me again. Hey, James wanted me to tell you that he's really a good guy."

I take the phone from him and end the call, but I can't get mad at the kid.

I put the cell in my pocket and walk over to the window to watch for the police cars.

"He was nice," says Chapman.

"Sorry I grabbed the phone."

"It's yours."

"Look, I'll stay for a bit, but I've got to leap out of here when the police come, okay?"

"Are you running from the man?" he asks. This kid watches too much television, I'm thinking.

"Sort of, but don't mention that when they ask about me, okay?"

"Okay," he says. "Will you wait till they get here…like you promised?"

I look over to him, and I want him to smile at me one more time, like his picture on the cup. I really want someone to keep one promise to this kid.

"Yeah, Chappy. I'll wait until I see them."

He does. He smiles and wipes his nose, comes over, and sits on the bed so he can look out the window with me.

"Jimmy, do you think my dad loves me?"

"Well, they both love you, right?"

"That's what they say."

"Don't you believe them?"

"They're supposed to be together, you know? Whoever's house I'm in, I'm always thinking of the other one. And they both promise me stuff, but I don't know which one to believe."

"Right," I say, "but they both love you."

"Yeah. I believe them both. Just it's hard knowing which believing is which."

"Right."

We wait. We eat Cheerios. We kick our legs.

But it's only minutes till three squad cars with lights flashing come screeching up outside the apartment building.

"Okay. There they are, Chappy."

The boy hugs my leg. Cops pour out of their cars with walkie-talkies and guns drawn.

"I got to go, kid."

"Thanks for sitting with me."

"Sure," I say. "Stay back from that door when they're breaking it down, all right?"

"Okay."

I hold my watch up closer to the light. I catch a reflection, and I'm thinking very intense thoughts about my good card table and that good empty carton of good fries. I hear the police pounding on the front door of the apartment.

Chapman says, "Hey, James. You did real good."

"Thanks," I say.

"I'll tell my mom you said hello."

"Right. See you around, Chap…

I drop on the floor outside the bathroom door. It's exhausting, this doing good. I'm not good enough at good, and I'm taking the rest of the evening off. Retired or sick leave, I quit. It's enough for one night.

I sit on my floor for a while, catch my breath. I hope Chapman's fine. By now, the cops must have busted down the front door and unlocked the door to his bedroom. I imagine how he must feel, listening to the doors breaking in.

I hated leaving him there scared, but I had to go when I did, right? Poor Chappy. I can't imagine what it's like being whisked out of your home and carried off to some strange room where you spend all of your time.

Wait a minute… Yes, I can.

I get up, go brush my teeth, gargle, drink a glass of water. That's good for you. I check the front door, not that it locks, but that it's still there. I push a small barricade of boxes into place. Then I get ready for bed. When you wear the same clothes, both in and out of bed, getting ready for bed merely involves the emptying of pockets. My cell phone blinks with messages. Three, in fact, which is remarkable seeing as I didn't know three people knew my number.

I dial voice mail, press a jillion buttons.

First message: "Hey, James. This is Kevin. Just giving you a call. I thought you ought to know that Charlene came in. Monica and I tried to cover for you, but you know how Mike is. He pitched a fit till she had to pitch one too, and now she's kind of mad. You ought to call her. Make up something or let her know what's up, you know? I mean, give me a call if you want to talk. Sounds like you could use a friend right about now. And, you know, so could I. Bye."

Next message: "Hello, James, this is Father Chavez from Saint

John's downtown. I just called to say thanks for dropping by yesterday, and I'm interested in finishing our talk when you get the opportunity. It was fascinating, especially the Aquaman parts, and I'm sure there was more we didn't cover. I don't know precisely what God is doing in your life right now, James, but I'd love to help you out if I can. Stop back by or give me a call at the church and leave me a message. Take care. Good-bye."

Now that's precisely why I like Father Chavez. Any other priest would've made that creepy, or not done anything at all. Kevin's message, slightly creepy. Father Chavez, as I've said, he's a good man. Maybe I should tell him about leaping?

Superheroes need a moral guide, right? A confidant. A wise mentor to call on when they're bloodied from fighting. A really wise mentor might tell me how to keep away from bloodied fighting altogether. We could work out a special signal between us for times of leaping need. Come to think of it, do I need a secret lair? Does the cathedral have catacombs?

Last message: "Okay, James, don't hang up. It's me…and I'm calling to say, you know, the kids wanted me to tell you thanks for the Popsicles. Emma smeared her Bomb Pop all over her cheeks before Chunky took it out of her hand and swallowed it whole. Stick and all. Then Ponzy licked the poor girl's face till she screamed, giggling. You would have liked that. I mean, thanks. It was really great of you… Oh yeah, and this guy called. Early this morning. I meant to tell you, but well, you got a little strange, and I forgot. Said his name was Goss, I think. A detective. Something about a grocery store? I think your new credit cards might be giving you problems. You know how that store is. But he asked for you, so I told him, you know, that we're divorced. I hope you don't mind. And I told him where you work. He wanted to ask you something. I guess that's all."

I will never understand how that woman draws a paycheck as a lawyer. She rambles, digresses wildly, and wanders blindly off the point. She rarely has a point.

But I got the point about the detective. This is how he knows where I work. Great job, Meg. She gives out little cards that say she's a lawyer, but what lawyer does that? Spills out personal information to a guy over the phone simply 'cause he says he's a detective? I guess I'm not her client, but isn't there some sort of attorney–ex-spouse privilege?

I turn off the lamp, drop onto the bed.

Bedtime is my usual worry time. Tonight I'm thinking how much I don't like the Goss bit. Who is this guy?

It doesn't make sense, even to an unstable, neurotic person, for him to obsess over me. Is he really bent over a lippy moron in a grocery? Can he find me here? Maybe I should check into a hotel. No, even though Goss called my work, even though I accidentally called him on my cell phone, I don't think he'll find me. No one but Meg knows where my new apartment is. I changed my address in the computer at work so they'd be able to send me my tax stuff, but Charlene won't let him into the computer. All my mail still goes to Meg's house. And he can't want to find me that badly. Why? If he did, how's he going to catch me?

And if he catches me, I yawn, how's he going to keep me caught?

've figured it out.

How this all started. I know why it's happened to me.

It was at Mass, a couple of weeks ago. Father Chavez wouldn't remember it because he wasn't there. He was off at some conference, so we had a substitute priest. They do that, like baseball. Maybe he's the designated priest or a relief priest.

Father Somebody.

Regardless, not the usual priest, and this guy added stuff. He added to the Mass, but I don't mean heretical, more optional. Bonus liturgy. He chanted everything, sang parts I've never heard sung. From what I heard, I'm not so sure they should be sung.

He read all the pieces in the book. If he started a reading, he got every last crumb. He prayed extra prayers, longer prayers, fancy, surprise prayer endings with more hand gestures. I promise you, he snuck in as much Latin as he could, right in the middle of plain English, like, "Dear Lord, *O Dominus Domino.*" I don't know if he was just improvising or putting things back in the liturgy that Father Chavez always took out, but either way, the substitute priest added bits.

Meanwhile, an old guy is sitting across the aisle from me. We're both on the central aisle, but this old guy, he's on the groom's side, and I'm on the bride's. He's also one row ahead of me. There's nothing wrong with this old guy, but I notice him, right?

He's eating it up. All the extra bits. He's really old, like eighty-eight old, and digging the Latin and the bad singing.

So I watch him because he's more interesting than the ad-libbing priest. He's into it more than the relief priest, who is adding motions, but they're still just motions. For the old guy, it seems they're not just motions but connected, meaningful, a real thing he's part of. I think he's going to have a fit, he's so…what? Happy? Engaged? He's certain.

I don't know what it is about me, but I'm bugged. This stems back to my childhood, because I remember feeling this same sort of thing all my life. I'd see a kid on the playground, he's having a great time playing marbles by himself, and I'd get bugged. Being just a kid, on that same playground, I'd think, *Hey, I'm not that happy.*

It's not so much that I want the kid's happiness. I don't really want to work on it and fetch my own, either. Just bugged that this kid's so happy. Over-happy all on his own, you know? I want him to come down a bit, and I've always been this way. I get bugged.

No one has the right to that much happy. Not in front of everybody else.

No one deserves all that.

I'm watching the old guy, and he's kneeling, praying, singing, and responding. I'm definitely not in a holy frame of mind because I remember thinking, *Somebody needs to dunk this guy's head in a bucket of ice.*

But I ignore it, start to get over Happy Old Guy, and go back to focusing on the Incredible Singing Priest.

Then, the time comes for the Mass. You know, the get-in-line-go-down-front-to-receive-the-host part, and I've a place I need to be afterward. So I post up, get ready to box out people, rush the aisle the moment we get the signal to head for the front.

The kneeling part is over, the rows farthest front begin to empty, people shuffling their way into the aisle. And I keep my eye on this old guy. If he looks like he's about to move, I'm going for it.

I didn't have to worry, though, because it turns out he's a bonus kneeler. In the aisle, he has to drop down on one knee, genuflect toward the front, before he jumps in line.

This is my chance. Nobody will look at me funny for slipping past a guy who's bonus kneeling. I step out, cutting off the lady behind me, and as the old guy stands back up, I jump ahead of him. Leap in front, so to speak. I shove into his shoulder a tad, not hard, and bam—I'm in his place in line.

It's only one spot farther ahead in a very long line, but it feels good. I've accomplished something, one place farther along than the other guy. Now I figure he'll have something to say, at least a cough or a grunt, because I jumped in front of him.

But he does nothing. He's just as happy as he was before, and it's disconcerting. I had my blank, unconcerned, young-person face all ready for a comment. No dice.

Old Guy's completely content to be behind me. I glance at him, give him a nod, and he pats my arm and smiles.

I lose. I cut him off, and he's courteous, and I feel like dirty gum stuck under a bus seat. We progress through the line, slowly moving forward, one by one, and as we do, I feel worse and worse. Hanging on the wall above the Mass table, there's a crucifix. Christ on the cross in agony, bleeding, head bowed and bethorned.

And I wish I hadn't done it, taking the guy's place, because it seems small. I have this intense desire to let him have his place back. In a gallant sweeping, Elizabethan gesture, I want to let everybody see I let the old guy take the host first.

Because you're supposed to be free, right? Free of guilt, sin, and line cutting before you go, free and clean to take the host. No time to confess now, we're getting close to the front. I think of excusing myself from the whole ordeal, check my watch and get out of line, but I'm sure that'd be worse. People will definitely notice, definitely stare then. The priest will stare, and no one wants that kind of attention from God's man, even a substitute. You don't get in the Mass line, then hop out close to the front. It's just not done. People will think you're playing games with God.

Just kidding, God. No body and blood for me today. Just checking the menu. Thanks, but no.

Now I'm in front of the priest, who's looking at me and wondering why I won't kneel. I turn to this old guy and whisper, "Really, you were first. You go ahead. I leapt ahead of you."

I remember saying that exact word. *Leapt.*

But when I turn to say this, I realize Old Guy's praying. He's out-religioned me at every turn. He's really good. So there's nothing left to do but kneel.

"The body of Christ."

The substitute priest lays the wafer on my tongue.

And then I feel it. The same weightless, bony hand that patted my arm, now presses my shoulder. The host is on my tongue, and the old guy leans toward my ear, to avoid disturbing the priest.

"Christ leapt into both our places," he says. "You should have mine." He says this but not mean or vengeful, not like he's sticking it to me. He's thrilled.

My eyes open on the crucifix. They hang those at an angle so the dying Christ stares right at you when you're kneeling, because I'm eyeball to eyeball with the bloody One on his cross, with the old guy's breath on my neck and his whispering.

And it happened.

I didn't leap. Not bodily, but something inside did. Something that wasn't mine, it wasn't there before. I remember now.

I felt that leaping sensation for the first time, like sand falling upward, filling my head, then out through the top.

I felt joy.

Like the old guy slipped me his joy. Like that first leap into Meg's garage, this happens suddenly. I'm not in a rush anymore. I'm not feeling guilty or afraid. I'm not feeling bugged. I'm thrilled to be where I am. I've got his joy, and I don't know what he's got of mine. Frankly, I don't know what to do with it.

Everything changes. I'm not me, but I am—just with this extra part that messes up everything James would've done with a joy that James doesn't know how to deal with.

Is this what bumping into God is like?

At first, I think, *I feel great.* It was great, but it began to wear off, just as quickly it moved, it passed, almost immediately. It wouldn't stay still, or I wouldn't. The more I messed with it, the more it slipped through my fingers and jumped under my last thought.

As it began to wear off, I caught hold of it for a minute, because I remember thinking, *Thanks.* I was grateful, even if it was leaving, that I had felt it at all. Never before had I been grateful at Mass. It stayed still inside my gratitude for a second.

Until the old voice scared it off, my voice. The voice that told me to kick through that kid's marbles on the playground.

"You know you're going to have to pay for that, right?" it said.

I feared the voice, though I've known it all my life. Afraid of the answer, afraid of what I'd owe for my glimmer of joy. That quickly, I was back to being all thumbs, excuses, and anxieties. I knew then, when the joy had gone, in the hole it left, that something else was coming.

I had no idea what that might be, and I made myself forget the whole thing.

Now I remember. Tonight.

I woke up remembering all of it in the dark, sweating and afraid. I could feel that blank place the joy left, the empty feeling after the sand has fallen up, the weight of a thin hand upon my shoulder. I imagine feeling the thick drops of blood running between those eyes.

God did this to me.

Part 2

11

The next day I woke with one fear: God.

Strange as it is, this is a step in a positive direction for me. It's work, but I can do it at home. Having the one thought that God is meddling in my life as opposed to the usual terrifying hoard of thoughts, I have to wonder if this isn't what it feels like to be well adjusted.

Don't get me wrong—I'm not particularly at ease. Pillows are piled on my head, and the bedcovers are drawn tightly up to my neck. This God-is-up-to-something fear is pretty huge, as far as debilitating fears go. I'm nursing a chilling sense of dread up and down my bunched-up, pin-starved spine. But it's just the one dread, see? One huge fear instead of a million little ones. Like debt consolidation, and I know precisely who's sending the bill.

On the other hand, this is precisely what's scariest about God. Okay, hell is scariest, but God showing up today is a close second. God actually doing something today, not confined to the long-ago past or a sickbed, or with some saint in Calcutta. Do you see? If God is really God, then he doesn't have to tell you when God's going to do a thing. What if God starts doing things to you?

Unacceptable. Horrifying. Inconvenient.

Divinia Interruptus. And you can guarantee if God gives you a hundred bucks, he's coming back around to see what you bought with it. That's in the Bible. The parable of the coffee shop shows that the kingdom of heaven is likened unto a man who goes into a coffee shop and orders an espresso.

As the man talks across the counter, the coffee guy makes his coffee and sets the cup and saucer on the counter between them. But the man doesn't drink it; he keeps talking, so the coffee gets cold, useless. The coffee guy pours it out and pulls another, sets it up. The man still can't stop talking. The next one goes bad too. So the coffee guy throws that one out too, makes another. And this goes on, see?

You may think you're the coffee guy in the parable, but you're not—you're the espresso. (It's like that in parables.) You're not for *you*. You're someone else's beverage. And God, the coffee guy, he's going to keep remaking you again and again, as many times as it takes until you're drinkable. God's pulling the shots, and he's got standards.

If God changes you, you'd better change.

I should be practicing all day. God himself has gotten involved. No leaving him at church this time. God's on the loose, and who's to stop God from doing it again?

Next time, maybe it's not leaping powers. How about a second head? Three cheers for the man with fish fins! Who wants everything I touch to turn to copper?

No, it's time to do good, I know that much. You think God's not gonna care if I don't get cracking on saving the world?

Would you risk it?

I put on a pot of coffee.

I grab a pen, a pad of paper, getting ready to make my list. I write:

Good Deeds List:

Then I sit.

You can stare at a coffeepot, but it won't brew faster.

What are good deeds? Is there a book on this or a Web site? There are vintage good deeds, like feeding the poor or helping old ladies across busy intersections, but God didn't turn me into a Boy Scout. My good deeds have to involve this leaping power, otherwise, that's just sheer ingratitude. Anything I could have done last week when still normal—understanding what I mean by that—that's definitely out-of-bounds.

I worry. I pace. I arrange boxes to allow space to pace around them.

You'd think the hard part would be the physically impossible stuff, but seems it's not. Why is it such a problem to find a few, measly good deeds to put on your list?

First, because good deeds are much harder than "not bad" ones. Not shooting people, not laughing at the homeless, not pocketing a tip left on the table when you sit down—these are easy to locate.

Second, I'm scared, and fear doesn't make you the least bit adventurous. I'm just hoping to get a cup of coffee in me before the locusts come. How am I ever going to seriously concentrate on do-goodness with God breathing over my shoulder?

Third, my good friend, Officer Goss, the obsessed grocery cop. Really...do I matter to this detective?

Which brings me to Meg... I should call Meg. No, I should yell at Meg about talking to Goss. I write that on my list:

Call/yell at Meg re: creepy cop.

I need to explain that, for future reference, any detectives calling about any ex-spouses should be rebuffed and lied to.

I pour a cup of coffee, then sit with my pad of paper. I write:

Truth, Justice, and the American Way

This looks remarkably foolish on paper. What does that mean, the American Way? Under that I write:

Truth, Goodness, Beauty

I write it because the phrase is similar; then I remember why I dropped out of Philosophy 101. Being American, I might have a guess at the American Way, but not being an old, dead Greek guy? This is the worst list I've ever written.

I need help with this list. I should call Father Chavez.

Call priest/good deed suggestion.

Brewed coffee is clearly not going to be potent enough to help. This calls for espresso. A leap to the coffee shop. Coffee is a noble motivation, isn't it? God will understand, right? It's coffee, and I need it. It may not be yanking stray puppies out of traffic, but doesn't finishing a good-deeds list qualify as a good deed itself? Besides, coffee's good for me; I'm a more wholesome person when I'm properly caffeinated.

Coffee is good.

I shove this pitiful list into my pocket on my way to the window. I rip aside a curtain and look at my watch. High noon. The sunlight from the window is bright, so I twist my arm until my watch catches a beam. I catch it so suddenly that I squint, sunlight glaring sharply off the watch glass.

I wonder who's at the shop near noon on Sundays. I imagine

Charlene sitting in her back room, doing paperwork. That's definitely not where I want to appear. I concentrate on the trash bins behind the coffee shop. I look at my watch, twist my wrist so it catches the glare again, as I squint and try hard to picture those trash bins. Huge, green-gray plastic tubs that stink when you lift the lid. I imagine smelling down inside one.

Nothing happens.

I move the watch closer to my face till I see myself. I look at my reflection, my own face, and nothing seems good enough. I move my watch closer, and like before, I see my own wet, rolling eye, but this time it just looks trapped on the watch face. It leaps around trying to see itself, but it can't get free. I realize: my strongest desires are only strong because they're for *my good.* Not even that, they're for my own comfort, my habit. My desires are not desires but habits, strong only because they're so thoroughly mine.

I drop my hand to the windowsill. Such a bright, terrifying day.

The coffee shop's not far. I picked this apartment so I could walk to work. Maybe Monica can give me a ride home. She's usually there on Sundays.

Or maybe Kevin.

Suddenly, I feel awful. If I had any decency, I'd write Kevin on my list. He's a little needy for my tastes, and that doesn't inspire confidence that it'd be a good time, going somewhere with him. Besides, he wears these weird flip-flop clogs and rolls his pants legs up too far. The kind of guy who always wears two shirts, a normal one and an undershirt, no matter how hot it is. Sure, this coming from a guy who doesn't change his pants, but slobby and strange are different. Kevin always wears his nametag on his apron. I mean, they give everybody a nametag, but no one except Kevin wears it.

I can see it pinned, just so, to his black apron.

Inadvertently, I turn my wrist. A bright flash bursts off my watch, bright and blurry, and I'm falling upward outside myself…

A nametag.

When I stop squinting, I look down at the black apron, bunched on the counter at the coffee shop. I'm staring at Kevin's nametag.

"James!"

I turn and see Monica. I'm there, at the coffee shop, and incredibly glad I put on pants. Monica pushes me out from behind the counter, trundles me toward the front door.

"You know Charlene doesn't want you behind the counter in street clothes…come on."

In her desperation to help me, to hide me from my manager, Monica grabs my hand and leads me outside. It's almost romantic, this moment. Her hand is warm and soft, albeit dabbed with steamed-milk foam. I half hope we keep on walking down the street, hand in hand, but she turns and looks at our clasped hands. She releases mine, blushing twice in a row.

"Who's working today?" I ask.

Before she can answer, she has to stop blushing, which she can't seem to do, and Mike sticks his head out the front door.

"Hey, Jimbo, some tough-guy cop came by this morning asking for you." Mike, he's a tough guy in an apron. He's iron tough in his short black apron and his rumpled khaki shorts, with his coffee-stained white golf shirt.

I look to Monica, and a sad blush confirms that Mike is telling the truth. She has an entire blush language.

"Yeah," Mike continues. "He asked me what I thought of you, if you seemed distracted lately, or exhibited any unusual behavior. Did anything noticeably strange." Mike glares at Monica. He's always had his eye on her, but is clearly not her type. He needs someone more along the lines of a she-bear or a robot that empties ashtrays.

"What'd you tell him?" I ask, fearing the worst.

"I told him you'd been fired. Told him you weren't coming back."

Truthfully, I hadn't expected Mike to have my back like that. It seemed loyal, decent, almost friendly, and so I'm pleasantly surprised.

"Thanks, Mike. Thanks for ditching the guy for me."

He says, "I didn't ditch anybody, Jimbo. You're really fired. And I hope you don't come back."

Yes, this Mike I know.

"Good job, Mike. Just inches away from that merit badge, buddy." I wink at him.

He did what he wanted to do, so Mike shuts the front door and goes back to not working. Good deed or not, I consider leaping into his room while he sleeps, kicking over his food bowl, and showing him some amateur acupuncture.

"Oh, James," says Monica. She's about to burst with compassion at this scene of general animosity. She can't abide conflict. I've seen her serving sleep-deprived customers who are demanding more whipped cream, less whipped cream, blue whipped cream. She smiles and looks for blue food dye. She's the employee of the millennium. Really, I've seen her plaque and the commemorative pen.

Monica wants to hug everybody when there's trouble: me, Mike, Charlene, Kevin, the homeless guy who drinks out of the half-and-half pitchers. Everybody needs a hug right then, but nobody's there but me. She doesn't hug me; she's just thinking about it and blushes.

"I wanted to be the one to tell you, James," she says. "I'm so sorry. It's all my fault."

This is pure Monica, I think, *but completely unreasonable.* I cannot fathom anything that could be Monica's fault, anywhere. I can't imagine her doing a wrong thing. When I try to, I still can't. I can only imagine her nursing wet butterflies back to health and flight; I can imagine her dabbing the hot foreheads of earthquake victims, carrying stir sticks and a camp stove through gunfire to tiny villages of customers with tepid lattes. I cannot, however, imagine anything for which she could accurately take blame, let alone me losing my job for ditching a shift.

"Monica, it can't be your fault."

"Oh, James," she says this and shakes her head miserably. "I couldn't lie! I just couldn't."

It takes a minute to adjust for what Monica thinks is lying, but I begin to understand.

"Did Charlene ask you if I came in yesterday?"

With a gasp, she stops breathing like I just suddenly appeared in front of her. For a moment, I wonder if I have.

"What did Charlene ask you?" I ask, hoping to let her off the hook.

"She asked me, 'Did James look sick?' "

Honestly, she starts crying. Big, sad, broken-up-about-everything tears. Now I want to hug her, the detective, Meg, and everybody myself. I open the coffee-shop door, step inside, and grab a stack of napkins off the condiment bar. When I come out, as if being tortured, Monica breaks.

She confesses in a torrent of words and tears: "Mike told her! Maybe he didn't mean to, but he told her you came in. And you did, you came in, James, but not to work. You did stop by, James! I couldn't stop him. Then Charlene knew all about that, and Mike told her, I'm sure he didn't mean to get you in trouble, but he said you claimed to be sick. He said 'claimed' with this big shrug, because I guess he didn't believe you. I believed you, James, but Mike said that you looked fine to him, and then, 'Ask Monica. Monica was standing right there when he came in, Charlene.' And, James…James, he pointed at me! Mike raised his arm up, with me looking right at him, and…he pointed at me…like this!"

She tries to demonstrate, but it's just too much for her kind heart. She raises her arm, tries to scrunch her pretty face into a scowl like Mike's, but she can't, and she tries to point at me. Her thin hand never makes it up that far; it just won't make the requisite fist. She drops her arm and the halfhearted scowl, then sobs afresh.

"It's all right, Monica. He's a real pointer, that one. Don't worry about it, there wasn't anything else you could do."

It's too poor consolation for this girl. She's truly too good. Who knows why, but she believes in the good in me just as she believes in the good in Mike and Kevin.

"I'm so sorry, James," she cries. "So-so-sorry!"

She bunches up the napkins in a fluffy wad and wipes her entire face. Her entire face needs wiping, so many are this girl's tears. She smears tears, makeup, stray coffee grounds, and snot all over the napkins. She's a complete mess. I can only think that she's prettier without the makeup. She's kind even when she's crying, an angel in a coffee apron.

She blubbers, "What are you going to do now, James?"

I shrug. I've got God problems as well as superhero anxieties. This is not an answer I'm anywhere near having at this moment.

"First, your wife leaves you, now you lose your job. All because of me!"

And I wonder, does Monica think she made Meg leave? I can't imagine what series of her far-too-good actions she's translated into home wrecking. Has she really had a crush on me for a while? I consider how that might be, at all, possible.

Maybe I've always had a crush on her, but Meg didn't know. Monica didn't know. I didn't even know until Meg left and I had a nervous breakdown. No, Monica and I never did anything, never went anywhere, we weren't even flirty. I'm not sure I'd recognize flirty coming from such an innocent person, so maybe I missed it?

We certainly never went anywhere. Not even for lunch. Does Meg think we did? Did we? Not that I can remember, but I'm thinking about it now. "Monica?"

"Yes, James?"

"You and I…have we gone to lunch?"

The sound of this girl's sobbing stopping, suddenly, is like a tube at the bank drive-through. A quick intake of air, a distant whoosh and rattle, then silence.

"Today? No, thank you, I just had a really big breakfast and—"

"No, not today."

"Oh!" She corrects herself, sniffles again, looks down and tries to fold the ruined napkins neatly, thinks hard, frowns, then corrects me. "Yes, I did, this morning…pancakes."

"No, I mean…"

Nobody involved in this conversation seems to be in charge of it, but the girl's no longer crying, so I'm pleased.

"I'm not sure I understand," she says.

"Me neither, but all I'm asking is…do you remember anytime when…I mean, us…we…a lunch or a dinner?"

"Well, I guess, James," Monica says this slowly, looking for any helpful signals that I might be giving. Which I am not. I am currently broadcasting my idiot face, leaving her to say, "if you are asking for sometime…then yes, I'd love to."

That first leaping moment, with the cutting board, the towel, the pins, when I realized I was suddenly in the middle of my former garage—it felt just like this. Monica's looking at me, wearing a flattered smile, wondering what to wear, and I have no idea how I got here.

She sniffles. "If not today, when would you—"

"Today's fine," I interrupt. It seems I can't stop any of it now.

"Oh, I'm not hungry for lunch yet. And I'm kind of…still at work."

"Right, not lunch. Would you like to go to dinner?"

And I'm thinking this is a good thing, when this confused shock wears off, I'll be excited, and that this will work out much better than the garage thing. Getting to this place, I've exchanged the ex-wife's bawling-out for a dinner date with a pretty girl. But my face must show the slow progress of my thoughts, because Monica begins to suspect something.

"James?" she says.

"Yes, dear?" I say.

"Did you mean to ask me out?"

"I do now."

"Oh," she says.

We let a few customers pass; I hold open the door.

She says, "If you do now, then…I think I've accepted."

"Always good to double-check."

"Then I'll give you a double yes." She says this, turns to go, then turns again. "Oh…and yes!"

She turns to go, turns again. "Wait! You're unemployed, James, you can't afford to take me to dinner…but…I could make you dinner?"

"You're perfect," I say.

"You'd let me cook for you?" She blushes. "Oh, my parents are having some people over tonight. But I could make a dish of something and bring it over to you? Do you like lasagna?"

My mind tailspins. Not about lasagna, I love lasagna. Frankly, I love any cooked food right now, but my mind spins because she lives with her parents. I panic.

How old is she? I'm not a creep, but I haven't dated in a long time and haven't adjusted, in my mind, for my own age. I mean, I can't look at people and guess their age anymore because I forget how old I am. I'm usually off by about twelve years.

Maybe the girl I thought was at least twenty-two is actually fourteen. But, I correct, she works here. Aren't there child-labor laws? She can't be fourteen. No, I've seen her drive without help, so she's at least sixteen. But that's still no good.

Her dad will tell me it's a school night, and I've already got a detective watching me. Which reminds me—my detective came snooping around my workplace? Is he in the parking lot right now, hat pulled over his eyes, waiting to follow me home? To my apartment with no lockable door. This is where the possibly nineteen-year-old girl wants to have lasagna together. My disheveled apartment with the duct-taped door and the fixated detective. Maybe she's twenty.

Monica senses something wrong. "I know, I'm a little odd. Lilies for lullabies!"

I have no idea what this means, but she laughs, shakes her head back and forth so her ponytail swishes.

"It's silly, a twenty-five-year-old living with her parents, but my daddy has some health problems. I help Mom with his therapy. It's good training for me, as a physical therapist. I mean, for when I finish my degree."

I imagine this pretty twenty-five-year-old therapist layering pasta with ricotta while cheering her ailing father on at his treadmill. I can't stop myself from saying, "I love lasagna."

We stand there. Outside the coffee shop, a bright, gorgeous summer day, like we're romantic leads in a musical and the orchestra's playing a swoony instrumental bit. We're looking into each other's bloodshot eyes—hers from crying, mine from, you know—standing face-to-face in front of the coffee-shop door. Customers can't get in or out.

"Well, James," she says, stepping out of an angry lady's way. "I should get back to work." She sniffles, straightens her apron.

"Sure, Monica. I should go too… How do I get to your house?"

"Oh!" She giggles, touches my arm.

Maybe I am a superhero.

"Heavens and help!" she says. It sounds like that lullaby-lily thing, but no head motions. "Let me go write you directions."

I follow her inside and walk over to the end of the counter. I'm not really worried about bumping into Charlene if I'm already fired, but Mike's up to no good. He's milling around, eyeballing me, like he wants to cause trouble.

"Hey, Mike!" I call out. "Pull me six shots of espresso."

He spins around and grins like a dizzy cat or an addled monkey. He looks delirious with thoughts of antagonism, and he's not about to give me free coffee. Instead he saunters over, leans against the pastry case, and twirls a pair of sugar-crusted tongs.

"Hey, Jimbo," he says this loudly, loud enough he hopes Charlene can hear him in the back. "What's with the cops…you in trouble with the law, Jim?"

"Yeah, Mike. Killed a man back in '84, about your height. Murdered him with pastry tongs and buried him in a coffee bin. Been running all these years. Now, as they say, my fears have found me out."

"Sorry to hear that, Jim-Bob," he says. He isn't and neither am I, and we both know it.

Mike starts again. "Hope you don't mind, the nice policeman asked so many questions, I just wrote down your address for him. I found it on the phone list in back. The cop said your wife—excuse me, your ex-wife—wouldn't give it to him, but I'm a good citizen, so why obstruct justice, you know?"

"Thanks, Mike," I say. "While I'm thinking about it, you should really think about shaving that neck."

Mike snaps the tongs viciously at me, but Monica saves us both.

"Boys, boys." She's way too happy for either of us to mess it up by fighting around her.

"See you later, Mike," I say.

Monica brings me six shots of espresso and hands me a slip of folded paper with directions to her house. Both written directions and a detailed map with lots of well-drawn, manicured little arrows.

"Seven sound good?" I ask.

"Seven will be wonderful," she says.

"Then I'll see you later. Tell Charlene I apologize and tell Kevin I said, 'Hey.' "

"Omigosh!" says Monica.

I've never actually heard someone say, "Omigosh," so we're both having a moment of surprise. She puts both her hands on her cheeks.

"Kevin quit!" She whispers, leaning in and looking around to make sure no one is listening. She touches my arm like this is a huge event. Her hand, her fingertips really, pinch at my dirty T-shirt sleeve and pull ever so slightly, like she's removing a stray thread. This pulls me closer, and when she leans in, her eyes become plaintive—sad and true—I can see all the way into them. She trusts me completely, for who-knows-what reason, and she leans her face close to mine to whisper, to confide in me, as if we've known each other forever. We hardly know each other at all. How can someone just choose to know you... to be known?

"When Charlene said that you were fired, Kevin took off his apron and threw it there." She points at his apron on the counter, the apron I saw when I first appeared in the coffee shop.

"Kevin took his apron off, right after Charlene said you were fired, and he told her, 'I was thinking of quitting anyway. Let James have my spot.'"

"Charlene let him do that?" I ask.

"She couldn't stop him. He just tossed his apron there and got his stuff."

I pick up Kevin's apron, the one with his nametag that made my last leap successful. In a way, I have a date with Monica because of this nametag, because of Kevin.

I owe the guy, I think. Although I don't believe he quit because of me, he made a sort of gesture on my behalf. Half on my behalf. He said he was quitting anyway, right? There's a strange camaraderie to it. *I should definitely call Kevin,* I think. *Put him on the list.*

"Hey, maybe Kevin wants to rob banks with you?" Mike shouts. He's been listening to everything.

"Mike," I say, "why don't you—"

But Monica saves me from my mouth again. Clearly a morning full of pointing and firing has pushed her beyond what she can bear, and she wants no more disagreeable business. She's collected herself while she's writing out the cute map, and she's brave now. She kisses me lightly on the cheek.

"I'll see you at seven, James."

Monica walks to the back. Mike is dumbstruck. Mike is dumb, so this is not a difficult adjustment for him. For a girl who lives with her parents, that showed some moxie.

I walk out and down the street. I walk into the street, waving at the honkers. I spin around. I walk back toward the coffee shop and arrive merely to stand there. I walk in a circle like a sleepy dog. I should be practicing. I should be heading toward the trash bins in hopes of leaping home unnoticed. I should do so many things.

But that kiss: when you've been divorced by a woman you were married to for five years and dated for three years, and you've been the faithful sort so you haven't kissed anyone but your former wife-slash-girlfriend for a very long time, not even kissed her for quite a while there at the end of your failing marriage, and you find yourself suddenly being kissed on the cheek by a beautiful girl, a beautiful girl who's thinking about her lasagna recipe and who looks great even after she's cried her makeup off into a handful of napkins, well—I have a date.

I leap home…

12

Do you have milk?"

Standing in the middle of my apartment, I admit it, I scream. I'd write out the "Ah!" but there would be too many *h*'s. As soon as I appear, I hear that question behind me, and it's rattling after my otherwise smooth demeanor.

It's Nelson. He's standing in my kitchen with the refrigerator open.

"What are you doing in here?" I yell.

"Perhaps you've heard... I was looking for milk."

"In my apartment?"

"I don't have any in mine."

"You came in my apartment when I wasn't here!" I walk over and give him a little shove, slamming the fridge shut.

"Right. You weren't here, so I couldn't ask your permission."

"So you just push inside and snoop around?"

"The door was open," he says and shrugs toward the door.

"It's open now." I walked over and slam that too.

"It was open then, too." Nelson looks disapprovingly around my apartment. "You've got nothing I'd want to steal. Relax."

I'm being told to relax by the resident drunk.

"Not to be a pest, but about that milk—"

"Nelson, I just caught you trespassing and staring into my fridge. Did you see any milk while you were in there?"

"No."

"Do you think there's another place I'd keep milk if I had any?"

"You have a stereo in your bathtub…"

I push past him into my bathroom, throw back the curtain, and do a quick inventory.

"Why were you snooping around my bathtub?"

"Let me repeat myself for one last time: I was looking for milk. I need some milk 'cause I have to write a letter."

I stare at Nelson hard because I'm beginning to suspect that he says things like that just to deflect the conversation from unwanted questioning.

"Okay," he says, like he's talking to a dim-witted guy and he has to slow down so I can follow. "The lady in 304 has this laptop she lets me borrow, but she's out of town, and she's got this cat—"

"Stop. No more."

"Geez, okay," he crosses his arms like he didn't think our relationship would sour this soon. "If you ask me, the real question is about the bathtub pawn shop you're working back there."

"Look, Nelson, I'm sorry I don't have any milk. Not in the fridge, not in the tub, not on a plane, not on a train. But, Nelson, when I'm not here, even if the door is open and there's a reserved sign with your name hanging on my fridge, don't just come into my apartment. I don't care what excuse you got or what you need. I don't care if you're drunk or dying, don't—"

"I don't drink."

"Please tell me you do, because otherwise I don't see why I shouldn't take off a shoe and hit you."

"You think I drink, don't you? Have you ever seen me drink?"

"I've never seen Alaska with my own two eyes, but I—"

"Why are you bringing up Alaska?"

"Big drinking state," I answer him.

"I wouldn't know because I don't drink."

"I bet you're drunk right now."

"No, I'm not. I'm Protestant."

"Is that like being drunk for you?"

"Are you insulting me?"

"I'm thinking about it."

"You're not very kind."

"You're probably right about that."

"So we agree. Fair enough."

We both stand there. There's this standing. Finally Nelson says, "By the way, how'd you do that?"

"Do what?" I say, and immediately I'm nervous.

"You just appeared in the middle of your apartment, like whoosh or something."

"I've been meaning to talk with you about that," I say as I open the front door for him.

"Let's talk now," he says, and he sits on my floor.

"I'm not so sure I want to talk now."

"Why not?"

"Talking with you hurts."

"Do you treat people who like you this way?"

"Excuse me?"

"Do you punish everyone with your lack of trust?"

I look at Nelson. I don't like what he's saying to me, but I think it's an experiment, and I think, *I'll show you, why not, just to see how it goes. He's probably not much smarter than a guinea pig.* "Right, okay. You won't remember this if I do tell you, so listen carefully. I…can… leap…through…space."

I say this, putting a little space between each word for emphasis and do a foot shuffle to help the announcement. "Space," I say. "Through it. Leaping. Bodily. Instantaneously. God made me do it."

"Cool," he says, getting up, then he walks out the door.

"You okay with that?" I ask.

"Yep," he says, walking down the hallway.

"Why?"

Nelson stops, turns. "I don't tell God what he can do. He doesn't like it."

"Doesn't believing that cause some problems?"

"There're always problems."

"You're okay with what I'm suggesting?"

"You? I think you might be crazy." He comes back down the hall, waves for me to come closer. When I do, he whispers, "Or drunk. Or maybe some liar who lies for the need of his own lying, but I don't have problems with God doing whatever he feels like."

"You really believe that?"

"For a while now, yes."

"But what if God starts doing things to you?"

"He does things to me all the time."

"Really? Like what?"

"Like sunrises and air that somehow fits my lungs and the twinkling light from long dead stars, and people you meet on subways that you don't really want to talk with but God tells you to, so you do, and it's the best thing that happens to you all week."

"What kind of Protestant are you?"

"Re-reformed Protestant."

"What does that mean?"

"I'm working on that."

"Oh...okay, then."

"But you," he says, "you're saying believing causes problems?"

"Exactly."

"What's wrong with problems?"

"I don't like them. They worry me, they hurt, and they're problematic. Too similar to actual suffering."

"What's wrong with suffering?"

"Primarily...it's suffering."

"So belief causes suffering?"

"Right." It seems we agree again.

"You're wrong, Seamus."

"How on earth do you get to Seamus from James?"

"Oh, sorry. I spell the words out in my head."

"What—"

"Look, you're Catholic, Irish Catholic, right?"

"So?"

"So, J-a-m-e-s...S-h-a-m-e...S-e-a-m-u-s."

"Do you know how often your mouth forms word groups that don't mean anything?"

"Okay, Jameson, look, you're saying believing causes suffering, right?"

"Right."

"Wrong! It's the exact opposite. I have to go." He walks toward his apartment. "My TV shows are coming on. You're welcome."

"Thanks," I say, but his door has already closed.

I put off practicing the rest of that afternoon.

Funny how another person seeing your apartment makes you see the apartment just as it is. It's a wreck. No, not even that—if I unpacked, it'd be a wreck. I need to clean up. Love is in the air, but not the air of my apartment. I don't know what that is, but it's not love. Again, I consider checking into a hotel, just abandon this life, and check in to another. But my credit card's already soft with heat, so I start tidying up.

I'm not joking about having no furniture, which is something one should think about before inviting a guest over for dinner. I have large boxes of largely unorganized, largely useless stuff. If it's truly useful, Meg kept it. I caught her, physically, taking things out of boxes I'd packed and remarking, "You're not taking this. This is useful!"

That's how I know, and it's part of the reason I haven't unpacked. I know I don't actually need any of the things in these boxes. I'm also not sure how long I want to stay in this apartment. In my pre-date-with-Monica era, I enjoyed living in a cheap, garagelike apartment with the boxes and a bed. My depression thrived there. Now, however, I long for chairs, rugs and carpet, lamps, for any two matching plates, and an object people can gather around socially, for a table whose legs don't collapse.

I try to work with what I have. I tidy the stacks of boxes. I put smaller boxes atop larger boxes: for stability, for neatness, for general eye-pleasing-ness. And the stacks look better. They're more symmetrical, and it looks more like I understand gravity. I also don't want a big box to fall on sweet Monica as she tiptoes through the cardboard maze to wash up.

I talk to myself and decide to attack the duct tape. One window is still in a shamble of tape and curtains from Meg's visit yesterday morning. I try to extricate duct tape from the other window and only succeed in pulling curtains and rod down on top of my head again. Pulling at the tape, I tear the curtains; I bend solid metal curtain rings; I remove paint; I dislodge a wall socket; I rip plaster off the wall—a big chunk of it comes off with a piece of duct tape no bigger than my thumb.

Then I remove the barricade from the front door, which makes me look at best hermitlike and at worst homicidal. The door still doesn't lock, and I recall that Mike has now given that detective my address. I merely move the barricade slightly toward a corner because I might need that barricade yet.

Except for the tidied stacks, the apartment looks mildly worse for my having straightened it. I sit down on a box and sip my espresso at the card table. I think about a vase for the center of the table, maybe some flowers. This table wobbles dangerously.

I grab my cell phone.

"Hello?"

"Hey, Meg, this is James."

"I know. Are we done?"

"Hey, do you have our table?"

"Nope. I sold it to gypsies."

"Really...why?"

"No, James, I have my table. My table says, 'Hey.' "

"Yeah, the talking table. Can I borrow that?"

"My table says absolutely not."

"I taught that table to talk. Put it on the phone."

"Where's your card table?"

"It's right here with me, wobbling in the wind. Would you like to speak to it?"

"James—"

"No, probably you shouldn't, I think you're why it's nervous."

"Is this really why you called me?"

"Meg, I need a table, and I was hoping you might—"

"Do you have a phone book? Look under *F* for *furniture,* which will follow *freakish* and be right before *furthest thing from my mind.*"

"Come on. I'll bring it back tomorrow."

"James, you break into my house, then you—"

"I need one table, just one night. I'll take a speechless one."

"How's the leaping today?"

"Pretty good. Thanks for asking."

"You're welcome. And why is a cop looking for you?"

"Pass. My turn. Can I borrow a table?"

"I'm serious, James. The detective who called yesterday stopped by today and asked some weird questions. He asked if you'd been acting strangely lately."

"Being my lawyer, I hope you were vague. Did you say anything?"

"Nothing, James. What have you done?"

"Nothing, Meg, but next time, please tell him you've never met me."

"James, I have a friend. He works at the university in the psychology department. I could—"

"I have friends too, Meg, thus, the need for nonwobbly tables."

"If you want, I could get you in to see this guy—"

"Sorry, didn't mean to bother you, Meg," I say, snippy. "I just thought if you weren't cooking tonight—"

"Don't start on my cooking."

"I wasn't starting—"

"Is that all?"

I think of leaping there and taking the cutting board back. Or stealing another one of Dougie's laundered shirts. Or the table. Just a table! I just wanted a safe place for flowers, for one beautiful thing.

"James?"

"Have a good night, Meg."

"James—"

I hang up, but I don't know why I do that. Yes, I do. I like hanging up abruptly sometimes. It feels like I'm in control of something.

Regarding divorce: it's no picnic. Actually, it's all the ants and spoiled potato salad without the Frisbees and the endless supply of chips and sweet tea.

Divorce is very hard on those who need some sense of safety and control. I've been forcibly stripped of dogs and home, sent packing with all the useless items. I live in a ratty apartment without doorknobs.

And the worst part is…how do you know? I mean how do you ever know anything again?

If you swear before God, family, and friends, and you mean it and she means it and it goes south anyway, how do you know it won't again? How do you ever say "I know" again to another living soul? I don't know if Meg ever worries about that. Maybe I should call her and ask her, but I've already used up today's annoying-phone-call-from-ex-husband. I know it worries me. Divorce is all about worry. If you get behind in your worrying, will you ever catch back up?

It's like this: Meg's no worrier. She couldn't worry her way out of a paper bag. She leaves doors unlocked. Doors to her car in the drive-way, unlocked, overnight. Doors to the house, the front and the back.

Once, I woke up in the middle of the night to get a drink of water, plus check the doors, and a draft blew in through the kitchen. The door from the kitchen to the garage had wafted open, and a shopper's-guide newspaper mailer was blown all over the floor. When I looked into the garage—wide open. The garage door was open. I hit the floor and crawled back to the bedroom for the baseball bat. I crouched and turned on lights, jumped across doorways. I checked every corner of the house systematically from back to front so that no intruder could have slipped past my search and hidden again. I checked the icebox for very small intruders.

I triple-checked that my wallet and my keys were where I'd laid them, exactly at the angle I remembered. This is the angle I always use just in case something like this happens. I went outside the garage to see who'd opened it, if anyone waited for me to come outside with a bat so they could shoot me. There was no one.

Finally, I realized, it was Meg. She had come home late, after I'd already gone to bed, and she had simply left it open.

Somehow, this intelligent woman I'd married couldn't see the problem with that even when I shook her awake at three in the morning. She couldn't work up even a smidge of polite worry.

"What's wide open?" she muttered, rubbing her eyes.

"Yes, wide, wide, wide!" I said.

"The garage is open?"

"All of it!" I won't say I screamed, but she asked me if I'd been hurt.

"Wide open to the world, Meg!" I trundled her groggy body out of bed, pushed her down the hall to make her see this outrage for herself.

"Yes, James, I see. The garage is open. Can I go back to bed now?"

"Did you do this?"

"I don't remember leaving it open."

"Do you remember leaving it closed?" I asked.

"Not exactly."

"Well, exactly! You have to remember doing a thing exactly or you can't really say you've done it, now can you?"

"James—"

"No, Meg, either you remember distinctly pressing the button and watching the door until it bumps closed, or you just left it open."

"The batteries in the garage-door opener in my Jeep are weak. Sometimes I have to press it two or three times to get it to open. Maybe it opened by itself?"

And she thinks I'm the crazy one.

"We both have jobs, Meg. We both get paid. I would have sprung for the three-dollar packet of fresh batteries if you'd told me you were planning to leave our sleeping bodies open to assault overnight. I'd buy you a bucket of double-A batteries if you'd mention your total lack of concern for our well-being—"

"James, it's late. I did mention it, told you my garage opener was acting funny."

"Funny? Acting funny? You think inviting roaming criminals into our lovely home for a shopping spree is funny? Funny is when our dogs bark at each other at cat noises on television. Funny is climbing a tree to get on our roof because we've never bought a proper ladder. Funny is when the right front wheel falls off our lawn mower every time you pull it backward. Okay, that's not funny either, but you get what I'm saying."

"Events with no personal risk are funny." I was warming for the big finish. "I can crack up like the next guy. I'm good with the funny stuff in life. Leaving the garage door wide open all night long, this we do not classify under funny."

Meg just looked at me, the half-asleep way she does. This time, she's actually half asleep. She hit the button on the wall, and the garage door creaked and moaned as the gears ratcheted away. She opened her eyes wide and stuck out her neck, watching the garage door slowly shut. Once closed, she scratched her backside, then turned to go back to bed.

"You can't leave," I said.

Meg turned, and her look that night—I understand it now. That was months and months ago, maybe last year. But what I saw and did not understand that night, the way her hair fell into her eyes and she didn't smooth it away, the way her shoulders slouched, the resignation or the beginning of it, the way she breathed deep and sighed, shaking her head and saying, "I don't know, James. I don't know anymore."

I realize now, she had already thought it. She thought about leaving before that night. She'd already begun to leave.

You can never worry too soon.

As I leave to pick up Monica, I hang the doorknob gently in place and push at the duct tape until it stays, making it look almost like a normal doorknob. A little piece of tape sticks to my hand, so I place it like the one I did last night. I place it low on the door, across the crack between the door and the frame. Then I leave, a little early, so I won't get lost and be late for Monica. Besides, I want to stop off.

I want to bring her flowers.

13

James! They're beautiful."

Monica takes the flowers, the white daisies, and goes into the kitchen to look for a vase. They have vases, these people, and they know where they keep them. Different sizes of vases for different amounts of flowers, all kept in one place for easy locating and quick flower putting.

"Thank you, James." I think she's about to kiss me on the cheek again, but she stops herself. She's unwilling to seem too forward. And her father is sitting in a nearby easy chair.

"James, this is my daddy."

He turns in the chair but doesn't get up.

"Nice to meet you, Mr…" With my hand extended, I realize I don't know Monica's last name.

"Oates. Robert Oates. James, isn't it? Good to meet you, James."

"Good to meet you, Mr. Oates."

"Bobby…Bobby, please."

I look around to see who he's talking to.

"Bob, great!" Nervously excited, I scream this.

He ignores my volume because these are polite people.

"My Monica's good at the lasagna, James," he says, then he coughs a short fit.

"Daddy, don't get up," Monica says.

"You're a lucky man if she makes lasagna for you, my boy."

Monica blushes. She sweeps away to the kitchen again.

I've fallen into one of those television shows my parents *would* have let me watch. Her mother comes down the hall. I expect studio-audience applause.

"Mrs. Oates, nice to meet you."

"Are you the James we've heard so much about?"

"I hope so," I say.

Monica hears this and laughs, smiles back at me from the kitchen.

Monica Oates. I couldn't have guessed that, no sir, but horse-food last name or not, she's positively stunning tonight. She's wearing this long, dark green skirt that kind of wrinkles and flows. Like her eyes and her hair, her blouse is dark brown, and the sleeves go all the way to her wrists, but the neck is cut low enough to see some of her shoulders, her necklace, her tapered neck. She's put her hair up in this pretty pile of silky brown with two chopsticks through it, holding it all up.

"Did you see my flowers, Mama?" Monica asks.

"Oh, James, they're lovely. Thank you for brightening up our little house."

I think if it got any brighter around here, we'd nova into a whole new solar system.

"The Petersons won't stay too late; they're old," says Mrs. Oates, leaning over her husband's chair from behind him, kissing him on the forehead, and he laughs. He reaches up and rubs his wife's arm. She turns to me. "So you two are welcome to come back here after dinner, if you'd like."

"Thanks, Mama. Ready, James?"

Monica, in pink oven mitts, holds either end of a foil-wrapped casserole dish. It smells wonderful. She looks wonderful. Her parents are wonderful. A house with furniture, so wonderful.

In the Volvo, I hold the lasagna while she puts on her seat belt.

Regarding dishes recently removed from ovens: I'm holding the dish wrong, not wearing the pink oven mitts. I've scalded my fingerprints off, and maybe that's better with the detective in pursuit. My eyes water, I exhale through my nose like an angry bear. No, I don't have any idea how angry bears exhale, just take this dish away, I'm thinking. But Monica's having trouble with the seat belt because she is still wearing the oven mitts, and I think I'm going to cry.

"Thank you, James." She places the dish gingerly on her knees. "And thank you again for the flowers. They're lovely."

This time, I think I'm going to lean over and kiss her on the cheek, but my eyes are still teary from the lasagna, and I don't want her to think I'm overemotional.

We drive.

Slowly, I become aware of Monica. I mean, quietly aware. The two of us driving, with no radio or rush, just a nice silence between us. How she makes it nice, how her kindness makes such a slow, nice silence, with her hair pulled up in these unfathomable loops and sprigs. She sits so primly, smiling in her silence—she's beautiful.

"Monica," I say, "I need to apologize."

"Whatever for, James?"

"My apartment, my car, my plates, my wobbly table… Did I mention my apartment? I wish we could go somewhere else. Maybe—"

"James," Monica stares at me, waiting for me to be still and to see that she's already happy. "Don't worry about things, James."

She means it. I don't recall anyone ever saying don't worry and it actually meaning something.

I look at her, puzzled, until she asks, "What is it?"

"It's just," I say, "why are you so nice? So…perfect?"

On cue, she blushes. "Please don't say that." Her fingers fidget with the latch to the glove box. "I'm not so perfect."

"No, really, I've been imagining perfect people to talk to, and every time I do, they ask if I've met you."

She laughs at me, then frowns at the latch and shakes her head.

"Really…you look great. The food smells great. You're definitely the kindest person I've ever met. How do you work at the coffee shop—with Mike, for instance—and stay kind?"

She doesn't answer for such a long moment, I think I may have offended her. I look over, and she's tilted her head down a bit, not laughing or frowning. Maybe she's thinking too hard about something; if she's still smiling, it's the quiet afterglow of smile.

She deliberately removes her hands from the latch and puts them in her lap.

"Monica, are you all right?"

She looks up and I've never seen softer eyes.

"I had a baby once," she says. "She didn't breathe very long. Daddy had her christened at the hospital; he drove the priest over himself. Seventeen hours, that's all her little lungs could do, and then she left. During those hours I made every promise I could think to make. I promised God the whole world, but she died just the same. I was angry with God for a while, but it passed, and I've always tried to keep those promises anyway. It wasn't a this-for-that deal—they were promises. It's always been the good thing to do. And God's so surprising. Every time I try to keep them, God seems eager to help me out, like Daddy being able to run down the hospital stairs to get the priest. Even when I forget or I mess up, or when I feel all wrong and break down, just sobbing, God plops down next to me and squeezes my knee."

She switches her hands around in her lap, changing which hand holds the other.

"Oh, lilies for lullabies, sorry about this sadness. I didn't mean to say all that. That's why Mike doesn't get to me, because things aren't perfect. Since that time, whenever someone doesn't like me or whenever I want to be mean and angry, whenever I wonder where God slipped off to, I remember those seventeen hours watching my beautiful, breathing girl."

We drive for a while in silence, before I say, "I'm sorry, Monica."

She smiles and shakes her head.

"Did you…were you all alone?"

"I had my family there," she answers, then understands my question. "Oh…the baby's father? He didn't really want me. He just wanted one thing, once."

I look at her and wonder why she'd trust me enough to tell me all that.

"Well, I definitely don't want that," I say. "No way. I mean…"

Monica raises her eyebrows and laughs.

"Wait—" I'm glad she's smiling again, but it's definitely at my expense. "I mean, of course I want that, but only…"

She laughs again.

"No, I don't. Not at all. I mean…not *want* want."

"James, it's okay," she says.

"I mean, sure, maybe I've thought about it, but I don't want—"

If Monica has a worried look, I've found it. I grip the steering wheel and grit my teeth to keep myself from speaking. Finally, I manage, "Without further comment, I'd like to change this subject… May I change, please?"

"Yes," she laughs. "You may certainly change."

Night has fallen by the time we arrive at my apartment. It's a cool night, a proper evening with its stars, rising moon, and Monica. As we walk up the stairs to the second floor and down the hallway to my duct-taped door, side by side, I carry the lasagna regally, like I'm escorting a princess, carrying her box of jewels in my pink-oven-mitted grasp.

Then I see it.

After I see it, I wish so hard I hadn't seen it that I actually turn a full circle in the hallway, with the lasagna, trying to take back my seeing it. I hate when I see.

The scrap of tape. The one I put over the crack of the door, down low to signal intrusion, isn't only out of place—it's not even on the door. The tape is a foot or two away from the door, as if it fell off and was tracked out into the hallway by someone unaware of it.

"Monica," I say.

"Yes, James?" she says.

"Don't be alarmed."

"Omigosh…what?" she gasps.

"That sounds like alarm. Isn't that alarm?"

"Omigosh…yes!" she says, alarmed at her own involuntary alarm.

"That's definitely alarm," I say. "Easy."

"I'm sorry," she says. She holds her hands out in front of her, palms down, like she's trying to keep a beach ball under water. After a moment, quietly and controlled, she says, "I'm better, what is it?"

"Someone has broken into my apartment."

"Omigosh!" the girl gasps. She points at the duct-taped doorknob and gasps again. "James, they've taped that back in place."

"Actually, I taped the doorknob like that." *Don't explain*, I tell myself, *you always explain.*

"I locked myself out the other day and had to break in. I thought if I taped the doorknob back that it wouldn't look so obviously broken."

"Perhaps a transparent tape?" she offers.

I shrug. "Let's forget the doorknob. Do you see this piece of tape?" I pick the scrap up. "Since I couldn't lock the door, I put this piece on the crack of the door to see if it'd been opened while I was gone. It's been moved."

"So someone moved it?" she whispers and points toward the apartment.

During the whispering and pointing, it occurs to me, for the first time—someone might still be inside the apartment. Now I'm alarmed and whispery too. I don't know how that escaped my naturally instinctive panic-response. Perhaps I was too happy or in love. Perhaps my nerves are slipping because I think I'm superhuman.

Regardless, I make up for it now and panic. My lungs stop working, lungs that are too scared to extract the oxygen from the air going in and out my nose. I set the lasagna by the door. With one pink oven mitt I push Monica behind me, and with the other I grab the dangling doorknob.

"James."

She doesn't mean to, but that scares me witless, and when I jump, I inadvertently shove the door open.

"Oh!" Monica yelps, grabbing my elbow. "Stop, stop, James... Shouldn't we call the police?"

"Shh!" I put an oven mitt lightly to her lips.

She nods calmly, then to encourage me. She's an expressive nodder.

I look inside, scan the room, and crane my neck to look into the kitchen. I see no one. I wonder how long I can stand there before it becomes clear to Monica that I'm a terrified coward, so I step inside.

"Hello!" I call out. No answer.

Monica bumps me from behind. "James, look! They put everything in boxes. James, they've boxed everything up."

I thought I had covered that in the car. "It's all right."

She pulls at my arm, "James, what if they're coming back for another load?"

I grab her by the shoulders, a pink oven mitt on each petite, beautiful shoulder. "The boxes are mine. I left them that way... We're okay."

Monica nods as if she understands. I nod as if asking her if she's all right. She nods as if to say go ahead, check the rest of the apartment. I nod but only because I've gotten used to nodding. I'm reluctant to check the rest of the apartment, and I pat her shoulders a little.

But there's no turning back, and I look for something to pick up, a makeshift weapon to wield. All the good possible weaponry is still packed. The only thing I can find under the rushed circumstances is a copy of *Coffee Grinder's Monthly*.

Try this sometime. Try rolling up a magazine into a threatening shape while wearing oven mitts. Thus armed with a poorly rolled *Coffee Grinder's Monthly*, Monica and I edge toward the bedroom.

Hoping to regain an element of surprise after calling out hello at the front door, I jump quickly into the bedroom doorway and suddenly yell, "Ha!"

However—and very unfortunately—this only succeeds in surprising Monica. She screams.

Instinctively, I turn and hit her.

Just once, but a good hit with the magazine, centered on the throat; a deft, sure blow. That fast I pop her one good in the throat, then I watch my dream date gasp, stagger, gulp, and reel. She grips my shoulder like she's gagging on an apple, mango, or a whole grapefruit. Her eyes fill up with water. In the mirror of the closet door, Monica squeezes her cheeks and checks that her facial features are still in place. She has to shake out her fingers thoroughly before she can swallow again.

"You will never fully imagine how sorry I am at this moment."

I say it, but I've swatted the girl. I've hit her so hard her hair has fallen from the pins. She tries to smile but can't; she's too busy rubbing the red welt on her neck.

"I will apologize forever, and then I'll—"

She shakes her head, trying to communicate. Somehow, she understands.

"You understand?"

Yes, she nods. Nodding seems to hurt, but she's still nodding. It was assault, yes, but, she shakes, an accidental assault. Voicelessly, she shakes and nods till I understand. It's her fault. She accepts that; she shouldn't have screamed. Regardless, she won't scream again, not with that welt. We both should just hope that she'll speak again.

Gulping, she points toward the bathroom.

We edge forward. *Dear heavens,* I think, *please don't let whoever broke into my apartment be in a compromised situation in my bathroom. Not on my first date with Monica, please!*

I push the bathroom door, and it swings open slowly.

"If you're in there," I say, "come out with your pants up."

Nothing happens. I pull back the shower curtain, exposing my television and stereo.

"Did you do that, or the bad guy?" Monica coughs. She's catching on, but the poor woman, I've probably injured her vocal cords. I run her a glass of tap water.

"He didn't do that," I say. "I did."

Her eyes widen as she sips the water. "Who is he?"

Then I catch it, just a trace, but it's definitely there—Old Spice. Officer Goss. My starched nemesis. Here in the bathroom, which really scares me. What do I say to Monica?

Oh, that's just my detective. I'm wanted at the Shoppy Mart. I like to scare old ladies on weekends, then steal beef jerky.

"The intruder," I say. This is safe, noncommittal. "Are you all right?"

Monica checks her neck in the bathroom mirror. It's swelling.

"James, shouldn't we call the police?"

"No," I say.

I don't want to tell her I think it was the police, the grocery detective who's investigated my bathroom while I'm gone. I don't want her to know that I know what cologne the grocery detective wears.

"No, we're fine. Maybe that tape just fell off, lost its sticky."

Part of me wants to believe it's true. Not the part that lost hair earlier while wrestling with that tape, the part that knows *that* tape will never *lose* its sticky.

It's the part of me that wants, recklessly desires even, to believe anything causing a happy ending. Nothing's been moved. No one's been here, why do I think someone's been here, just because I think I smelled Old Spice, that doesn't—

Nelson.

I sigh angrily, but I'm relieved. I'm just imagining supercop. Nelson, he wears Old Spice. He comes and goes as he pleases, and showed interest in my bathtub pawn shop. Of course, it's Nelson.

"Monica, it's nothing," I say, with more conviction this time. "We're fine."

But Monica doesn't look very confident. I can tell this was not the kind of date she expected. Candlelight, maybe. A nice loaf of buttery bread warming in the oven. Music wafting from the stereo in the tub.

A bottle of wine on a picnic blanket on the floor. A healthy swat to the throat as we Scully-and-Mulder our way through my scary apartment? No, she never expected that.

"If you think it's okay," she says.

"I'll get the lasagna," I say. I go out into the hall and bring it in, setting it on the card table. I'm humming a sprite little ditty, feeling calm and casual. I get out the two plates, the forks and knife, perfectly place them, and pull out a chair for her.

Monica sits, but she's still unsure.

"James—" she says.

"We're fine," I say. I shrug, very carefree, nonchalant. I take off the oven mitts and drop them on the table, as if saying, "All done with scary!"

"James—"

"How's that throat?" I say.

"James, what if the intruder comes back?"

"Who?"

"The intruder," she says.

"Oh, him. Monica, I overreacted. Which I sometimes do... Maybe you've noticed."

"No, James, you didn't. You worried that someone might break in, and you put that tape there—"

"Monica, me and the tape, we've had a long afternoon, and I overreacted."

"But, what if you didn't, what if—"

"There's nothing to worry about. I apologize for—"

"But the tape."

"Monica, there's this crazy guy down the hall. Earlier today he—" I stop midsentence.

"James…James, what's wrong?"

I just stare. She traces my staring until we're both staring at the cheap, plastic grocery basket on my kitchen counter, the basket full of stolen items that I leapt out to my car with the other day. Monica doesn't know why we're both staring at a grocery basket.

I do. I didn't leave it on the counter. I'd put it in the shower so it wouldn't get stolen—technically not being mine. So maybe Nelson needed a basket for his shopping-in-my-kitchen needs. But maybe the detective came snooping and found a basket with Shoppy Mart printed on the side. Maybe I'm not imagining supercop. Maybe he's seen the basket and left the proof out for me to see that he's seen the proof. Maybe he's coming back… Maybe he's down the block getting a sandwich… Maybe he's on the stairs right now… My naturally instinctive panic-response is at one percent now.

"We have to go," I say, picking up the lasagna. Somehow it's still incredibly hot, and I quickly set it back down, don the pink mitts, hoist it up again.

"Omigosh! What's wrong?"

"We need to overreact again."

"What did you see?"

"Nothing. We just need to leave, right now."

"Where are we going?" Monica asks.

"Somewhere else. I've got a backup plan." But I don't; I'm desperate now.

"Why were you staring at that basket?"

"I'll tell you while we go." I grab her hand and pull her up.

"But where?" she asks innocently.

"Plan B," I say.

"What's B?"

"Please, let's argue at the next place. Let's go."

"I don't know enough to argue… Where are we going?"

"A hotel. I thought about checking us into a hotel anyway. Come on."

Me and the lasagna go out the door.

In the hallway, a number of important things flash through my mind in a quick ten-point list:

1. *Monica is not following me.*
2. *I just asked Monica to go to a hotel.*
3. *Monica's father, albeit unwell, strikes me as potentially handy with a rifle.*
4. *I just asked Monica to go to a hotel.*
5. *After swatting her in the throat, I asked Monica to go to a hotel.*
6. *After she confides in me about her past, I insinuate carnal thoughts, then visibly repress them.*
7. *I just asked her to a hotel.*
8. *If I try to explain, I will only further cement my stupidity.*
9. *Monica is still not following me.*
10. *I've finally found something that offends her.*

I peek back into the apartment.

It's sad. She's standing with her back to me, one hand resting on the chair I've pulled out for her, like no one ever has done that for her, and her other hand rubs her throat. I've hurt the kindest person I know.

"Monica, I didn't mean…"

She won't turn around, and I'm afraid she's crying again. I want to explain to her, trust her, even with my craziness. Tell her why we need to leave, about the tape and why a hotel, come absolutely clean to her.

I want to lay it all out: the crappy grocery basket, the overzealous detective, the old woman's purse. Tell her that something strange has happened to me and trust her with that. Tell her that I can leap through space, that maybe I'm crazy, and ask her if she thinks I am crazy. If she says I'm not crazy, I want to ask if she would help me pick out capes. Tell her I think God did this to me and ask if she thinks that's possible.

But she's not talking to me.

"Monica, maybe it would be best if I took you home."

She looks up, and perhaps I've hurt her twice, but she nods, tries to smile, then walks past me down the hall.

"Monica, wait…"

She stops but doesn't turn. Another thing broken, a thing lost.

"Yes?"

"Nothing," I say. "I'll take you home."

She nods. For the first time, when I see her face, I know she's listening to my words but without her eyes.

14

You don't have to walk me up."

Monica says this before I even stop the car. She's been quietly looking out her window, not looking at me, but I fish in my pocket for a hanky, just in case. A guy sporting a hanky doesn't actually exist anymore. Somehow I forget this in the impossible hope that I'll have a hanky for her to wipe her eyes. Instead, I find a crumpled scrap of paper.

When I do pull the car into the drive, she opens her door herself, or she tries. Volvo doors are too heavy, cranky, and temperamental. I jump out my side and run around to help her, but there's a garden hose running the edge of the yard, and I catch it with my foot. I don't fall, but I do catch my balance on her door. Which slams closed.

"Ouch...James!"

It's her hair, that hair so admiringly piled. Part of the pile is now caught in the closed door. I open the door.

"Monica, I'm sorry, I—"

"I'm fine." She announces this, shaking her rumpled head. "All good."

"It's my fault," I say.

"It's nobody's fault, James, really."

Unassisted, Monica slides out of the Volvo with the cold, uneaten lasagna.

"Have a good night, James," she says. She tries to smile. "Thanks."

I wait, watching until she's disappeared inside.

After her front door closes, it stays closed. Driving away, I feel the crunched paper in my hand, so I uncrumple it:

Good Deeds List:

Call/yell at Meg re: creepy cop.

Truth, Justice, the American Way

Truth, Goodness, Beauty

Call priest/good deed suggestions.

Coffee is good.

There it is, in writing. My laughable best effort at doing the world good. God's reminder that I shouldn't be busy with Monica's lasagna, that I should be busy with doing good and I deserve my wreck of an evening. In all the time I've known him, God gives me one thing to do, and I get distracted.

I muffed it, sure, but here's my real question: why did I think if I had a superpower that I'd be supergood? Automatically, you know. Why did I believe that—are these things similar? If so, what's a supervillain?

In fact, what is good? I'm not good. I don't even think I want to be. Desire for the good—that's the phrase isn't it, from all the philosophical boys. What do I desire? Who knows, least of all me? To desire a thing, you have to have the time to think about it, to sit in a chair with yourself and not have your hands shake. What do I actually desire? Does God really want to know that? If God asked you straight, would you tell him the truth?

The truth is, here you go: I have no desire. None whatsoever. Nothing strong enough to earn that term, and certainly not for someone else's good. If God's suggesting that am I expected to do good and also obligated to manufacture a genuine desire for it, this boat's sunk, still sitting on the trailer in the driveway. A stack of things need to happen before I desire to be good.

We've got to talk me out of me first.

Now God's gotten involved, at least with one life. Frightful to think about, he may be waiting for me to return the favor. Involvement—maybe God thinks that's happiness, the answer to desire?

Waiting your turn for the coffeepot. Leaving the last banana for someone's breakfast. Figuring out how to share a bathroom. Imagining how for someone else, is that the good?

Maybe that's why Meg left. Maybe I never figured it out enough, I kept waiting for her to figure me out while she was on the other side waiting for the same. We imagine one person, one love, will be enough to balance the differences. That one love will outweigh a world of worry that loads the scales, but it never does. Maybe that's why she left: my world of worry outweighed her love.

"It's my fault," I say.

"It's nobody's fault, James. It's not about blame," Meg says. "Irreconcilable differences is what the paperwork will say."

"There are already papers on this?"

"I'm a lawyer, James."

"You've already started the paperwork?"

"No, not really. Nothing's been filed, but I've pulled out the forms and filled them out, in my spare time."

"You have spare time for divorce paperwork, but you're just getting around to telling your husband?"

"Be reasonable. I'm not conspiring against you. I've been considering this for a while."

"Why? Irreconcilable differences? I don't know what that means, Meg. Differences are usually irreconcilable, aren't they? If they're real differences, and not just watching baseball instead of *Law & Order*. Real differences are the point, aren't they?

"It's your differences that remind me I'm living with Meg instead of some other woman. I want the woman who has spent years trying to build a compost pile in the corner of the backyard but doesn't realize it's just an unsightly heap of rubbish. I'd miss the way you separate garbage for recycling, though you never take it anywhere, and it ends up thrown out with the rest of the trash when you're not looking. How could I go to bed without that perpetually cold someone piling on blankets when the house is burning hot? One of my favorite argument openings, 'If you bring that fan in here, I'm going to a hotel.' How could I sleep without that?"

"James—"

"We see eye to eye on the important things, don't we? If we even talk about important things. What are the important things? We usually vote the same, or we vote differently for the same reasons. We don't have kids because we both agree the other wouldn't be able to handle it, but we agree, right? I make dinner on days that start with *T* and *F*. What's so freaking irreconcilable?

"If you're just mad about the little stuff, well, give me a chance. Tell me what little things are irreconcilably huge, and I'll adjust. But the huge things, potentially huge, don't seem to be what's nagging you. What is it?"

"It's the whole thing, James. Not this issue or that. It's all of it together, too often, too long."

"Too long...five years, what is that? We haven't made it to the pewter anniversary gifts yet. We're back at burnt paper or broken glass or other meaningless compound."

"That's it," she says. "Meaninglessness. Five years, one after the other, one year compounding the next with meaninglessness. I want my life to mean more."

"Well, I'm so sorry I'm not a guru chocked with pithy little proverbs to make your life stunning with purpose."

"It's not you—it's us. What are we? Just two people who got married and started living in the same house. Do we even remember why? That's meaningless; we don't mean anything, James. We don't mean anything to anyone, to each other, to—"

"I don't mean anything to you?"

"James, that's not what I'm trying to say—"

"You just said it. You said I don't mean anything to you."

"Of course, you mean something to me. It's just that it's not enough, not anymore, all right?"

"Right."

"Okay," she says.

"So. Did you have a list of things I haven't lived up to? One you've been secretly checking off in your spare time at the office?"

"James, stop. I don't have lists."

"Actually, I've seen your lists. You're the most list-making person I've ever met."

"I didn't marry you with a list in mind."

"Your list either changed, or you finally got one, and I don't add up."

"Yes, James, I've changed over five years; you've changed. We both want… I don't know what you want, but I want more. I didn't know I would or mean to, but now I do. I want more out of life than what we have."

"Like what?"

"I can't answer that. I just know it's not enough."

"Not enough—that's rough. No chance of me ever making that grade, huh? Just not enough. No matter how I shuffle myself around, I'm never going to be enough since you've already decided, am I?"

"No, James. I'm afraid not."

"You're afraid not?"

"Talking with you is like arguing with an echo. I'm tired of that."

"Irreconcilably tired?"

"I'm afraid so."

I drive slowly.

No reason to hurry home, me and the Volvo. I can still smell traces of lasagna.

On the floorboard, on Monica's side, I see a daisy. It must've fallen out of her bouquet on the way over to her house. A white daisy with a broken stem.

"Good night, Monica," I say. I put the white daisy in my pocket.

15

I pull into the parking lot of my apartment.

Perhaps I've mentioned the wonderful view my apartment has of this particular lot? It means parkers can see directly into my apartment from aforementioned parking lot. Especially at night when the curtains have been yanked down by a duct-taping fool and a bright bulb glows inside of aforementioned apartment.

Funny thing, though, I didn't leave a light on. I know how lit I leave a place, paranoid neurotic, remember? My toaster faces north. I know which floorboards creak in my hallway and can navigate around them in case of terrorist invasion. I've named the boards alphabetically—Alpha, Bravo, Charlie…

So I don't park; I keep driving. I drive out of the lot, circle the block, do a drive-by, and look into my apartment. That's when I see him.

Just a glimpse, but I'm sure it's him, my detective—the close-cropped hair, his inflated chest, a starched white shirt. I see him walking past the window, and I coast down a side street to park the Volvo where it can't be seen. I climb out, slip into the shadows of the building, and cross the street to watch.

The light clicks off in my apartment, and I figure he's leaving again. After all, who'd want to spend the evening in my apartment? There's nowhere to sit. But he never comes out the front door of the apartment building. I watch, fifteen or twenty minutes, and he never comes out.

Goss, a trap, is it? Supercop lying low in my apartment, lights out, just waiting for me to come home. I'm crazy, and this behavior strikes me as odd. But I can locate illegality in this situation, that guy being in my apartment.

I walk down the block to a pay phone.

"911 hotline. This is Ellen, what is your emergency?"

"Ellen, hi." I say.

"This is 911. Your location, please?"

"Yeah, um, Ellen, was it?"

"L-N," the woman enunciates. "What is your emergency and location, sir?"

"My current location, um…Ellen, right?"

"*E* as in emergencies only, *L* as in liar, another *L* as in we'll lock you up for lying, another *E* as in emergencies only, *N* as in not in the mood. What's your location?"

"Oh, Ellen!" I say as if I've finally placed her role in my life. "I'm at a pay phone at Barksdale and Peabody."

"What's your emergency, sir?" She's efficient, my Ellen.

"My emergency? Well, I—"

"Sir, please don't do this. Okay, just don't. Either hang up or get to it. I've got call lights flashing all over the place here."

"Sorry, Ellen. My emergency is that I came back to my apartment—"

"Where is your apartment?"

"Number 208, Barksdale Manor. Right across the street from this phone, Ellen."

"Your name?"

"Don't you want to know about what's happening in my apartment?"

"Not right now; now I want your name."

"My name?"

"Your handle, partner. Spill it, or I move on."

"James. James is my name."

"Did you just make that up, sir?" she asks.

"Do you get training classes for this?" I ask.

"If you say your last name is Smith, I hang up."

"I'm not telling you my last name. I'm telling you there's a guy wandering around inside my apartment."

"Do you know this guy?"

"Not really, Ellen."

"Not really the right answer, James. Thank you for calling 911—"

"Wait, Ellen, please! I've seen this guy at the grocery store, but he's not a friend or anything."

"How did he get in your apartment?"

"Well, thank you, Ellen, it's kind of you to ask. I went up to my apartment just now and found the doorknob busted off the door, and a bunch of duct tape all over everything. Fearing ne'er-do-wells, I immediately left to call 911 from this pay phone."

"If you left immediately, how do you know the ne'er-do-well is a he?"

Ellen is good, so I stall. "Do you mind saying that again?"

"How do you know who the 'he' is?"

"Now say it faster."

"Sir, you do not sound—even remotely—like someone concerned about your apartment being robbed."

"And you, Ellen, do not sound remotely like an emergency hotline operator."

I could tell she liked me.

"You can hang up and call again for a different, more believable operator. Would you like me to disconnect you, sir?"

"Ellen, a guy I saw at the grocery store is in the window of my apartment. I saw him from the parking lot. My door had the knob bashed off, and he's sitting in there, with the lights off."

"Is it your birthday?"

"No, Ellen, this is not my surprise party."

"He turned the lights off?"

"Yes. I saw him walking around; then he turned the lights off. He didn't leave the apartment building because I'm watching the only door out right now."

"Well, sir, that's the first believable thing you've said in this entire conversation."

"Wow, you're tough."

"Tough job. You got to be."

"I'm just glad I'm not bleeding."

"I'd know if you were bleeding. We'll dispatch a car immediately, sir."

"Excuse me for asking, but how do I know you'll actually do that?"

"You doubt me, sir?"

"Like I said, you're tough, Ellen. We've gotten off to a rocky start."

"I'll get into big trouble if I don't dispatch on a criminal call."

"We wouldn't want that."

"And, Mr. James, if this is a prank call, you'll be in big trouble as well."

I hang up the pay phone. Detective Goss is still in there, but I don't want to be standing around here when the cops find out it's a cop in my apartment. I plan to be around, just not next to the suspicious pay phone.

I have my special ways of being around.

I get back to the Volvo and speed away.

I calculate ten minutes for the cops to show up, another five for them to get together and make a plan for entering the apartment—then the mighty Detective Goss must explain himself. That's what I don't want to miss. I'm hoping to get a read on this Goss fellow, why I'm so important to him, what's his next move. In the meantime, I got twenty or so minutes.

I don't know how this works for normal people, but being a basically paranoid-delusional person who finds himself with someone actually following him—well, most of my life has been lived talking myself out of such imagined plots. Now it's happening. There is a guy, and he is following me. An actual emergency.

In a way, it's like an "I told you so" to the universe. I feel prepared. I have been practicing for this sort of thing all my life.

I go to the ATM near my house, withdraw a few hundred bucks. That should get me through a few days in a hotel. I catch the interstate and take it downtown. It's 8:52 p.m. on a Sunday night, so no traffic. I want a nice hotel, you know, the kind for businessmen and their conventions. Something busy, full of out-of-towners, something with a steam room. Great for the sinuses. I want my own copy of the newspaper in the morning. If I'm getting a hotel room I can't really afford, I'm popping for a good one.

The Hometown Suites will suit me fine. Ellen's phone interrogation has got me on my toes now, and when I check in, I pay in cash and don't use my real name. Gabe Oates. My name is Gabe Oates.

I'm a big, cash-paying guy named Gabe Oates. I tuck my shirt in so I'll look decent. I leave my backpack in the Volvo so they won't think I'm homeless. (Even tucked, I look homeless.) The recorder, I have, as it's very important for recording Detective Goss.

"The only room available, sir, fourteenth floor."

Fine. Gabe Oates is fine with heights. Wake-up call, I need not; please tell the staff not to disturb. Gabe Oates, a late sleeper.

My room is great. There's a huge bed, two ice buckets, Dish Network, clean towels. I should have checked into a hotel years ago. No time for the luxuries, though.

I lock the door, pull it twice to make sure it's locked, flip the dead-bolt. I turn on the TV, ease the volume up so it sounds like someone's alive in here. I take my hotel key card, put it in my pocket, and my recorder as well. My car keys, my wallet. I've got my glasses. I clean everything off the table next to the TV and pull the table out from the wall. Very deliberately, I put the white daisy in the center of it. Very deliberately, I look at it, recording a mental image.

I turn the light on in the bathroom for added glare. I sit on the edge of the bed. It's 9:23 p.m. by my watch, but that's not why I'm looking at it. I start to stare intensely until my vision blurs. I see the hands, then just the glass of the watch face. I turn my wrist until the glare from the bathroom catches. I squint and stare and blur and turn my wrist till I see the light fixture from the bathroom reflected on the watch face.

I want to leap into my bathtub, back at my apartment, behind the shower curtain. I'm sure the cops Ellen sent have arrived, and I'm hoping they've already checked behind the curtain. If they've checked once, why would they check twice? So if I appear behind there…

It's not the worst plan, come on. In a pickle, I can always leap away. I get the dreamy eye focus thing working; I know my port of destination. All that's left is the intense desire. Oh boy, oh boy, oh boy, oh boy! I intensely desire to hear Detective Goss explaining to his colleagues why he's breaking into apartments.

Then I remember, there should be some good reason for my leap.

And here's where I do it. I think, forget goodness! I'm mad. My home, that hole I've been forced to make my home, has been invaded.

My wife hates me, my one date hates me, I've lost my job, I've eaten nothing but old meat strips for days, and I desire a little satisfaction— I'm letting the mad out. Come on, madness!

I'm still staring at my watch, doing the blurry focus bit with the reflection, but the more the reflection hits my eyes, the madder I get. That rolling crazy wild eye. This isn't to prove anything to anyone or help anyone out; I'm not anybody's hero. My intense desire is for myself. I want to leap into that shower because I want it.

I won't take no for an…

"No!"

"Explain to me again, Bill. Where did you meet this guy?"

"I told you already," says Detective Goss.

I can hear them through the shower curtain, my detective and the other cop. They both sound irritated, and they're both close. Not in the bathroom, not that close, but they must be in my bedroom.

"I saw him steal groceries from the Shoppy Mart while I was there. He also tried to steal an old lady's purse. So I got his license plate, and I tracked him here."

"You just break into his apartment, Bill?" says the other tough guy. I'm glad they sent a tough guy for me. Thank you, Ellen.

"Look around this place, Arnie. Just look for yourself. The guy's a wack job."

I take offense to this, straighten my back, and nearly fall over my stereo. There's not enough room in this tub for a TV, a stereo, and a hunched angry man to hide. My foot is actually wedged between the appliances. My ankle's twisted at a painful sort of angle, but I'm afraid to move or to breathe.

"Okay, Goss. Your boy's a wack job. You still don't get to break into his apartment just because—"

"I told you...I didn't break in, Arnie. The guy's doorknob was taped, actually taped, to the front door. I knocked; the door opened. I went in when I saw the curtains on the ground, the boxes, the wads of tape all over the floor. Looked like somebody could have been dead in here. Or worse! Tell me, Arnie, what's all the tape for?"

"Still, Goss, you don't just—"

"He's a wack job, Arnie. Look around...it's like a creepy psycho's basement in here. He's planning to kidnap somebody or something. His ex-wife. A co-worker, who knows? I think he was involved in that boy's kidnapping, the one we found last night."

"Yeah, you told me, but the kid said he's the one who called in the boy's whereabouts to the police. That's not—"

"But how did he know the whereabouts, Arnie? If he was there, why was he there? And why does he leave before the police he just called arrive? No, something's cracked about this guy. Or cracking. I found out he got fired from his job this week, he lives alone, early thirties. Arnie, he's the classic profile of a guy skipping over the edge."

"You went to his job?"

"Yeah, and they even said he was nuts. Said he stopped showing up for work. He's just been divorced. He stole seventeen rolls of duct tape and hostage rations; he hides his valuables in his bathtub...look in here."

My entire body spasms. My knee knocks the remote for the TV

across the top of the stereo. Somehow my spastic hand catches it before it rattles down into the tub. I try desperately to stare at my watch, but there's no glare behind this curtain. No glare! No glare! A wack job with no glare! *How on earth am I going to leap without a glare!*

"I saw," says the other cop.

On the bathroom tiles, Detective Goss's steps stop, turn, and scuff away.

"All's I'm saying is that it's our job to stop crime. To stop it, not just clean it up, Arnie. It's too late when someone's dead, some kid, maybe? Can you sleep when you know you could've stopped a criminal before he slipped over the edge? And this guy is gone, he's crazy, Arnie. I talked to him and saw it in his eyes. And he's already broken the law once—"

"A guy loses a crappy job, so he steals some groceries. That don't mean—"

"Okay, it's petty theft, but he's on his way."

"Listen, Bill—"

"I just wanted to talk with him, Arnie. Just a little chat between the guy with the badge and the guy with the duct tape. Okay? Let him know somebody's watching. Even crazy, he'll think twice if he knows someone's watching. That's all."

"Why do you always assume the most horrible thing possible?"

"I don't always."

"Did you hear what you just said? He's over the edge, he'll hurt a kid…"

"No, you're not listening. We're checking out a suspicious character."

"And you just assume he's guilty until proven otherwise?"

"What's your job again?"

"I know, I know. I've seen the same sick cases you have, so I get it. But I don't do this, and you can't either, Bill. You can't judge the whole world as depraved just based on a few rotten ones. It'll eat you up."

"Right, you've seen rotten. Answer me this: how often do you see the good?"

"I've seen good and bad."

"No, answer the question. How often does the good surprise you like the horrible?"

"Bill…you got to hope it might, geez…or how else do you get up every morning?"

"I get up. I have hope, but I don't get up blind, and you're asking me to be blind, Arnie. My hope is not blind. I have hope when I see it happen. Every day I hope that I'll see it happen. Meanwhile, I'm not blind to what's around me."

"Wow, man. You're due for a vacation, you know. You can't crash around believing—"

"I believe nothing. That doesn't mean I'm hopeless. In fact, I don't believe, so when I see real hope, the genuine article, then I'll know it for sure."

"Come on, just admit you look foolish and you were wrong this time, and—"

"I was cautious. Smart…proactive. That's not wrong."

"Bill…let's go. Let me buy you a beer."

"No, thanks."

I hear steps moving toward what I imagined was the front door when Goss says, "Look, when I was in my third year on the force, my partner and I took a call, domestic abuse case, right? No idea who called it in, but we go over there. There's a beat-up blue Monte Carlo parked half in the yard, half in the drive. I'll always remember that color, that car.

"So we ring the bell, and the door opens and this woman—no, girl—this young nineteen, twenty-year-old, stringy, sick-looking girl in a thin sundress answers the door but won't let us in. I can see the guy through the inch of door she opens. He's a bruiser strutting around the house with his shirt off, swigging from a beer bottle, talking loud to her or nobody, oblivious to us. Beer bottles line the TV, the windowsill by his easy chair, and she won't let the door open wider than a crack. She tells us to go away, that she's fine, no troubles here. She's got red marks on her shoulders and neck, Arnie, fresh, finger-shaped ones that hadn't turned to bruises yet. Meanwhile, this guy's yelling at the game show on the TV, drunk off his butt at two in the afternoon.

"No, she says, she didn't call us. She's fine. She doesn't want any trouble, and so we write it up, we go.

"The very next day, we get a second call, the same house. But this time, the pretty, sick-looking girl is wadded up in the Dumpster in the alley behind the house. She's naked. Her fingers are twisted, broken, every one. Her nose is flattened and swollen at the same time, bruised all black and crusted with blood. That sundress was shoved down her throat. And the Monte Carlo is gone. The house was in her mother's name; who knows where the mother is. None of the neighbors can say anything useful about the guy other than they were afraid of him. He's gone. Never found that guy, Arnie. Pictures of that dead girl's body were shoved in the unsolved box and buried on a basement shelf. That animal probably drove away with her purse and a six-pack on the seat beside him. And you know what? The day before, when I snickered at how that jerk had parked the car, I stared right at the license plate and didn't bother to remember it. I didn't even read it, write it down, call it in, just to see.

"So don't tell me I've fallen prey to a soured disposition. I have hope, Arnie. I hope that punk got a bullet in the back of the head in the next town, and I hope that little girl woke up in a miracle heaven where they feed her right and give her a decent dress. But I've never seen that miracle place. I don't often see miracles, and my job is to do something about the evil that is happening, not hope that it won't. My job is to watch. Watch for the worst before it happens, and if somebody I'm watching turns out to be less evil than I assumed, well, that's one less report to file."

"Looks like your crazy man was watching you this time," says the other cop.

I can't see from the bathtub, but he sounds like he's grinning.

"What?" says Detective Goss.

"You said the guy's name is James, right?"

"Right."

"Well, one Mr. James, no last name, called you in to 911."

"Don't mess with me, Arnie."

"I'm not. He told the dispatch there was a burglar in this apartment. Said you busted off the doorknob and taped it up again."

"Said I did that?"

"He said he was afraid some guy was waiting in the dark for him. He called about a half an hour ago, from the pay phone across the street."

"Why, that son of a—"

The other man laughs, but not Supercop. I hear his feet running to my den window.

"That pay phone right there, huh?" Goss calls out.

"He may be losing his mind, Bill, but what he's got left works better than yours."

From the loud footfall, pacing back and forth, I guess that my detective is gathering his stuff.

"Bill, don't leave in such a huff."

"Got to go."

"Listen to me, you leave this guy alone."

"Sorry, it's personal now."

"Sounded like it was personal before."

"No, now it is."

"Goss—"

I hear the front door open, then slam. My detective is gone, but he's coming for me. Ellen's tough guy is still there, talking with one or two others. I open the shower curtain an inch so I can get light on my watch.

"Lieutenant, how do you want me to write this up?"

A new voice says this, a young one, one I haven't heard yet. It seems my tough guy is a lieutenant.

"No report."

"Sorry, Lieutenant, what'd you say?"

"I said forget it."

"But, sir, we can't just—"

"Aw, don't worry about it. We caught a cop being a cop, tipped off by a guy who knew he was a cop. The fact that we caught him will make that guy far happier than a write-up that won't amount to anything."

"So we're done here?"

"Yeah, we're done," says the lieutenant. "Let's go. Let me just take a leak."

I catch a glare.

White daisy, white daisy, white daisy...

16

Back in the hotel, let's review.

The good news is that I can now leap whenever I want, bend it to my will, leap for my own reasons. And I recorded Goss red-handed. The bad news is coming right up.

More good news: this is a really nice hotel. I'm feeling crazy, but I'm doing so luxuriously. I take off my shoes and socks, stretch out on the bed. The TV's still going; I turn the volume up. I flip through the channels. This room gets approximately two million channels.

A robe hangs in the bathroom, and I wonder if it has been left by the previous patron until I see the Hometown Suites logo emblazoned on the front pocket. Swanky, I think. Soft like a good towel. I've never owned a towel this nice, let alone a robe. I strip down to my skivvies so I can lounge around in one. When you don't tie the belt it's like a cape. I run and jump onto the bed, and the cape thing works. I check the room-service menu and look for when the steam room closes.

I feel super. Maybe it's not confidence, but it feels like I'm wearing shoulder pads. Maybe it's the robe-cape. Because I usually feel nothing remotely resembling confidence, this is worth noting. I bent my leaping powers to my will. Something feels different inside. Harder, stronger, higher, like an aerial view.

This may seem like grandiose thinking, but it's exactly the kind I went for at that moment. Though neurotic, I've a superpower. I've done a fair bit of ruin to my chances with my dream girl, but I plan to bully forward. The superhero plan. I'm counting heavily on this unhatched egg.

Doing good is going to earn my way back to lasagna.

So I'm thumbing through channels again, way too many channels. I'm seeing the world, all of it with many disastrous goings on—the world ripe for superpicking. Floods, riots, poverty-stricken villages, assassinations, kidnappings, derailed trains, and so on. With this power, the perfect leap anywhere, the nick of time will be my specialty. I'll be the news. I'll be on all the channels. Special Announcement: the world can sleep sound tonight. Better than a bird, better than a plane, with me, everything happens faster than a speeding bullet.

I imagine, sitting on a hotel bed in this soft robe, watching myself on the television:

Man Carries Fifty to Safety as Hurricane Crashes into Coastline.

Twelve-Year-Old Girl Returned Safely to Parents, Kidnapping Ring Foiled.

Hero Removes Getaway Car at Bank Heist.

And once I'm on all the news channels at once, Monica's got to see me.

Now, it occurs to me that I'm saving the world to look good for my intended girlfriend. A little swagger is a good thing, right? Whose motivations are pure? My best intentions are bifurcated at best. Yes, I want to make Monica admire me, even adore me, but I'm also stopping the speeding train. The people on the runaway train don't care as long as they don't smash into another train.

If I wait to be purely good, I'll never leave the house, right?

I'm watching disasters, and I fetch the stationery pad and the complimentary hotel pen and take some notes. Hurricanes again. Dangerous leaping involved but people needing nick-of-time deliverances. I still don't know—can I carry a person with me when I leap? I should try with something else first, I think, like a sack of potatoes. A mannequin. Where do you get a mannequin? Can you buy one, and do people look at you oddly if you do? I put a question mark beside mannequin.

I start to get drowsy. Holding the pad in my hands, in that warm comfy robe, I close my eyes a bit. Just resting, and I try to think of a supername. This matters, you know? Leaper Man is nice…short, to the point. Maybe too bland and a little lame. It doesn't evoke anything. If you're not paying attention, it sounds a lot like Leper Man. Leper Man is not good. I don't want people screaming, "Unclean!" when they see me coming. Maybe just Leaper.

I close my eyes again.

Names matter. Like Monica. How beautiful is that name? Mellifluous, that one. Three sweet syllables. Oates, that's harder. But I genuinely do like it, and I'm smiling while lying there thinking of her name. I can feel my face smiling.

I check my watch: 10:04 p.m. Four minutes past polite calling hours, but this is an emergency.

Because I've decided to do it. To call and tell her everything.

"Hello?" It's Monica's voice. She sounds asleep.

"Hello, Monica? It's James."

A terrible, terrible pause.

"Hi, James, how are you?"

"Fine." I should really think things out before I start talking. "How are you?"

"I'm okay," she says. "What's that noise?"

I realize the TV is loud enough for her to hear. I wrestle the robe and the bedspread to find the remote and mute it.

"Just watching the news," I say.

There's another weird pause. She asks, "Are you in your bathroom?"

It takes a second, but I figure that one out.

"Oh no, I'm at a hotel." I am positively the dumbest person alive. I should really think these things out before speaking.

"Then I don't want to bother you—"

"Monica, wait! I'm at a hotel because I was afraid to stay in my apartment. Monica…"

It's now or never, I tell myself.

"Monica," I say, "I was afraid—which is why I wanted to go to a hotel. Not because, well, you know…but because someone broke into my apartment."

"But you said you already had been thinking of checking into a hotel."

"I did," I say. "For the past two days, I'd been thinking about a hotel, before we even made our date. Because there's someone following me, Monica, and I think I know who broke into my apartment."

"Really, James?"

I can't tell if she believes me, only that she wants to believe me. She's that good of a person. "Really, Monica. It's a long story. I do want to tell you, but it's a little crazy in places, and I don't want you to think I'm crazy in big places.

"Suffice it to say, there's a guy following me, for two days now. A detective. I didn't do anything wrong, not really, but he thinks I did. He's gone by the coffee shop, called my ex-wife, and rummaged through my apartment. He was there again when I went home."

"Oh, James!"

"Right…so I'm at a hotel."

"But why is he following you?"

"Well, it has to do with a Mass I went to a couple of weeks ago."

"I didn't know you went to Mass."

At this point, I'm thinking, *Excellent. This is sounding perfect.* Monica may be the one in whom I can confide all my weary leaping woes.

"Monica, let me ask you a question. If you were suddenly offered an ability to do something others couldn't, let's say someone offers you the ability to fly—"

"Who just offered me the ability to fly?"

"For the sake of this example, let's say God."

"God offered me the ability to fly?"

"Right…or you're pretty sure it was God. You didn't actually get it in writing, but you think it sounds like God, okay?"

"Okay."

"Right. God offers you flying, and you think, since it's God, that you should fly for good reasons, not just for fun or whatever. You should definitely do good with whatever special deal you're given, right?"

"Right. You should do good."

"So…what would you do?"

"What would I do?"

"What would Monica Oates do?"

"Oh…well, I'd turn down the offer."

"What?"

"I would turn down the offer. I wouldn't want it."

"You wouldn't?"

"No. I'm not good enough."

"Really? But—"

Here it is. Everything that's happened to me, my whole life, everything I've ever done, thought, and been, it all leaps into what happens next.

"James, are you there?"

I'm there, but while I'm talking to Monica, trying to get out my questions, my eyes wander to the television. The volume is muted, so it's just images, and it's set on local news. The Breaking News logo flashes on the screen. Live coverage, from downtown at the hospital. Maybe three blocks from my hotel. Camera shots from a helicopter. Shaky camera shots looking down from the helicopter at the roof of the hospital. It's a big hospital, ten or eleven stories high. Blue police lights flash far below, down on the street. A red fire engine and paramedic lights flashing way at the bottom of the shot. They're all out of sync, light irregularly pulsing and flashing. There's a police team on the roof of the hospital, in bulletproof vests and helmets. They're all looking at another guy on the roof, a guy who has crawled over the side wall of the roof and stands precariously on a small ledge. I'm watching this. The police are nowhere near him. It seems he won't let anyone near him, that he's threatening to do it. On the ledge, his back is to the hospital wall, and he's edging out, looking down at all the flashing lights. A leaper.

His hair and shirt are whipping in the wind. His hair is in his face, and it's just a white T-shirt, so I can't see his face, and the camera can't get close enough. But I can see his jeans are rolled up a bit. I can make out that there's too much of his ankles showing. He's wearing clogs.

"James, are you there?"

"Hey, Monica, did Kevin ever come back to the shop today?"

"After he quit? No. Yesterday he told me he'd be at the hospital. His father's been really sick."

"I have to go."

"James—"

But I hang up on her. I have to go. *I need shoes,* I think. I jump to the floor, scramble around for my shoes. I've got to have shoes for traction once I grab him.

Once I get one shoe on, I notice my naked leg and realize I'm in my underwear and a robe. I yank the robe off and grab my pants, but I have to stop and take the one shoe off to get the pants on. Then I shove my shoes on, no tying. Forget the shirt. I sit back on the edge of the bed, leaning close to the TV screen so I can see what's happening.

"Hold on, Kevin. Hold on," I say. And I hold my watch up close to my eyes, turn my wrist, but I can't catch the light.

"Hold on!" I say. And I jump up, turn on all the lamps.

I sit back on the bed, raise my watch again. On the television, the news cuts to a reporter with a microphone on the street outside the hospital.

"Go back!" I yell.

I need another look at the scene. To see exactly where Kevin is standing so I don't miss. I'm focusing my eyes on my watch, but I have to keep glancing at the screen. Finally, they cut back to the aerial shot. The police are all backing up with their hands raised. Kevin has taken his hands off the wall, threatening them with his life.

There's a shimmer off my watch. I catch a glimpse of light and I focus on it. I make my eyes blur.

I think, *Appear directly behind him. Appear on the roof on the safe side of the wall directly behind Kevin. Throw both arms under his arms and pull.* I'm thinking as hard as I can. A good reason. A very good reason, but it's taking too long. I'm thinking of pulling Kevin to safety. My eyes are on the light. I can't stay focused. My mind flies around like a bird in a grocery. I think of too much, my mind flooded with thoughts. Kevin's on his ledge, and my life is passing before my eyes, and I can't stop it.

Everything: My apron at work. Monica's phone number. Meg's hair undone in the wind. The knobless gearshift on the Volvo. The detective's shiny black shoes. Father Chavez and that yellow slip of ribbon. I see Meg grin at me as she comes down the aisle. I see Monica blush as she puts her flowers in a vase. My mind rolls around like a wet, glaring eye. Everything, what I thought were good things, even the best things, even my loves, crowd in the way of the one thought I ought to be thinking.

In anger, I had bent my will my way. Now desperate, I couldn't bend it back.

I look up at the TV.

Kevin lurches forward. He's stumbled. A clog slips off his foot and vanishes as it falls toward the red and blue flashing lights.

Don't wear clogs if you're crawling out on a ledge! A good boot, a sensible running shoe with new treads. But not clogs. They aren't good footwear for ledges. For God's sake, Kev, you could…

And he leaps. Not like a superhero. Just spirals away as we all watch our screens.

Breaking news.

Up to the minute.

Live coverage.

We cut away from impact.

Part 3

17

I think I'm broken.

Definitely need ice. Proper numbing.

I'm numb most places except my toe—that's throbbing, stubbed badly on a chair leg while struggling to find my pants and my shoes. I limp over and pick up the ice bucket but never make it out the door. Sitting on the edge of the bed with my ice bucket in my lap, I stare at the television. It's hard to think. They keep replaying the moment of Kevin's fall. For how long, I don't know, I sit there and watch, for at least the rest of that news show. Then I thumb through the two million other satellite options till I find another local news just coming on.

And Kevin leaps again and again.

None of the reporters, the police, and the witnesses seem to know much about Kevin. They've found his name on his license in his wallet and, having nothing better, they show his horrible license picture on the screen, blown up and ghastly. It doesn't even look like Kevin. They've put together that his father was in this hospital. It seems his father passed away only a few hours before Kevin's jump.

They interview a nurse who'd seen Kevin by his father's bedside in the past couple of weeks. This nurse says that the leaper had seemed a little down, understandably, but she'd never guessed he was suicidal.

Are we still on for tonight, James…

It's Kevin's voice in my head. The guy asked to talk to me at least a hundred times, but I did nothing. I should have guessed.

Sometimes it's good to talk to someone when you feel out of your head…

And I'm definitely out of my head. No, that's not true. I've never been out of my own head. Like now, the voices in my head, like voice mail that won't erase, that won't shut off—the whole thing, me locked up in my head, so much so that I failed Kevin.

I was thinking of quitting anyway. Let James have my spot…

It should've been me.

Finally, this news goes off too, and there are no more pictures of Kevin falling. Or at least not on the screen, the image playing by itself in my head, again and again. My foot's throbbing. I feel sick. I see that image of Kevin falling so clearly that I fear I might leap off the side of that hospital myself, might leap into the middle of the air, grabbing for Kevin, falling with him.

I get up, limp, and pace. Try not to think.

I open a window.

Hotels go to great lengths to make it discernibly difficult to open a window. I figure it's because they don't want people leaping out of them—bad advertising. I have to use the complimentary shoehorn to snap off a piece of metal at the bottom of the window's slider rail.

Then I rock the frame, use my full weight just to force it open enough to stick my head and arms out. But I need it open, I need air.

This Hometown Suites sits right up against the river. The wind has picked up considerably, making the river below look cold and choppy. Looking down the city skyline, I can see the hospital lights where Kevin jumped. The helicopter's gone, but I can still see flashes of red and blue lights a few streets over. Kevin's hospital's that close, only a few blocks away. I could have driven to the hospital.

I need ice.

I limp over to my stuff, put on a shirt, a belt, grab my car keys, phone, key card, and drop them into the ice bucket and leave my room. I'm taking the key card, because there'll be no more leaping. From now on, this James is limping back to hotel rooms the old-fashioned way. I swear it off. Right there in the hallway, barefoot and gimpy as I am, swear a promise—no more leaping. If I can't use it to reach out to a guy on a ledge, what good am I?

In the elevator, I thumb the button for the lobby. It lights up yellow, bright like that ribbon at the church when I made my second leap, when I prayed.

Hey, God? I punch the button with the lit up *L* a few more times. *Lord, until further notice, I'm out of this leaping business, unless you send someone to tell me what it's for, someone to put the pieces back together in my head, 'cause I can't do this. You interrupted once, and, well, that's been surprising, so just someone to believe me would be nice. Scratch that— just someone who wants to believe. A sidekick, maybe. Anyway, this is my floor, God, so amen.*

Stepping out, I watch the elevator doors close on my prayer, watch the little numbers above the door take it upward and away.

"May we help you, Mr. Oates?"

I do a double take looking for Monica's father. He shouldn't be out on a night like this. He's not well.

The concierge is talking to me. "Sir, you can call our desk if you need ice," he says, behind his counter. It's then I realize I'm barefoot in his lobby.

"What? No, I'm good, really," I say. "Just taking my ice bucket for a walk."

"Do you need me to call for a cab, Mr. Oates?"

"What?"

"A cab, sir." He glances over at the security guard. "Do we need to call anyone for you, Mr. Oates?"

"Do you have ice?"

"Yes sir. It's down this hallway, by the kitchen." He says this and points politely, but he's giving the security guard another glance.

"Thank you," I say and pat my ice bucket. "We'll want some when we get back."

I walk out the front of the hotel, limping. The wind, Kevin's wind, the one that blew his hair, his shirt, it's bringing rain now. A light, steady rain, but enough to soak you if you stand in it. I do just that. With my foot throbbing, I stand in the dark parking lot till I'm soaked.

The Volvo starts, and I set the ice bucket on the passenger seat. It seems I'm not only taking the ice bucket for a walk but also for a drive. It's raining, and my wipers have never been the best. Really, they're less wipers and more simultaneous smudgers.

My foot shoots with pain every time I use it. It's my left foot, my clutch foot, and it may well be broken. My foot, not the clutch, which is just spongy. I turn on the heater because I'm soaked to the bone, clothes, everything—a pneumonia waiting to happen.

On the dash, I find the directions to Monica's, and I've got to talk to someone. Probably Monica won't believe me, about the leaping, the superpower, the God parts, so despite our progress earlier, I won't be mentioning that. Maybe, though, since she's lost a kid and she's gone through that, maybe she can understand this, this having loss inside you.

I check my directions, pull out of the parking lot.

These driving conditions: rainfall, slick oily streets, simultaneous smudgers, darkness, Volvo, crappy Volvo, crappy '88 Volvo, bald '95 tires, driver in shock, having a nervous breakdown, knobless gearshift, no shoes, broken clutch foot, images of suicide, falling, falling, falling. Let's say I'm driving erratically and swerving occurs. Frankly, it's a wonder I stay on the road as well as I do.

But not well enough.

In the rearview mirror, I see a car behind me, one that gets way too close. Why would someone drive up on a car that's swerving?

Do you climb frayed ropes?

Do you get in the elevator marked Danger?

Do you buy the discount cheese?

I slow down a bit. Swerve to one side so he can pass, but he doesn't. Now I'm a little peeved. I swerve back in front of him and start to speed up. But I pull too far, swerve into the oncoming lane. Just a tiniest bit of overcorrection—cut me a little slack, it feels like the clutch pedal is welded into my shinbone. But the oncoming car in that oncoming lane, he's understandably startled. He honks, swerves, and I swerve.

We avoid collision, no worries. The car behind me turns on its blue lights. Blips his siren a few times to get my attention.

"License and registration, please." The cop has his flashlight out, beams it in my eyes.

I squint and turn away, but hand him my information. He doesn't seem pleased to be standing in the rain.

"Can I have you step out of your vehicle, sir?"

I'm already wet, so why not. I step out and follow the officer, limping to the back of my Volvo where I stand. He shines his flashlight in my eyes a second time.

"Have you had any alcoholic beverages this evening, sir?"

I should have just slurred and belched out, "Loads to drink. Bottles and bottles." It would have saved everyone time, but I shake my head no.

"I'm going to ask you to take a field sobriety test. Is that all right with you, sir?"

"Peaches," I say.

"Can I have you stand on one foot, sir?"

"I already am."

The officer shines his flashlight toward my feet. He sees I'm holding my left foot a few inches off the ground like an injured dog.

"Would you like to get your shoes, sir?"

"Are you going to wait here while I go back to the hotel?"

"You're driving without shoes, sir?"

Before answering, I try to remember that booklet I studied when I was sixteen to get my driving permit. I can't remember if shoeless driving is an illegal act, but I risk it.

"Yes."

"Can I have you touch your fingertips to your nose…first the left hand, then the right."

I do this. This is not hard. I imagine someone drunk enough not able to locate his own nose probably shouldn't be driving.

"Now can I ask you to walk this white line here on the side of the road, one foot in front of the other?"

"You can ask me, but it's not happening."

"Excuse me?" Written down, I'm sure this looks polite, but don't you believe everything you read.

"I have a bum left foot."

"You're driving a manual in the rain without shoes and with a hurt foot?"

"Changes your perspective on what is bad driving, huh?"

"Are you refusing to complete the sobriety test, sir?"

"I'm not refusing," I say. "It's just that walking hurts right now, so the foot-in-front-of the-other deal's probably not going to work out the way either of us wants it to."

"What's the problem with your foot?"

"I kicked a chair. Saw some bad TV. It might be broken."

At this point, I think I'm aces. The officer may think I'm just an idiot with a bad foot.

"Were you driving to the hospital?"

I turn on him, stare at him. How does he know about the hospital, about Kevin? I look at him like I want to shove him. Feigned aggression is not lost on a policeman. He takes a step back, flexes everything, before I realize he merely means about my foot.

"Oh…I might need someone to look at me."

He shines the light one more time in my eyes.

"Look," I say. "I'll be glad to breathe in one of those thingies. I haven't had a sip to drink."

"Were you aware you were driving erratically?"

"I'd just mentioned that to myself before you drove up. Yes, I was aware. I'm superaware right now. But it wasn't intentional erraticism. My foot hurts. I thought you wanted to pass, and I'm destined to overcorrect."

The officer thinks for a minute. He says, "Sir, if you'd be more comfortable waiting in your vehicle, you can have a seat inside while I run your information. Just keep the engine off."

"Fine."

He watches me like he's afraid I'll make a run for it. Honestly, I'm thinking that I've used up today's Volvo starts, I'm going to have to ask for a jump, and I'm not in the mood. It occurs to me I could go back to my car, turn on the dome light, and leap out of there. Although, they'd have my Volvo then, and cops—like others—don't like you to

vanish when they tell you to wait. That, and I've sworn off leaping. So
I just cross my arms and lean against the back of the Volvo in the rain.

The officer gets back in his cruiser. There's no siren, but his blue
lights are still flashing brightly. I can see his black silhouette in the car,
talking on his police radio, calling in my license. Someone's definitely
telling him something. I should have known when it took so long.

This time, when the officer climbs out of his car, he puts a hand
on his service revolver.

"Sir, I need to ask you to put both hands on your vehicle."

"I paid my insurance—"

"Sir—"

"Are we going to turn the car over, because I'm definitely going to
need help—"

"Sir!" His voice sounds different now, more official. In fact, that's
a bark. "I repeat, I want you to put both hands on the back of your
vehicle right now!"

I do it. What choice do I have? I see my arms in front of me, see
my watch, the blue lights flashing off it, my eyes flutter and blur. I am
aware of an intense desire to be somewhere else. For good this time.

"I've done something wrong…" I say.

He comes up behind me with his flashlight raised. The officer's
right hand grabs my right wrist. The handcuff metal is cold and slip-
pery. Now his flashlight beam bounces off my watch face, and I focus
on it. It's 11:48 p.m. Let the eyes blur, but he grabs my other hand,
cuffs them both behind my back.

"It seems you've done a bit more than swerving lately," he says, as
he pats me down.

"Probably. Remind me, would you?"

"Shoplifting, attempted robbery, prank call to the emergency hot-line, and now reckless driving."

The blue lights pulse on the Volvo's slick hood. I focus. I see the soft robe in a pile on the floor of my hotel room. I could have gone, right then, because who can stop me? Then Kevin's clog slips, and his foot falls toward the flashing lights in my mind again.

"I've done worse," I mutter.

The officer didn't expect that, and he doesn't seem to appreciate it. He pulls me hard by my arms toward his cruiser.

"Well, you'll have plenty of time to tell us about that at the station," he says.

He leads me limping to the backseat, opens the door, guides my head down into the car. Before he shuts it, he says, "There's someone who wants to talk with you."

I sigh. I've been summoned. Twisting my legs for more comfort, I try to ease my foot.

"Do you mind getting my backpack out of the backseat? It's got important stuff in it."

He stares at me in his rearview mirror.

I cough.

"What's left of me is in that backpack, do you mind? Please."

He does it. He walks over to the Volvo in the rain. He takes the opportunity to shine his flashlight all around the inside of my car. He checks the glove box, under the seats. I feel a twinge of revenge knowing that whatever's under the seat can't be nice to find. He locks the door, slams it shut. But he's got the backpack. My recorder. My note-book. I'm going to want those.

Only a few things left.

We sit while he fills out papers and calls things in. My cough is pretty strong now, there's a distinct after-wheeze. I watch the wrecker pull up to tow my car, and I'm just thrilled with how this date night's turning out. We make a U-turn, follow the wrecker to the downtown station.

Finally, he turns off those awful flashing blues.

'm alone, and it's cold in this cell.

Okay, I'm not totally alone, if you count that guy. Even the passed-out drunk guy looks cold, although I'm sure he's far too sauced to actually feel anything. I'm sure of this because he's drooling copiously, and he never moved when they clanked open the metal door and shoved me in with him. He also did nothing when I took off his shoes and put them in the far corner. There was this putrid stink that I thought came from his shoes. Turns out, it was his feet. The stink is much worse now, with his shoes off, but there's no way I'm going back over there. I think it's on my hands now. But he looks cold, he keeps reaching for a pretend blanket, grumbling and pulling at comfort that's just not there.

I'm definitely freezing, being soaked head to broken toe with rain. There's a puddle on the cement floor where I'm sitting. And the toe of my throbbing foot's the size of a baseball, or a racquetball, maybe. A squash ball, but a very purple one. Why do we compare injuries to sports equipment?

It's definitely broken.

When they booked me, they took my picture and thumbprints

and asked if I had any medical conditions they should know about. I mentioned my toe. Then I told them that I'd recently been having trouble with inadvertently beaming my body through space.

I told them that's what happened at the grocery to cause the shoplifting. Told them I'd be more than happy to pay for the jerky. The lady filling out the paperwork, she enjoyed this information and read it back to me, making sure she'd got it just right. She'd done fine.

They also let me have my one phone call, so I called Father Chavez. I didn't speak to him, just the answering machine at the church. I kept it short, mentioned being in jail, and hung up. Then they trundled me back to this holding cell.

Holding cell. That's perfect. Everything is put on cold, numb hold here, adding a special cement-gray jail perspective. The drunk holds his collar up around his ears and his knees up to his chest. I hold on to this notebook, trying to hold on to my grasp of things. I'm on hold for whatever's coming next, something heavy waiting to come down on me. No matter what I hold, no matter what happens next, Kevin doesn't come back.

It should've been me.

The cell door opens.

"Get up."

It's a new officer I haven't met before. I've been huddled in here so long they've probably changed shifts for the night. I stand.

"What time is it?"

"Late," he says, surly. "Come on."

"That guy smells really bad," I say. The drunk pulls at his clothes again.

"He always does. Come this way."

"You shouldn't arrest people who smell that bad," I say, but this guy's not in the mood for me.

"Where are we going?"

"This way."

My humorless officer leads me limping down a gray hallway. All the hallways are gray here. They should pump in music, put up travel posters, and bring in small café tables. He stops and pulls open a heavy door.

"In here." I hesitate, but hesitation is really more for those who have a choice.

"Hello, James."

I'm surprised. "Hello, Father."

Father Chavez sits at a table by himself. There's a chair for me, a metal folding chair. It's cold looking, and my clothes are still soaked, but I actually feel hot.

Father Chavez is in his civvies; no collar, no black, just a yellow button-down shirt, a rain slicker, and jeans. The room is bare, blank. White walls, gray table, gray chairs, gray, scuffed floor. They've done a lot with the place.

I cough.

"How are you, James?"

"In jail," I say.

"Are you all right?"

"Not really."

"Would you like to talk about it?"

At this, I bust a gut with a fit of coughing.

"You're soaked." He takes off his Windbreaker and hands it to me. It's light, not really a coat, just something to shed the rain, but I put it on. I shiver and sit down.

"Sorry to bother you. I wasn't sure who else to call." My bum's so cold from the metal chair, it starts another coughing fit.

Father Chavez waits for me to finish. "Do you feel all right?"

"Feel? Me? I don't know. I feel guilty."

"Why?"

"I'm in jail. It seems to fit."

"Do you want to talk? Why are you here, James?" He was trying, God bless him. I'm freezing and burning up both, so I try to pull together the most sensible voice I can find.

"The truth?"

"Absolutely," he says.

"Truth then…you ready? God."

He pauses, then asks, "God?"

"Yes, God put me here. Well, maybe he didn't drive, but he sent a car, if you know what I mean."

"No, James, I'm sorry. What do you mean?"

"Look, you think I'm crazy—"

"No, not crazy, you're just—"

"Yes, you do. Or you should. I would…in fact, I do. Perfectly crazy. It's reasonable to think that my overwrought condition has led me to an insane tussle with the authorities. If we could unscramble this craziness, perhaps we'd placate the powers-that-be, right? No deal. It's the powers-that-be, or the Power-That-Is, that's done this. That I deserve to be locked up, totally my fault. But that I am locked up… God's fault."

Father Chavez frowns, puzzled. "Let's take this in pieces. Why do you feel you deserve this? Did you do anything wrong?"

"It's what I couldn't do, Father, what I should've done. I'm better locked away."

"What couldn't you do?"

"The impossible."

"What's impossible?"

"Impossible to lock me away, I'm afraid."

Father Chavez looks at his shoes, which are tennis shoes. I've never seen a priest in tennis shoes, and it takes something away.

"Father, how do you deal with it when God does a thing to you?"

My priest leans back. "All right, what do you think God has done to you, James?"

"He's changed me, Father. Zap! I'm not who I was, but I didn't ask for it. I think maybe I just got too close to the God areas. I don't think I can undo it. And that's what landed me here."

"Are you referring to the story you told the police? Is that what you are talking about? They said…you claim to be able to…um… transport yourself."

"It's not a story. Leap, Father."

"Yes, that's what you told them. You claim to be able to leap through space."

"And?"

"That's all they said. About that, and what seems to be a misunderstanding at a store. An elderly lady, some groceries."

"The old lady's nuts, but I stole the groceries."

"James, if you're ever short on money for food, you can come ask me anytime—"

"No, I got money and I didn't mean to steal them. I had them in a basket, and it happened. A leap, I leapt out to my car. I wanted to come back and pay, but the day went a little crazy."

"So…you…you really believe…" He clears his throat. "Leap through space—you believe you can?"

"Like a butterfly in a bad breeze, I'm all over the place. I thought I could control it, but then…" I squint up at the air-conditioning vent. It's like you can see the cold air coming down to get you. "I know what's happened to me, Father. I've repeated it a bunch of times. I was almost creamed by a Popsicle truck. If I borrow your watch, I could probably disappear right now. But I've sworn it off. There's no uncertainty in my mind as to whether or not I can do this, or whether I've gone mad or not. Madness is number two on my worry list. Unruly leaping superpower, it's number one. Because I'm no good at it. I don't want to be a hero, save the world. And I don't want to be changed."

"Tell me what happened." He hasn't left, so I'm hopeful.

"Okay, yesterday, or the day before, what day is it? That day I asked you about Aquaman?"

"That was Friday afternoon. It's early Monday morning, James, still night."

I pause and see blue lights flashing in my head. I close my eyes to rub them, but I see Kevin's flip-flop.

"James…where'd you go?"

"Sorry, Father."

"I'm right here, go on."

"I discovered that if I saw one thing, focused hard and I lost myself, I could leap to the place of that one thing, where I most desired to be."

He waits, but I'm finished.

"I see," he says.

"It's not stunningly believable, is it?"

"No, James, it isn't."

"Okay, crazy, right, but humor me for a second. Pretend, *imagine,* I'm telling the truth. Let's say for a minute that my transspatial leaping ability is a fact. If God did zap me, and I'm different—what do I do?"

"I'm not sure."

"Isn't this where the faith comes in?"

"Faith?"

"Right. You got faith, got it in spades. Give me a chunk. Cut me a slice of what I'm supposed to do next."

"What do you mean?"

"Where's the list? Faith, the five-easy-steps version? You're a priest, God's point man. Maybe God will tell you."

"Are we talking about faith or instructions?"

"Exactly! Instructions, right."

"Faith isn't a set of instructions, James."

I unzip his jacket because now I'm sweating in it.

He tries again. "I'm not sure I understand."

"Let me put it this way. Let's say I know a guy who plans to leap off a building. I don't know if I could stop him, but I should be able to if what I'm telling you is true. If I'm any good at all, I'd be able to leap and save him. But I'm *not* good! I'll try harder next time, I promise, if someone will just give me the instructions, a list to tell me what to do, step by step."

"Slow down... What's this about a guy who plans to leap off a building?"

"Because some guys do. And I couldn't stop it."

"James—"

"God's changed me, and I didn't ask for it! I'm just so very blessed, I guess. So now I'm sending in my cereal box tops, asking for the God-list, and whatever I can do to get God off my back."

"Why would you want God to give you a list and then leave you alone?"

"Wow...does anyone really warm to the idea that God sees them?"

Father Chavez takes off his glasses. I didn't know he had bad eyes; he must usually wear contacts. I've kept him from his sleep.

"It's just a list. Is that so hard? I'm not saying I'll become good with a list, but I'm utterly lost without one. I don't have to understand, just mark through the step I've done and go on to the next. That's what's gorgeous about lists. One-two-three. Like the Ten Commandments—there's God doing something in a way I can understand. What a fabulous list! Not a difficult go-and-do list, but simply a stay-away-from-these-places list.

"Thou shalt refrain from these possible violations—ten total. God bless Moses. Maybe it was Moses's idea. God can't expect people to simply desire good and strike out and do it right some morning. No sir, people aren't any good at that kind of living."

"James, I don't think that's faith. Faith is more like trust between people."

I fidget uncomfortably.

"If you trust someone, you want them to see you and know everything about you. That's what faith is: trusting God better than any person. That trust gives you courage to keep going along *with* God, despite evidence to the contrary—only *because* you trust and you've seen God himself doing the best things, and you want to stay near that."

"Whoa…I like you. You're a smart guy… But are you sure that's faith?"

"I believe so, James."

"So because I want instructions, a list, making this whole God thing more manageable—what is that?"

"I'd bet trying to pin God down to a list feels frustrating."

"Right…feels closer to madness, actually."

"Well, I'm not sure I'd call it madness—"

"I may be going crazy, Father. The leaping's happening for God's reasons, and God won't identify those. I'm not doing well with the not-knowing aspect of this superpower, but it's either crazy or—"

I stop and shiver, drop my head. Father Chavez reaches over and rocks my shoulder so I can feel he's really there.

"James," he says, "you tell me you can leap through space, and

I'm not sure what to do with that confession. But God will definitely always be God, and we never get a blueprint for what God is doing. It's too wide; there's no way we could understand all God does even if he did reveal it. We have to trust. We're made to."

Father Chavez leans back, puts his glasses back on. "Since you've been to Mass, we've gotten to know each other. I've enjoyed you and our talks, so listen…that's how it'll be. You and I will talk about what's going on with you, about God, and then we'll talk to God. Listen to what he has to say. He hasn't left you, James. We'll get through this. We'll trust God together."

"Thank you, Father. That's what I needed to hear."

"You're welcome."

I should've just stopped talking, let Father Chavez think he's fixed it. And I do feel better, like a weight lifted or a decision made, but not for the reason he might think.

"Father, I just figured something out. What's driving me crazy."

"Yes."

"You said, this God bit… It's all about trust."

"Right."

"Yeah. I don't want that."

"I'm sorry?"

"No, I'm sorry…for wasting God's time."

"What do you mean?"

"I mean I don't want that God."

"James—"

"No, Father, I don't eat sushi, I don't bowl because of the borrowed shoes, and I don't trust. I want a divorce."

He pauses. "I thought you and your wife—"

"From God. I want a divorce from God, right now."

"I'm a priest, James. I don't support divorce, certainly not from God."

"You got to get me out of this. There's got to be some magic la-la backward spell you can use to get God off me, okay?"

"James—"

"I want a God divorce. We're irreconcilably different. He's a deity, for God's sake. God wants me to trust him when I have no idea what he might be up to? No, thanks, that's just not safe."

"James."

"No, come on, you're a priest. Sling a little water, say fancy Latin words. Can we do it right here, or do we need a church?"

The air conditioner kicks on again, and I cough so hard my eyes bulge. I should never have unzipped that jacket. Father Chavez stands, walks over next to me. He places the palm of his hand on my forehead.

"That cough sounds nasty. Do you have a fever?"

"I'd put money on raging fever—scarlet, yellow, two-tone green."

"You're burning up. Tomorrow we'll get you to a doctor, okay? You'll be out of here soon. I'll go with you."

"Tell me," I say and grab his hand. "Do you believe me?"

Father Chavez sits again, takes a deep breath. It's bad to make a good priest pause so long.

"I believe that something's wrong and you're torn to pieces. Truthfully, James, when you tell me you can actually beam yourself through space, I have to ask if you're okay. Are you? I know you've been through a lot and you're hurting. You're fevered. Is it stress? For-give me for asking, but it's possible, right?"

I smile at his tennis shoes. "At least you're not saying my leaping through space is not possible."

"Honestly, I'm having my issues with that, yes. Don't want you to think I'm a hundred percent on that one. I can't leap through space, and I've never seen it happen. But I'm trying to understand. I'm try-ing to answer your questions about faith. And with God, I stopped discounting the impossible years ago. I've seen stranger things be true. But if it is pain and stress, I'm here to help, okay?"

"If it's true? If I can leap through space?"

He looks worriedly at me. "Then God has put you in a place I don't know anything about. So I'll listen and pray for you. Maybe together we can find out what's happening to you."

I reach out, try to rock his shoulder like he did mine before he goes.

"Thank you, Father," I say.

"Thank you, James," he says. "Maybe I need to believe more."

"You believe just fine."

"No. I haven't believed one new thing in years, James. I need to think about that."

I hear footsteps coming down the hall, outside the door. Keys clatter, then fit and open the lock. The officer who led me in here holds the door open as Supercop enters. He comes into a room like he owns it.

"Sorry, sir, but your time's up," Detective Goss says.

"It's Father," I say.

"I don't care if he is your father, visiting time is over," he says to me. "Sorry, sir, but you'll have to go."

"No," I say. "He's a father. A priest."

"Oh," Goss says. He looks like he's trying to care, trying to find a problem with what he's done but can't.

"Father Chavez," says the priest, offering his hand.

"Detective Goss, nice to meet you."

They shake.

"Technically, I'm a captain, but since you're not a cop, I won't hold you to that," he says. "Perhaps you'll forgive me if I don't call you Father?"

"No problem at all, Captain. Have a good evening."

Detective Captain Goss sets his coffee down on the little table in front of me.

"Captain, may I ask why James is being held?"

"Reckless driving and refusal of a field sobriety test. We can hold him overnight for that—not to mention a few other things."

"I see," Father Chavez says, turning to go. "Oh, Captain, my friend here is freezing. He's been in a cold cell for hours, soaking wet, and he's probably caught something. Is there anything we could do about that?"

Goss looks as if he sees Father Chavez for the first time. "I'll see what I can do."

He says this dismissing Father Chavez, but my priest is stubborn.

"Perhaps a warm cup of coffee?" he says, waiting for an answer. "A little mercy?"

Goss thinks his answer, a nasty one, I can see, but it's hard to be nasty with a priest in the room, even is he is in street clothes.

"Eddie, bring another coffee, please, after you escort Mr. Chavez out."

They leave and the door shuts.

Maybe it's my fever, but I feel like I've leapt into a cop show.

"At last we meet…" and all that.

Goss stalks, paces, leans, pulls at his belt, flexes his neck in neck places that shouldn't do that. No kidding, that's the way this guy acts, like now that we're alone, he's going to start laughing from deep in his chest or remove his head. He doesn't, and instead, Goss drops the file he's carrying smack onto the table, spilling a bit of the coffee down his Styrofoam cup. The folder has my name on the tab. I feel a cough coming on, one good deep bark from the chest, but I swallow it.

"Good morning," I say.

Silence. He's trying to unnerve me, but I'm pure steel.

"Hey, you guys should think of chipping in for a coffee grinder. How many of you are there? Fifty, sixty? For a couple of bucks each, I can get you one heck of a grinder. You'd be amazed at the difference freshly ground beans will make. Look at this coffee. Look at the way it ran down the side of your cup. It's got no legs. Like a good wine, there ought to be legs. More like a thick wood stain, not this watery, sour, thin, insipid—"

"Having fun?" he asks.

I look up at him. He's still standing to make a tough impression. It's working.

"Is this funny to you?"

"No sir," I say. "This is not funny at all. Nothing even slightly funny about people drinking water steeped with pencil leads. I'm deadly serious about this stuff. I bet we could go to the kitchen right now and find calcium deposits lining your coffee maker, and if that doesn't make a difference to the bouquet—"

"I heard you were fired from that job at the coffee shop."

He looks at me. I look at him.

"You work there awhile?"

I nod.

"So that's all you do, sell coffee?"

"I also drink it."

"Why were you fired, James?"

"It seems I missed a shift, Officer."

"Why'd you miss it?"

"I had more pressing matters."

"Such as…"

Now, I may be shivering, I may be sweating, I may be crazy and a lot of other things, but I'm sure I don't have to take this macho stuff.

"Why am I here, Officer?"

Detective Goss sits and then leans on the table. "You're here because I want to talk to you."

We stay like this, him leaning, me shivering, and he's just staring at me, all *Law & Order* gorgeous.

"What time is it?" I ask.

But Goss never takes his eyes off me, he just stares, leans, like he's waiting for something. I try to look at his watch. I can't see the time but, boy, it's shiny, reflecting the bright lights in this room.

The door opens, and Officer Eddie comes in with my cup of coffee.

"Just put that in the trash for me, thanks," I say. I try wrinkling my nose cutely at the cop, but it sends me into a coughing fit. He leaves with the cup, slams the door. I hope he drinks it. Please, please, drink the cup—

"Okay, James, why'd you steal the groceries?"

"They only had one register open, and the line was so long…"

"And the purse? Line too long at the Social Security office, so you just grab an old lady's money while picking up a few groceries?"

"Old is rude, you mean elderly. And you walked up as I was giving the purse back to her."

"So you're a good guy then?"

"No," I say quickly. "I don't think I'm good."

"That makes two of us."

"You're not good either, Captain?" I ask.

I figure I've just earned another lean-and-stare part, but he's enjoying scratching the back of his neck.

"How about the phony call to 911?"

"How about the dude in my apartment, sitting around in the dark?"

"When I was there, I wondered, what's the tape for?"

"Tape…right!" I remember the recorder in my pocket. I take it out and set it on the table. "Please talk clearly. My lawyer's got a bum ear."

Now he's not quite so sure of everything. I'm glad, because I'm not sure of anything.

"I was referring to the duct tape."

"Love it. Big fan of duct tape."

He picks up my file and browses through it. "Yeah, but why so much of it, all over your apartment? What are you trying to do there?"

"My apartment's drafty. I've positively caught my cold of death."

He glances at me. "Sorry." I sniffle. "My death of cold."

"I'm just looking for answers, James. This doesn't have to be difficult."

Could this be some Neanderthal version of kindness? Like he means it or like he's putting the spiked club behind his back and he was only accidentally threatening. But if he wants answers, he needs to get in line. I say nothing.

"Okay, then, difficult. Your wife's concerned that you've been on edge lately. I'm sorry…your ex-wife."

My back spasms, and I adjust my seat. Goss sees me wince.

"Is that why she left you?" he asks. "She did leave you, right?"

I thump the Styrofoam. "You should drink this before it hardens back to shoe scum."

"It's amazing she put up with you for five years." He turns the file, like he's looking at a picture. "She's good looking. Why was she with you?"

Another coughing fit throws off my timing. "I exercise regularly."

"How? By beaming through space?"

"Most often I do that just sitting in a chair. It's not physically strenuous."

"You weren't sitting in a chair at the grocery."

"What can I say? They need more chairs. I can't tell you how many customer-comment cards I've filled out about the poor seating—"

"You're sitting now," he says. "Go ahead. Go beaming out of here, right here and now, and I'll forget the whole thing."

I think about it, that possibility—a final leap.

Instead, I say, "I've already forgotten the whole thing. Was there a thing? Honestly, I can't make heads or tails out of any of this."

"Your wife's a lawyer. How's that work when you're divorced? Do you lose a soul mate and legal representation?"

I want to leap badly, his watch is just glaring, and no, it's not for any good. It's an evil, evil desire. I want to leap into his supercop supermobile and puke on the seats, but I still see Kevin falling.

"All right, James. What do you know about Chapman Collins?"

"Who would that be?"

"Little kid, disappeared two weeks ago from his mother."

"I've misplaced a lot of stuff, but never a kid."

"He was kidnapped. We found him last night, tipped off by a cell-phone call."

"Great. Those cups with missing-kid pictures pay off occasionally."

"How'd you know his picture was posted on a cup?"

"It was?"

"Yeah, like the one on your kitchen counter."

"But the kid's fine, you say? Back with his mother?"

"What do you care?"

"I don't. You brought it up."

"Kid's fine, back with his mom. We staked out the apartment and arrested his deadbeat father. He's just down the hall, if you'd like to visit."

"Is there an espresso machine on the way?"

"Strange, though…the kid told us that someone with your height, your build, and your description miraculously appeared in the locked room with him."

"I get that all the time. I'm criminally average, I guess."

"Chapman said he used that guy's phone to call us. Called you Jimmy?"

"Wow, I haven't been called that since—"

"Last night?"

"Let's see, last night… I can't remember that far back."

"What if I said I traced the call, James?"

"I'd say you're bluffing, Chief."

"And what if I subpoena your cell-phone records?"

"On what grounds—I'm a heavy duct-tape user?"

"The kid said you vanished as soon as you saw the police arrive. He said you asked him not to tell the police about your being there."

I laugh, which is too close to the coughing reflex, so there's coughing.

"Here, let me show you something," I say. "You'll be interested in this."

I run the recorder back. It takes a minute because I have to start and stop it. I hear my own voice dictating to myself, and it's like coming unglued from my own body. I cough. I know I'm close to where Goss's voice in my apartment should be, but I can't find it.

"You wanted to play me something?" Goss crosses his arms.

"Hold on."

"Let's get back to the kid."

"You were in my apartment, and I was there. I leapt into the shower. I recorded the whole thing."

That makes Goss uncross his arms.

I give up on the recorder and reenact it for him with my best Goss impersonation:

"That pay phone right there, Arnie?"

"He told the dispatch there was a burglar in this apartment."

I use a slightly smarter-sounding voice for Arnie. "He may be losing his mind, Bill, but what he's got left works better than yours."

"Shut up, Arnie, it's personal now!"

I stop my performance, although I'm quite good with the multiple voices.

Goss shifts his weight back and forth, a little speechless.

I run the recorder ahead to the present, start recording again. "Any comments, commander?"

Goss looks at the recorder suspiciously, confused, teaming with questions. "You say you heard all that?"

"No comment, perfect. Guilty cops always go for no comment." I tap the recorder. "Remember, speak up."

"You were definitely not in your apartment—"

"Not when you searched it. Not then."

He seems worried. "What's to keep me from taking that recorder right now and losing it?"

I smile and say, "Because I made a file, Cap'n. Loaded it up onto the Internet. E-mailed it to my lawyer. E-mailed one to my ex-wife lawyer and one to my other lawyer and two more lawyers I've never met. Heck, I e-mailed one to the pope. But if I'm smart enough to have recorded your conversation, I'm smart enough not to show it to you unless I've passed it around. Your move, Sarge."

Of course, I'm shaking. I haven't done a thing, haven't touch a computer in months. I've got nothing, nothing but pneumonia. And the fearful shaking is indistinguishable from the feverish shaking.

I don't know why I want to make him so mad. And I do, I wish him ulcers and gas and insomnia and unquenchable anger at me. Since the ulcers haven't taken him yet, Goss just shakes his head and picks up my file again.

"Let's see. Swiping groceries, a defenseless old lady's purse, making mock phone calls to 911, accessory to kidnapping, lost your job, fired from it, divorced, pretty lady left you. Hey, tell me something, do you know this guy?"

He throws a picture on the table right in front of me. It's a blown-up, black-and-white, faxed copy of a driver's license picture, but I recognize it. It's the same picture the news used of Kevin.

I feel dizzy again. "Can I go now?"

"I asked if you know him."

"I want a lawyer."

"I believe your lawyer's in bed with another man. Should we wake them? How about the guy in the picture?" he repeats.

"Yeah, I knew him." I shove the picture back at him.

"You *knew* him? So you know he's dead then?"

"I watch the news like the rest of America."

"What can you tell me about that?"

"About what?"

"Did you have anything to do with that?"

"I have the right to remain silent—"

"Now you don't feel like talking, is that it?"

"If I give up that right—hey, Captain, just jump on in here any time."

"Were you two up to something, and he backed out?"

"Anything I say can be used against me…"

"Did you have a plan?"

"…in a court of law. Help me here, I don't know much more, Cap'n…"

"What's the duct tape for? Was he going to help, but something went wrong?"

"…I have the right to call you a monster, a moron, a misogynist, and other derogatory words that begin with the letter *m*…"

"James, I thought you said you could leap through space?"

"…misfit, monkey-loving miscreant, malevolent malefactor."

"So maybe you leapt up to the top of the hospital and pushed him?"

I can't think of any more words that start with *m*.

"Did you do that, James? Did you push him off?"

"I'd like my coffee now."

"If you were watching the news and you can jump through space, why didn't you do anything?"

I can't think of words. I cough again.

"What's wrong? Did I touch a nerve?"

I stop coughing, swallow it down.

Goss waits. "James. Did you have anything to do with his jump?"

I look my interrogator straight in the eyes. It's the best lean and stare I can do from a sitting position.

"No," I say.

"That the truth?" he asks.

"The truth," I say, "is that I had absolutely nothing to do with him."

"I think maybe you did."

"If I had…maybe he wouldn't be dead right now. Is he somewhere in this building too?"

I couldn't say for sure, but the way Goss blinked at me, I thought Kevin's body just might be here.

Goss cracked his knuckles. "You're a hard man to believe, James."

"Yeah, well, maybe believing is just hard."

"Frankly, I don't believe a word you've told me." He shuts the folder and takes a sip of his foul brew. "But the thing is…thing is…I saw you."

I look up at my inspector.

"That's what's bothering me. I've concluded you're an idiot and you don't have the stomach for crime. Not yet. But in the grocery, when you stepped around that corner, I saw you… You vanished. You did and I saw it."

He says this, waits. It's my turn to answer, but this is one of those conversations you can't rehearse ahead of time, so I'm lost. I just shrug politely.

"How'd you do it, James?"

For a moment, the way Goss looks at me with his eyebrows raised and his face quiet, for just that moment, Goss reminds me of Chapman. It's in a good way, like he's really waiting for me, wide-eyed and waiting for whatever miracle the superhero might pull off. He wants me to get him out of there, like he's been kidnapped and locked in a small room for a long time, like maybe he wants to believe.

I say, "You'd never believe me if I told you."

Goss stretches his back. "Try me."

Why not? I think. *I'm pretty low on the dignity scale about now.* "A couple of days ago, something happened. God changed me and made me this…a leaper. I mean, I can do precisely what I said I can—leap through space. At least, most of the time. God wants me to use it for good, and I'm not good. Good is much trickier than it looks on television, so I'm giving up."

Goss wants to laugh, wants to ridicule, pull my ears, and call me a moron, but something stops him, and it isn't me or how well he's been raised. No, he's on the edge just like me.

"Don't give it up yet, James," he says, "Let's see ya."

He holds out his hands, as if saying, we have all the time in the world. I see his watch on his wrist, a glint off the bulb above.

I sigh. "It doesn't work that way."

"No, I'll drive you home myself, buy you dinner, set you up with a six-pack. All you have to do is leap outside this room and into that hall." He points at the door.

I stare at Goss, and I'm suddenly tired, my arms feel weak, and it's weird to say this, but I feel like Jesus must have felt when people kept asking him for miracles and he just wanted to sit down or go to sleep. I ask, "Man, what do you care?"

Goss slaps his hands down on his thighs and juts his head forward.

"Care?" he laughs, but it's an old, worn-out laugh. "You tell me you can appear and disappear, that you're some kind of hero. You tell me God made you this way, and well, I'd like to see it. Show me! I'd love to believe.

"Do you know how good it would feel to think that God was back, that he was doing something—anything? I can't tell you how relieved I'd be if God were back. God, *the* God, doing miracles again. Even if it's just you, a hero on the prowl for good. Wonderful—I'm tired of doing it all alone. Come on, James, you've almost persuaded me. But can you show me? Please, James, leap us both out of here."

My eyelids sag and blink. I'm exhausted, and I'm beginning to feel like breathing is too much for me to handle. Is this guy for real or not? What if I showed him—would I be free—or a whole different kind of trapped? I press my thumbs on the tabletop and shake my head.

"You said you saw it in the grocery. If you've seen it once, believe that," I say.

Goss looks at me, and I can't tell if he wants to beat me till I show him. Or thank me for confirming his doubt, all the bad things he already assumes, and for letting him off the belief hook.

"All right," he says, standing. "Despite my recommendations, James, the grocery store won't be pressing charges. They would prefer you shopped elsewhere, but no formal charges. Be that as may be, I do want you to know something."

He pauses for effect, but I'm not asking. I can barely hold my head steady.

"I brought you here tonight because I can, and I wanted you to know that. And I'm watching you—know that too—from here on out.

"Be an idiot," he continues, "but don't get too grand in your thinking or start thinking you're above the law. I'm keeping my eye on you, James. Do we understand each other?"

"Watching me. I got it…from here on out." It's my turn to blink and wait.

"You can go," he says. "Get up."

He collects my file, checks his watch, and he's done with me—on to thinking of driving home, paperwork, whatever's next for his night.

"The door's been open this whole time?" I ask.

Goss shrugs. "Try it and see."

I stand and cough, limp slowly around the table, reach for the door. It opens. It was unlocked and something about that just cracks me up.

"What did you say?" Goss asks.

I didn't realize I was mumbling, so I have to think about it. I mumble again and smile. Goss still stares at me. He wants his answer, and I should just go, but why not tell him?

I tried to give up the gift, but he's watching. I'm in whether I want in or not. There's only one way to stop the gift now.

So I turn and say out loud, "I said, 'Good luck.'"

"With what?" Goss asks.

"Keeping your eye on me."

19

What's the number here?"

I ask the police guy checking me out of the station. He gives me back my stuff—my wallet, my belt, my watch. I should've checked to see if they'd swiped my money, all that cash I'd just taken out of an ATM, but I was coughing too much, too consumptively, to worry properly about my wallet.

My coughing feels like I'm going to cough out something that's never supposed to be out, things I didn't know people kept inside, things hacking their way free. The guy makes me sign a few papers. The papers say that I agree that they did, indeed, give me back all my stuff, and that I checked it and everything was there. Clearly, that's when I should have checked my money. Some worrier I turn out to be.

I sign. I'm sure there's stuff missing, but there's no changing what's already done, no going back.

"This is the phone number for the station, right?"

He grunts. He's a real heavy grunter, this guy, but it's a communicative grunt.

"You should see someone about that grunt," I say, then I cough so wildly I have to hold the wall until I'm done.

He points me to a side door, with a pitying, semipolite grunt. Bless his heart, he probably can't speak. He lives in his sad grunt world with other grunters. I slide my pocket change on the counter to him. Everything but the quarters. I need my quarters.

This door leads out to a fenced-in parking lot, barbed wire coiled along the top of the chain link. I have a stub of paper that the grunter also gave me. It reads C-21, the parking space that contains my impounded Volvo. It's still raining, and it takes a while to find the spot, as there's all these cars parked on top of the numbers. I shiver uncontrollably, and I make a mental note: *worry desperately about health.*

When I find the Volvo, I kiss its dirty windshield, then spit. It's rained on my car for hours, but my windshield remains covered with dust and crud. I look around, search for something, any object on the ground will do. A nail, a pen, a beer can, anything. Something shiny. I see this candy bar wrapper, and that will do nicely, mainly the foil, although the red wrapper shines too. When I bend down to snag it, I realize I'm still shoeless. My feet look cold, a little blue. I zip up Father Chavez's Windbreaker.

I unfurl the candy wrapper, twist it, poke a hole through it and cram it halfway down the Volvo's antenna, take a step back, focus on what the wrapper looks like under the parking-lot lights. Nice. Bright red wrapper, foil flicking in the rain, midway down my Volvo's antenna. Very memorable, this is. I take off my glasses, wipe them free of rain, record a good image of that desire in my brain: wrapper, door, rain.

Then I limp out of the parking lot.

"Hey, you can't leave your car here. This ain't no parking garage."

The guard doesn't even come out of his dry, little booth to say this. He just yells into his microphone.

"Hey, Mack," he yells, sticking his face out the shack's window. But I'm not Mack, and I balance myself, taking a deep breath to crouch under the parking barrier. It's one of those up-and-down mechanical, orange-striped arms, that the guy in the booth presses a button and it raises.

"Pipe down!" I say. I'm soaked again and miserably cold, but giddy that I don't fall over while standing back up. "I'm not leaving it, I'm coming right back. I got to make a call."

"Yeah, well, you better not."

"What are you going to do, arrest me?"

He slams his little window shut.

A pay phone. I remember seeing one out front of the station when they brought me in this place. Not a booth, of course, they stopped making phone booths.

Why did they stop making booths for phones? I liked the booths, and I bet the phones preferred the booths. I bet Superman misses those spacious, seventies-style booths. This is a phone stand. A perch for a phone.

And I'm smart to have asked for the station's number, because someone's ripped off the phone book. The pitiful chain just dangles there. I've never seen a chain attached to its phone book except in movies, so what's it really for? If someone really wants to swipe a phone book, that's a flimsy restraint. Who steals the phone book right in front of the police station?

I dial the number for the station.

"Detective Goss, please."

"May I say who's calling?" ask the operator.

"No, just tell him a guy who de-naps kidnapped kids. He'll know who it is."

She puts me on hold. The police switchboard pumps Five for Fighting at you when you're on hold. It's very surreal, and I wonder if she's just filing her nails. With a fever, Five for Fighting starts to sound like—

The music suddenly stops with a click.

"This is Goss."

"Hey, Cap'n."

"Who is this?"

"I'm no hero," I say.

"James? Look, you little punk—"

"Nope, that's not my name anymore. And I've given up being a punk, too. Just Leaper from now on, thanks. As in one who leaps."

"James, if you don't think I'll throw you right back in the lock-up—"

"Oh, you'll never touch me," I say.

"I know where you live. I know the hotel—"

"Hey, Captain, does your gray police station have a window?"

"What?"

"I know it has a window, okay. I'm looking up at a window. Second floor. There's one on the third, too. Tall, skinny windows, built like they didn't really want people looking out. You know those windows?"

"What's your point?"

"I'm calling from the pay phone outside. Do me a favor, Sarge, and go look out one of those skinny windows."

Then I slap two fingers down on the hanging-up lever. That's what's classic about pay phones. Booths and hanging-up levers. I could get used to phone booths. Of course, you need a whole different set of superpowers for taking on and off boots in a booth.

I wait, staring up at the window. I get ready. I angle a bit so the street light falls on my good side, the side I wear my watch on. It kills my foot to pose like this, but it's worth it.

Standing in the rain, I pull up my sleeves like a magician, stretch my bare arms out, tilt my head onto the shoulder of the left arm, the arm with my watch, and twist my wrist around. With my right hand, I hold the phone receiver out as far it will go.

And I wait for him.

I see him step into the little window on high. He's looking down on me, and he seems cautious, unsure of himself, unsure of me. But he's really there.

Wait for it, I think. *Let him see you. Let him see you good.* I badly want him to see me good.

He does. He's there… He sees.

Red wrapper, red wrapper, foil flicking in the rain…

A minute later, when I drive past the guard booth, Goss is outside by the phone stand. Now he's getting soaked. He must've run down the stairs. He looks winded, flabbergasted, and he stands in the rain, watching the dangling phone receiver swing.

I drive right past him. Who's crazy now?

20

T he ice bucket.

There it is, sitting on the seat next to me. Hometown Suites. The name of my hotel is written in pretty cursive on the side, even the address. *They must really want these back,* I think. That's how Goss knows about my hotel.

I can't go back to that hotel. I shouldn't sleep there. Will I ever sleep? But no visitors in the night for me, thanks. (I wouldn't trust this night not to end that way.) Or is it morning? My stuff's there, but I can always leap in and leap out from a safe location. I need a place to hide, someplace new and safe.

I have to concentrate just to drive. More specifically, the wiggly raindrops nudging across my windshield are far more interesting than the road. Also, I'm burning up. My temples are beating, my neck is clammy, and my clothes are freshly soaked. Not sure if I should turn on the air conditioning or the heater, but certainly should not be driving. I slow down, but pressing the clutch sends remarkable pain up through my foot into my leg. Yeah, I shouldn't be driving. As bad as this, I've got to keep going until I know where I'm going.

Oddly, I'm not really worried anymore. There are things to be afraid of, but I don't *feel* afraid. I *see* the fearful things clearly as if they are right in front of me, and they remain ever-so-fearful, but I'm not afraid. Do you see?

I don't really feel my choices are going to keep me safe anymore. This evening—everything about it—it's moving too fast *and* too slowly, the way everything moves feels too certain *and* unknown, too wildly inevitable to do anything about. I can make my choices, but choices are made inside a bigger thing that I can't move an inch one way or the other. Strange as it is to say, that feels hopeful. I'm only responsible for the really small choices, the ones with me in them.

And that feels free.

Out of the ice bucket, I grab my cell phone, mash the speed dial. It rings forever.

"Hello?" Her voice is thick, husky, and addled. It's hard for me to speak. She says, "James? Is that you?"

I'm still silent. The wipers don't even smudge now. How do wipers completely miss rain on a windshield? If they do, technically, are they still wipers?

"James…that *is* you. Don't just breathe, please!"

"Hey, Meg…"

"What time is it?"

"Hey, let me ask you a question—"

"What time is it? For the love of…I have to be at work in—"

"Quick question and I'll be gone."

"Call me tomorrow. Try to sleep, please!"

"Meg, did I ever punish you with my lack of trust?"

"Dear God—"

"Seriously, Meg, I'm asking here."

"You're kidding, right?"

"Honey, I may never be this serious again."

"Okay, sure, yes, James, you did, since you're asking."

"What does that do to a person?"

"James, I can't—"

"Please, Meg."

"It robs them, okay? It robs them of being with you."

I hear her sigh—a sad, tired sigh.

Then she says, "James, I'm not doing this."

There's silence.

"I'm sorry, Meg."

She waits.

I say, "I guess I wanted to say sorry, and…if I had to go through all of that…I'm glad I went through it with you."

More silence.

"Don't mean to bug you," I say. "I'll go."

"James, wait—"

"Good-bye, Meg."

I hang up. And as I drive, I'm not angry or sad, and I'm not in need. I think, *How long till morning?*

I'm free to make the little choices. I drop the cell phone in the ice bucket, roll down the window, and toss both out into the rain. In the mirror, I watch them bouncing, flipping, shattering across the wet asphalt.

Slowly, I smile. I know where I'm going.

21

F or the record, I do not recommend leaping inside a dark church alone.

Shadows are everywhere. And I mean creepy ones.

You wouldn't think a long, cold room, *already* dark, could have so many shadows, but there's dark and darker. Moonlight through stained glass makes you think you can see, but there are too many corners, too many places under pews, too many columns that are just dark and darker on the side away from the moon.

Let's not forget what moonlight does to stained-glass people: they move, they jiggle, they stand up straighter, their doves rotate. You don't see the faces, just postures, hands in weird gestures, and I swear, they change when you look away. Trust me on this. Cold, dark shapes watching, and I'm limping down a long, unlit aisle leading up to the dark platform where God is. Dark, empty pews everywhere. I hope they're empty. Every few feet I pass through the gaze of another staring saint—pale moon blue reaching through frozen faces.

"Anybody home?"

I call out in the off-chance Father Chavez came back to the church, but my voice squeaks and breaks. I cough.

"Didn't imagine there'd be much hope of…"

A noise, from behind me, back at the door. I crouch in the aisle. I don't know, but I don't like it. Not the crouching, the noise. I know I didn't leave the door open because I leapt in here. But maybe church doors don't lock? Maybe sanctuaries works like convenience stores, 24/7…

"Who's there?"

A terrible, awful, wrenching, dumb question to say aloud to yourself in an empty, dark room. What's a crouched man's crazed mind going to do but scroll through all the bad possible answers to that stupid question.

Another noise.

I know I'm not making it up, but this time from the front. I lay perfectly still. Okay, relatively motionless, considering the various forms of shaking. Now I need to know about the doors—they have to lock, right? Haven't I seen Father Chavez lock up before, or open up, or swing a big, iron loop of rusty keys and yell, "Last call"?

I crawl back down the aisle, and my bare feet are a plus now. Like a nervous, lame, damp crab, I shimmy toward the foyer. I stop at the entryway and lean my back against the stone holy-water basin. Must I dab and cross? I don't want to risk it. I reach up, shoot my hand in and dab, pull back, quick and safe, but I hear another scuttle.

Then I see it.

Down the center aisle, in one of those pools of moonlight blue, I see a thin yellow ribbon. The yellow ribbon flips and jerks then in that blue pool. Nothing, just lying there brightly. Yellow isn't yellow under blue. Then it flips again. Am I mad? I lay on the floor of a church, in fear of what may be a three-cent piece of fabric, and I cannot fathom what to do except watch.

A mouse tugs it out of sight.

Crouched in fear, my superhero-self slumped limp, like old whipped cream sagging on top of a hot, hot chocolate. I think, *What hero is afraid of mice? What human?* But I'm only afraid of mice with yellow ribbons. Only one person knows about that yellow ribbon.

I look at my fingers. The dab of water has dried up before I used it.

Into the sanctuary, I call out, "Your here, aren't you?"

When I stand up, I cough so hard I swear that stained-glass guy with the axe scowls. He stares at me with his eyebrows raised. Maybe he's holding his breath, afraid to catch what I've got.

"I know you're in here…"

I wait, but no answer.

"It's not really fair, you know, your being everywhere, all the time."

Nothing happens.

"Look, I came to say…this isn't going to work out."

As I reach the front pew, I cough, and it doubles me over, my eyes watering. I think I've sprained a muscle in my neck. I cough what tastes like blood into my mouth—the taste of the blood on the tongue.

"It's like this: I'm sick, I'm wet, I'm tired, I'm cold, I'm feverish, I'm confused, I'm hot, I'm sick, I'm tired, I'm hungry, I'm afraid, I'm angry, and also I am sick. And I'm done, okay? Not good enough. You want from me what I can't give, and I want out."

I squint across the dark church, looking for lightning or a pillar of smoke or Morgan Freeman.

"Are you ready? Okay…"

I clear my throat for effect, but it leads to another coughing bout. I let myself down on the front pew, way up in the God area.

"I, the aggrieved, being of sound mind and—"

I listen to the dark.

"Right, skip that. I do hereby nullify all connection between God and this neurotic party, and further do solemnly vow to stay out of your way henceforth, and until further notification, on the condition that said God agrees to do the same and without consideration of up-bringing, parental expectation, obligation, guilt, hellfire, and brim-stone. In other words, all bets off. Eternal bets, all off."

I look up at the crucifix.

"Please don't interrupt me now. That's how we got in this jam."

Sitting, I feel dizzy, so I grab the pew seat with both hands.

"Let's just say we missed each other, okay? Two ships in the dark night, and call it a day. Irreconcilably different, you and I. You want trust; I can't trust. We're just not going to work out. No hard feel-ings… In fact, what do you lose, really? Not a thing, as I see it. So thanks. I'm really sorry, and I hope you don't take this the wrong way, but we're done. Really sorry."

There's enough moon to make the crucifix blue. He looks cold too.

"Don't be like that. Why am I leaving?"

Although talking to God, I hold up fingers and count them for effect.

"First, I am not good enough to do what you want. Second, I'm not smart enough to understand what you need from me. Third, I am not quiet enough to ever listen to you. And number four, I do not want this. I never asked to be wanted, not like this, not this way. No disrespect, and I certainly don't hope to hack off the Almighty with some display of ingratitude, but hey, I can't live up to this or even imagine how to try. So we're done, we're over."

The Christ on the crucifix, he doesn't move.

"It just wasn't what I expected. I can't live this way, wondering what you'll do next. With my kind of issues, I don't trust myself to wake up in the morning and know who I am, let alone worry about how you're going to show up and—"

A cloud must have passed the moon, because I lose his face, and the blue, the light, the pale saints behind me fade.

"Besides, this whole deal's been a fraud. This screw has been pooched from the get-go. I had no idea you even *wanted* trust from me. You really should mention that way up front. Like knowing you would actually matter…like you'd actually speak? I had no intention of trusting you like that.

"The truth is, I hoped to be on decent, comfortable terms with your Almighty-ness. It makes sense, like giving the cops free coffee in the shop. You want the guys with guns thinking happy thoughts when they see you, you know. If they pull you over, you want them to taste the free coffees while getting out their ticket pad…"

I cough again, taste more blood.

"See, God, I had no idea you meant to infringe upon my self-absorption, not this slicingly, not all at once. What kind of deal is that? You are absolutely the least-safe God I know! I don't open the door for the UPS guy even when I'm expecting a package. What possible universe allows for free access by God anytime, anywhere, in all things? Here's your house key, God; there's lunchmeat in the fridge. But no, not even that. You don't come over unless I'm home—that's when you come barging in. We Americans value our privacy, God. A little holy water on weekends, but let's not overdo this, shall we? What do you say? Let's split up. This is totally unsafe."

The hanging blue Christ doesn't even lift his head.

"Don't blame Father Chavez; he did what he could. In fact, I can't imagine anyone else showing up for me. But if faith is what he says, if faith is the courage to keep trusting, then I don't want to believe. Trust is crazy. You are a risky, risky God. I didn't sign up to be Amazing-Trust Boy, and I did not sign up for Danger God. I do not like surprises—birthday, happy little, tuna, or otherwise—and you're flatly not safe…"

The cloud's gone. I see his bowed head, his sad eyes, his torn beard in sharp detail again.

"I wasn't made for it, I guess. Every time I've come close to a genuine attempt, every little thing howls inside like a—"

When I blink, like blood pumping, the crucifix pounds my sight. So I close my eyes tight.

"Here it is: I've come to ask you to get out. I mean out of my life. This place, of course…kinda yours. No, I'll move out. I'm used to that. Let me sleep here tonight, and I swear I'll be gone by the morning. You can keep everything. But do you hear me? It's finished."

My ears are ringing, my tongue is parched, my spine shivers. Everything inside my head burns.

"I'm glad we had this chat, and when I wake up, I hope this little gift of yours will be gone." I gather my legs up onto the pew, take a hymnal for a pillow.

"Good doing business with you, God. I'm glad we could settle this amicably. You're all right in the end. I just can't live the way you live."

I zip the Windbreaker up tighter over my wet clothes.

"Good-bye."

The moonlight shadow of the crucifix seen straight on appears in profile—the dark shape of the nail-hung Christ in blue profile, depending on the light.

That stretched shadow captures something the crucifix itself does not. That shadow of the Crucified curves more beautifully. More beautifully, because you can feel the gravity he's pulling against. More lifelike because there's more suffering.

In shadow, you can almost see the chest's last rise and tremor and fall.

22

Sit up."

"What?" I ask.

"Drink this."

"What is it?"

"It's good for you. Come on, it's bracing. It'll put warmth back in your bones."

"How did you know about my bones?"

"That's it, sit up."

I can see the silhouette of a man sitting next to me. He has a cup in his hand, a chalice. Candles lit somewhere behind flicker. I pull myself up and lean my back on the armrest of the pew. My clothes are no longer wet, not even a damp spot where I'd been lying.

"Where am I again?"

"Right where you were."

"I came to the cathedral, right?"

"Apparently… Here, sip this." He holds the chalice up to my lips. One of his hands supports the base, the other holds the bowl of the cup. I take a sip. It burns all the way down.

But I don't cough. I don't need to cough.

"How did I get here?"

"That's better." The man wipes the lip of the cup with his hand-kerchief.

"How did I get in here?" I ask again.

"You know how." He smiles at me, just an easy curve of a smile. I'm seeing a little better now. My eyes begin to adjust. It's still dark, but lots of candles flicker. He's a thin, elderly man with a thin voice, dressed just like a regular guy: dark cardigan, old-man shirt, frumpy pants. He's holding a folded white hanky and a chalice.

"How long was I…"

"Quite a while." He doesn't seem to be going anywhere, just sitting and waiting.

"How did my clothes get dry? I was soaked when I came in."

"That's why you need to sip this, to warm you." He holds up the chalice again, the second time that happened.

"What's in that?"

"It's what you need."

I take another sip. This one goes down more smoothly.

There's something funny about this guy. He seems nice and smiling, sure, but I can't keep what I think about him in one place.

"Why are *you* here?" I ask.

"Oh, I come here sometimes, late at night. I like what quiet does to a soul."

"Me too. I'm a big fan of quiet."

"Is that why you came?"

I'm unsure of the question, my answer. "The quiet? Or my soul?"

The old man nods.

"Buddy, if you're working on commission for the devil, I'm fresh out of soul."

"Then why are you here?"

"The doughnut place was closed. How'd *you* get in?" I ask.

"One more sip, when you're ready."

"Did I leave the door open?"

Now he really smiles. It's in his eyes, like he knows the trick to my question. He doesn't answer.

"I don't remember leaving it open," I say.

"Do you remember leaving it closed?"

"Not exactly."

"Ah, I see," he says.

The candles flicker madly, and I'm not sure, but I think he might actually see—and I'm not sure I like it. He blinks slowly, patiently, like he's waiting for me to remember.

"I never leave things open."

"I know," he says.

I squint toward the flickering. I see the candles lit on the altar table up in the God area.

"Is Father Chavez here?"

"I lit them. Have another sip?"

"Stop it, okay? We both know this isn't real. I'm not really here, or you're not. And my soul? You're crazy. Or finally, I am, but I've got no way to tell right now. I feel a little…laid out on a pew, covers it."

"Sit up. You're good."

"That's rich. What would you know about it?"

He smiles, wipes the chalice. It's ready for me to drink from.

"I know you," I say.

"Do you?"

"Well, not know…but I've bumped into you, maybe? In real life."

"Maybe."

I check my watch. Not for the time, just that I have it. That I can catch the flicker if I need it.

"Fine watch," he says admiringly, dangerously.

"Just what I was thinking about the candles. They're a nice touch."

"Thank you. I always prefer candles here."

"You come here, light the candles…why, again?"

"It was dark, and I was praying."

"For what?"

What he thinks first, he doesn't say. He tucks the hanky into his sweater pocket, reaches out his frail hand, and places it on my shoulder in a grandfatherly squeeze. He pats my neck, then he sits back and gets out that hanky again.

"Why are you here, James?"

"Oh, I see… Did you get my name rummaging through my wallet while I was blitzed? Let me tell you something, old guy, that comforting leather bulge better be there when I check or I'm liable to…"

"You're liable to what?"

I look at my watch, the candles glinting off it. But I don't have any place I desire to be.

"You're liable to what, James?"

"Nothing."

He listens, taking that "nothing" in, with his forehead furrowing like Father Chavez.

"Rest. Here, take another sip."

"I'm so tired." I say this, but I'm not tired. Whatever's in that cup is working. I'm ready to fight, old guy or not. I'm dry, I'm warm, and I'm feeling tired, but in the most active way.

"You're tired?"

"All the time. I'm liable to tiredness, to fall out any moment and never find the next."

"You mean your soul? Is that what's tired?"

I ignore his question and ask, "Is Father Chavez here?"

"No, we're alone."

"That figures."

"What does?"

"It's a nightmare, right? The flashlight batteries go dead, but Jamie Lee Curtis heads on down the dark dock. Phone line snipped, but Janet Leigh takes the shower anyway. There's no escape, and the stupid guy opens his own fateful doors, leading straight to the final surprise."

"Careful, James."

"Stop saying my name."

"Please try to rest. Here, take another sip."

"Put your cup away. Just bring me my check, please."

"Easy, son. Think about this moment before you use it."

"Why should I?"

"Because you can bend a moment out of shape, and if you do that long enough, you can't bend your way back."

In my head, I see Kevin, his face the last time he spoke to me, asking me to listen, like this old man wears Kevin's last expression on his face.

"Here. Last sip."

"If I click my heels together, will you go away? There's no place like James, there's no place like James—"

"Look, I brought your book."

The book I left at the coffee shop. He has it. Coffee stains down the edges of the pages.

"How did you get this?"

"I stopped by your work, picked it up."

"Just happened by?"

"Well, I like coffee. C. S. Lewis, *The Great Divorce*. It's a fine book."

"You've read it?"

He nods. "Not terribly accurate, but you have to love the imagination."

I take the book, and it feels real. But dream or not, this is too weird. Time for me to go, one way or another. "I just remembered. Left the window open back at the hotel. Need to get back—"

"Stay. Wait—"

"Thanks, no. Let's do it again sometime."

"Here, take one last sip."

"Sure, give it here."

For the third time, he holds up the cup. I put the chalice to my lips, tip it, but I don't drink anything.

"Happy? Now I got a date with a window."

"You're not ready to go, not yet."

"Unless you plan to swat me with your walker, we have a difference of opinion."

"Why did you come to the church, James?"

"You know… You seem to know everything about this dream."

Now that he thinks I've taken all the sips, he sets the chalice down on the floor, folds his hanky away.

"When do I wake up from this? Answer that."

"Whenever you want," he says.

"I remember who you are, okay. That day at Mass. Your smile. And I'm sorry, okay. Sorry for pushing you aside, sorry for taking your bread out of the priest's hand, sorry for everything! All right? Just leave me alone."

"I will, but I have to show you something first. Get up. Follow me."

"I can't. My foot's—"

"You're not broken."

And he's right. I stick my bare foot out in front of me, wiggle my toes, roll the ankle both ways. No pain.

"First, you tell me…why'd you come here, dream boy? Better yet, how'd you get in here?"

Slowly, the old man pushes himself to his feet, stands. He's not smiling anymore.

"You know how. The same way you did."

"Perfect! You're a creepy nightmare twist—the elder leaper. You're…one of us!"

"I came here to see you, James."

"You should have called. I'd have put on coffee."

"Careful with yourself. This moment matters."

"Oh, okay," I say and laugh. My dream guide, he's not laughing.

The cathedral is so quiet. Creepy quiet. The old guy just smiles at me, sits and smiles, picks a little fluff off his sweater. My head is pounding, not with pain, but silence. In the pause I think I can hear the candles flickering. And something about it, this moment, this pause, his smile, something makes me want to slow down, stop fighting. Dream or no dream, I want to hear the quiet flicker of candles.

"You came here to see me? Then answer this."

"If I can," he says.

"Tell me. Tonight, the past three days, this whole thing—is this reality or madness?"

He stares at me, unsure. Not like he's unsure of his answer, but of whether or not I will believe his answer, no matter what. Finally he says, "Without God, reality is madness. Reason will tell you so. You either madly trust in God, or you trust in a world gone mad without him."

"Is there a third option?"

"Time to go," he says.

"Wait! Does God really do this? Does God get involved, really make people do the impossible?"

"He always has."

"But does he still?"

"Don't rob God of being with you, James."

"But I can't…," I start, but then say, "I'm afraid."

"That's why you can't see it. That's what happens sometimes. And when it does, trust becomes the only road home, back to love."

I have no answer.

He pats my shoulder again like he did that day at Mass.

"That's why I'm here, James. I came here to help you see—and to show you a few things. Come on." The old guy reaches into his pocket. He pulls out a shiny silver pocket watch. "My grandfather gave me this, last time I saw him. Get up. It's your time to see."

"See what?"

"You need to see moments without you in them, just as they are." He turns a bit, dangles the pocket watch by its long chain so it spins in the candlelight.

"It's a beauty," he says, eyes reflecting the light like his watch. "You've been changed, James. You've been given a gift."

"I don't want this gift."

"The gift's not for you. It's for others. Everything we're given is for others. God has already changed you, and you can't do anything about that now."

"But what if I don't want to be changed?"

"Well, that's why I was sent, to show you the ropes. Show you a few moments, and you'll be back. You can make your choice then. It'll take no time at all."

He takes the hanky out again, leans down, picks up the chalice. He sets both beside me on the pew. "Your choice...but no more faking it."

I pick up the cup and sip it. It's real this time.

The silver pocket watch spins in the candlelight. It's hard to look at it, but you have to look, it's so...

"Where are we going?" I ask.

"Come and see..."

understand now.

I've seen.

I've been taken.

It's like this: Meg's not a saver, no pack rat. She's just not sentimental. She likes empty closets, sock drawers that are orderly, and garages without boxes. She carpools plastic to recycling centers, shreds bills and papers, marks garbage pick-up days with bright blue. But tonight, leaping along, I saw Meg, with her snoring and her legs kicking every cover.

She's sleeping like she's only got so much time before she has to run again, only so much time to set her life straight. Beside her fitful sleep, on the nightstand, is her shoebox. Of the few things she keeps to touch, to remember, she keeps them in this faded shoebox from when she was a kid—a ladybug ponytail holder; a pink ribbon tied around a note in her father's hand saying "I love my girl"; a picture of her and me on this rickety wooden dock, laughing in the rain. Tonight, there on the nightstand, the shoebox is open, and lying on top is a piece of orange construction paper with the letters M-O-M, the *O* drawn in heavily with crayons, but the *M*'s are made with Popsicle sticks. Mostly, the Popsicle sticks are stained red and blue; a few are fudgy.

And she's asleep with her hand hanging near enough to touch the box, its contents.

In all the years I spent with her, I never made her feel that she would be a good mother, something that important to her, and she would be a good mother, she will. But now this, I played a small part of that Popsicle stick scrap, her hope tonight, her better belief.

She'll keep that part of my good in her shoebox. That's beautiful.

It seems doing good isn't *doing* good. It's desiring to be there when God shows up with the good. The truth is, you only need one beautiful thing to free you and talk you out of yourself.

Sleep sound tonight, Margaret. I'm listening now.

Father, I've seen you too. Your glasses on your nightstand; your prayer book on the floor, the page marked with a sock; the glass of water you meant to drink in your silent, lonely home. I see now, Father, that all heroes are unlikely, that the world doesn't need people to be more heroic, just less comfortable. More people willing to be less for someone else's benefit, eager to be used, to rush toward what's most needed and not away from it.

Imagined or not, your suffering only matters if it connects you to the suffering of others, if it heals them, too. You don't change the world by telling it what to do, sitting at home, and telling it what you believe. You believe by throwing yourself into it. Making a leap, getting involved, then waiting, taking some one person's place for a while, one suffering person at a time.

Thank you, Father. You visited me in prison; I'm not locked up anymore.

I understand what I'm supposed to do now. I'm going.

At first, God's gift was annoying, an interruption. When the interruption became surprising, then God was simply terrifying. But God was alive. Like Chapman kicking his legs, kidnapped and scared, somewhere deep down, I longed to tell God not to leave, to come surprise me and to do it again. God was, at least, interesting.

Then suddenly, tonight, not only was God terrifying and interesting, but it occurred to me that God might also be up to good. Not that I owed God good, but that God himself might be up to good—that God might be truly, quietly, surprisingly, tirelessly good.

God is beautiful. Why not trust myself headlong into that?

The moon sparkling on the dark river below—that is beautiful.

Even this reflection off my watch is as beautiful and blinding as talking to a stranger.

God help me.

I must be going…

I must be…

I must…

EPILOGUE

LETTER FROM FATHER CHAVEZ

I compiled the diary as I found it. Where it was difficult to read the handwriting, I did my best.

I've included Captain Goss's notes from his report. I contacted Detective Goss when James went missing, and he made me privy to what his investigation had found, helped me to locate the hotel.

James's articles were left without his checking out. His key card lay on the nightstand with his car key and a note donating his Volvo to our parish. The Do Not Disturb sign left on the door prevented any movement of his things until the police arrived. Due to the finality of his note and the broken, open window, the hotel management feared the worst and immediately alerted the police.

But I do not fear.

As for James, I do not share in the official deduction. I'm unsure as yet what I do believe. Not without any doubt. I don't know if true belief requires the absence of doubt. But I do know what I do not believe happened to him. Sometimes it's hard to believe, but I'm trying. So I leave his diary for each to decide for himself.

As for me, I will hope. I hope as strongly as I can. I'll do that for my friend.

And if it should be possible for you to read this some-day, then, Godspeed and be well, James.

Go in peace.

Father Francis Chavez,
Saint John's Cathedral

Acknowledgments

My heartfelt thanks to my editor, Shannon—a savvy woman of incredible skill and patience—along with my gratitude to the good folks of WaterBrook Press. And a special word to my dear friend, Gloria— a sparkling inspiration and a wise muse for all the many years I've known her.

To learn more about WaterBrook Press and view our catalog of products, log on to our Web site:
www.waterbrookpress.com

WATERBROOK
PRESS